BODY AND SOUL

Once inside her dark chamber, Sally turned to face him. Without removing his eyes from hers, he kicked the door shut behind him and greedily took in the loveliness of her slim body silhouetted against the firelight behind her. He moved to her, settled his trembling hands upon her shoulders, and gazed down into those soulful dark eyes of hers. His senses awakened to the rising and falling of her breasts, to her sweet floral scent, her warm breath. His head lowered to touch her lips, lightly at first, then with a deep and devastating hunger.

George gloried in the gentle whimper that shuddered through her as her arms came around him, as her mouth opened to him as hungrily as he tasted her.

This wasn't how he had planned their first mating. He was to be the master, patiently schooling his youthful bride in the ways of love. But he felt more like a green schoolboy than a master in the art of love.

AN IMPROPER PROPOSAL

Cheryl Bolen

ZEBRA BOOKS
KENSINGTON PUBLISHING CORP.
http://www.kensingtonbooks.com

ZEBRA BOOKS are published by

Kensington Publishing Corp.
850 Third Avenue
New York, NY 10022

All Kensington titles, imprints and distributed lines are available at special quantity discounts for bulk purchases for sales promotion, premiums, fund-raising, educational or institutional use.

Special book excerpts or customized printings can also be created to fit specific needs. For details, write or phone the office of the Kensington Special Sales Manager: Kensington Publishing Corp., 850 Third Avenue, New York, NY 10022. Attn. Special Sales Department. Phone: 1-800-221-2647.

Zebra and the Z logo Reg. U.S. Pat. & TM Off.

First Printing: February 2004
10 9 8 7 6 5 4 3 2 1

Printed in the United States of America

This book is dedicated to my precious son, Bo, who (regrettably) shares his mother's disdain for the mundane. Your father and I hope you soar on the wings of your dreams.

Prologue

Blanks had revisited every schoolboy prank he and George—now Lord Sedgewick—had ever instigated. Anything to keep George's mind off the grim lying-in taking place beyond the door to Lady Sedgewick's bedchamber. It had taken all Blanks's efforts to keep George from storming into his wife's rooms when he heard Dianna moaning in pain.

No matter how amusing Blanks was, George could scarcely attend to his words. A chilling, foreboding fear like nothing he had ever experienced gripped him. He thought back to when Dianna had given birth to their first, Georgette. The attending physician had deemed it a remarkably simple birth in spite of the nine hours his beloved Dianna had writhed in pain.

'Twas said the second one would come quicker, but already it had been ten hours and there was no sound of a babe.

With sickening apprehension, George was coming to believe something had happened to the babe. As disappointing as that would be, he could accept it. He could accept anything except losing Dianna.

The very thought of Dianna dying caused his stomach to restrict and left him feeling strangled of all life. He could not bear even the contemplation of it.

He looked up at Blanks and said, his voice splintering, "Something's wrong." As soon as he said it, he wished he could retract his words. Poor Blanks would be a father for the first time before the month was out, and George had no business alarming his friend. For Blanks was as besotted over his wife—George's sister Glee—as George was over Dianna. If that were possible. Though George was convinced no one could love anyone as much as he loved Dianna. Never had a more perfect, more beautiful creature graced the planet. Not even his sisters, Felicity and Glee, could compare.

"You're just imagining things," Blanks said. Though Blanks attempted a reassuring voice, his own fears caused his voice to crack.

George turned when he heard footsteps mounting the stairs, and he saw Felicity's blond hair. She was accompanied by her husband, Thomas Moreland. George could never look at Moreland without being struck by the resemblance between him and Dianna, Moreland's sister.

"Do we have a baby yet?" inquired Felicity, her face lifting into a smile.

George sighed. "Not yet. I'm frightfully worried."

Felicity set a gentle hand on his arm. "Don't worry. She'll be fine. I'll go check on her right now." Then she disappeared into the viscountess's chambers.

A quick glance at Moreland caused George to become even more upset. For Dianna's brother's face had become ashen. Thomas pulled up a Chippendale chair and sat beside George and Blanks. "How long's it been?"

George swallowed. "Ten hours."

Thomas's brows lowered. "I had thought it wouldn't take so long the second time."

"That's what I thought," George said.

The door to Lady Sedgewick's room squeaked open, and George looked up to gaze at Felicity. And his heart sank. Tears streamed from her blue eyes.

George leaped to his feet. "What is it?" he shouted. "Is it Dianna?"

She slowly nodded, then she burst into tears.

George did not hear Moreland's hoarse scream or Blanks's sharp intake of breath. He had entered his wife's dark chamber. He ignored his very-increasing sister Glee, who stood clutching Dianna's hand, tears flowing unchecked down her face.

They had to be wrong! Dianna couldn't be dead! He reverently approached her canopied bed and looked down at her lily white face, her dark hair damp around her temples, her long lashes closed as if she were asleep. Even after all this time, his heart clenched whenever he beheld her gentle beauty.

For a few hopeful seconds he allowed himself to believe her alive. His beautiful wife was merely asleep. With tears pooling in his eyes, he went to caress her face with his palm. As soon as his flesh touched her cold skin, he knew. A primeval sound broke from him. "No-o-o-o-o!"

He drew her limp body into his arms and sobbed.

He must have held his precious Dianna to him for an hour before Glee urged him to let her go. "You must come and see your son, George," she whispered.

With one last racking sob, George let go of Dianna's lifeless body and whirled at his sister. "I want no part of the babe! He killed his mother!"

Then George stormed from the chamber.

Chapter 1

"I declare, Sally, the only time my poor nephew doesn't cry is when you're present," said Glee, who was plaiting the hair of her own little toddler, Joy.

Sally Spenser dropped a kiss on little Sam's golden ringlets and continued to rock him. She told herself she had become attached to the little tyke because he had never known a mother's caress. More likely, Sally's affection for Sam was fed by his own father's scorn for his innocent son.

Sam's father, George Pembroke, the Viscount Sedgewick, was undoubtedly the most exasperating man Sally had ever known. His lack of interest in his heir was unforgivable. His propensity for tipping a cup too much was irresponsible. His predilection for gaming was unwise. And his taste in poetry was nonexistent. In short, there was not a single thing about the viscount of which Sally approved. They could not be in the same chamber together for five minutes without clashing.

Why, then, had she adored him for half of her two and twenty years? Ever since she and Glee had become best friends while attending Miss Worth's

School for Young Ladies, Sally had worshipped Glee's elder brother. It wasn't as if George had ever given Sally a crumb of encouragement. Quite the contrary. The viscount had never had eyes for any woman on earth save his beloved wife Dianna, who had been dead these two years past.

It hurt Sally to see George descend further into the grim valley of grief he had dug for himself since Dianna's death. It was evident he had no desire to live. There was no longer any joy in his life, save his love for his daughter, who bore a striking resemblance to her mother.

"I'm so happy you've come to Bath," Glee said to Sally. "Not just because I love you so dearly and am so thoroughly happy to see you—but because poor little Sam needs you. I've become quite concerned about him. He doesn't speak at all, and Joy—who's a week younger than he—is already talking in sentences."

Sally bristled. "Mama said girls always talk before boys do. She also said to never compare children for they each develop at a different rate, but they all get to the same place sooner or later."

Glee sighed. "I hope you're right—about boys speaking later. I worry so about Sam. I keep wondering if I'm doing the right thing by allowing him to continue under George's roof. My brother is such a brute! I truly believe Sam would be better off with me—except, of course, for missing his sister, whom George would never give up." Glee removed her daughter from her lap, stood her up, and gave her rump an affectionate swat. "I want Sam and George to grow close, and the only way that can happen is if George has to be responsible for him."

"You have no reason to feel guilty," Sally said. "George *does* need to exercise his paternal responsibilities." She lovingly ran her fingers through Sam's tresses. "Surely one day George will realize how precious Sam is."

Sally reached down to clasp Sam's bare feet. "This little piggy," she began. The little boy sat up and squealed with delight. By the time Sally had finished grabbing each of Sam's chubby, curled toes, he was giggling.

Then his sister strolled into the room, a great, fat, fluffy gray cat in her little arms. Sam scooted off Sally's lap and ran to take the cat from his sister. The cat, who was obviously immune to Sam's clumsy abuse, was almost as big as Sam. Sally was pleased that Georgette was willing to share her pet with her little brother.

Joy, her little legs churning, ran over to her female cousin. "See? Mama made my hair pretty. Like the maiden in the book."

Georgette hopefully looked from Joy to Glee. "Will you plait my hair, too, Aunt Glee?"

"I should be happy to, Georgette. Come here," Glee said, stretching out her arms.

Sally stared at Georgette. Though her name was a variation of her father's, she was all Dianna.

Sally still remembered her own grief when she had learned George had become betrothed to Dianna Moreland. How painfully difficult it was to abandon her dream of growing up and capturing George's heart. At first Sally was convinced George was shackling himself to Miss Moreland for her enormous dowry.

Then the seventeen-year-old Sally met the nineteen-year-old Dianna. And Sally was even more devastated. Of course George would love Dianna! She was not only wealthy, but elegant, gracious, and beautiful. Like her daughter was now. Georgette was tall for a four-year-old. Her mother had been tall, too. And Georgette was very fair of face with rich dark brown hair and eyes. Just like Dianna.

After Glee finished braiding Georgette's hair, she sent the children off with their nurse, then turned to her dear friend. "Now you simply must tell me what brings you back to Bath so soon after you arrived at your brother's house. What has he now done to cause you to be so out of charity with him?"

Sally, who was on her knees picking up after the children, sighed. "He all but promised my hand in marriage to the odious Mr. Higginbottom."

"Pray, why is Mr. Higginbottom so odious?"

"Perhaps the word 'odious' is unjust. The man may be perfectly amiable, but it is difficult for me to determine that because I'm so shallow a person I'm frightfully put off by his appearance. 'Tis no fault of his that he is fat and persists in wearing garments that fit him when he was a much leaner man. And it's terribly unkind of me to object to the fact that his head is as hairless as a billiard ball. Suffice it to say, the man has a granddaughter who is my age."

Glee's eyes widened. "Oh dear, that will never do! Does Edmund actually think you would be *that* desperate to marry?"

Sally's lips folded into a grim line, and her grip tightened on Joy's cloth doll. "*My* feelings were never considered, I assure you. All that mattered to Edmund was Mr. Higginbottom's large purse." She tossed the doll into a basket.

"I cannot understand why your mother would continue to live under her son's roof when he is so thoroughly mercenary. Did he not himself marry for position rather than love?"

Sally nodded. "But Mama is no proponent of love matches. Her father arranged *her* marriage. Besides, she is besotted over Edmund, and he persuaded her how advantageous it would be for me to marry Mr. Higginbottom."

"Oh dear," Glee said again. "And knowing you and your sharp tongue, I am persuaded you alienated Edmund dreadfully."

"I could hardly be expected to hold my tongue—" Sally shook her head and burst out laughing. "I daresay I've never been one to hold my tongue in my entire life."

Glee laughed, too. "I daresay you're right."

"But I'm now faced with the difficulty of my situation. I refuse to go back to Edmund's, and David is off who-knows-where in the navy. As the daughter of a deceased vicar, I obviously have no great fortune of my own."

Glee's smile widened and her eyes twinkled. "You'll just have to live with Blanks and me!"

"As much as I love you," Sally said, "I refuse to live off your charity. I shall have to take a position. I've been thinking . . . I was at the top of our class at Miss Worth's. Do you suppose she would engage me to teach at the school?"

Glee shook her head vigorously. "I shan't allow you to think on the matter! Why, you're the niece of Lord Bankston!" Her eyes surveyed Sally, who was putting everything in its place. "Though, I declare, looking at you now, one would believe you a parlor maid. Do leave that for the servants!"

"You know I cannot."

Glee nodded. "I know. Living with you at Miss Worth's was the only time in my life I had a tidy bedchamber."

"Then my neatness did not rub off on you?"

"Heavens no! I shouldn't wish to have everything tucked away for I'd never be able to find anything. But *that* is not what we were discussing. About your teaching . . . I daresay Lord Bankston would suffer apoplexy if he thought his niece would accept a position as a teacher."

"Grandniece. Then I shan't tell him," Sally said curtly. "My mind is made up, Glee. I wish to be independent. I refuse to live off anyone's charity."

"You were going to live with your brother. What is the difference between living with me—who loves you—and living with your wretched brother?" Glee challenged.

"Edmund was charged by our father with the responsibility of taking care of us upon Papa's death. All of Papa's money—what there was of it—went to his firstborn with that caveat. Edmund bought David's colors and was to make a home for Mama and me with him and Drucilla and their children."

"I am certain that if you stayed here in Bath with Blanks and me you would quickly capture a husband, and that would solve all your problems."

"You may be certain of it, but I'm not," Sally said. "You and Felicity and Dianna all easily captured agreeable husbands because you are beautiful. Unfortunately, I cannot aspire to such hopes."

"You *are* pretty," Glee countered.

"If one likes females as tall and shapeless as a beanpole. And add to that, I am possessed of hair that bears a remarkable resemblance to straw."

"That's not true! Granted, you are taller than average and slight of frame, but your face *is* pretty. Why, you have the nicest dimples I've ever beheld, and your eyes are lovely. 'Tis so unexpected to see dark brown eyes on a blonde. I vow, I would trade anything I have—save Blanks and Joy—to have your complexion."

Sally rolled her eyes. "You're the fair, pretty one. Why would you want skin that's bronzed?"

"It's not bronzed. It's . . . tawny. Like you. Shades of golds and browns. You're really very pretty."

"Would that men shared your views," Sally muttered. Her eyes narrowed as she watched Glee. "Speaking of men, I detect a marked difference of late in your husband. You have every right to tell me it is none of my concern, but I'm quite distressed over what I witness. Blanks had become so responsible, such an attentive husband, and now he's returned to his former ways, cavorting with that brother of yours."

Glee's little shoulders shrugged, and she spoke in a troubled whisper. "We shall never have another child, for he absents himself from my bed."

Other maidens might turn scarlet and avert their gazes when confronted with talk of what occurred between a married couple in the bedchamber, but not Sally. Her brows lowered. "I cannot believe Blanks has fallen out of love with you!"

"Oh, he hasn't," Glee said. "The problem is he loves me too dearly. Ever since Dianna died on childbed, my darling Blanks is determined to spare me such a fate. And—because he loves me so dearly—he cannot be close to me and not . . . well, *not* wish to make love to me. So that is why he is never around."

Sally sprang to her feet and glided across the carpeted floor to Glee. "Oh, you poor dear. We must put a stop to his ridiculous behavior." She hugged Glee to her.

"I cannot think of what to do. I have spoken to him any number of times and assured him the women in my family *are* good breeders. Felicity's already delivered two perfect children, and Mama delivered three. I told him I am positive I shall never die until every red hair on my head has turned white."

"And what does he say?"

Glee's lashes fell. "He says one in four women

die on childbed, and he'll not have me being one of them." A sob escaped her, and she turned to Sally with weepy eyes. "Oh, Sally, you cannot imagine how good it is to lie with a man you love so desperately."

Oh, but Sally could. Though a virgin, she was no blushing maiden. She could never behold George's muscled body and not long to have it stretched beside hers, to feel his solidness beneath her sweeping hands, to want to take him inside of her. Thinking on it now caused her heart to drum.

Shaking her head, Glee walked toward the door. "Our conversation has been far too draining. Come, let's go to the Pump Room. Perhaps I shall see my wayward husband there, and you can scold him."

Glee excessively disliked having to leave Sally on just her second day in Bath, but Felicity had summoned Glee to nearby Winston Hall. And since Felicity was the eldest of the siblings, neither Glee nor George had ever possessed the backbone to defy her. Not that there had ever been any need to, since Felicity's judgment was unerring.

So now Glee found herself in the Morelands' library facing Felicity and a solemn George, with both doors leading into the chamber firmly closed behind the three of them.

"Pray, what is all this about?" Glee asked.

Felicity's eyes flashed in anger, and her hands flew to her waist, elbows pointed outward. "It's about George. We've all been patient with him in his grief." She turned narrowed eyes on him, and her voice softened. "Don't forget that I know what it is to lose a beloved spouse. I never wanted to love another man again. I had known love with Michael."

"You cannot compare Michael Harrison to Dianna!" George snapped. "No woman can ever take her place. No woman has ever been created who could be her equal."

"Be that as it may," Felicity said, "I've brought you here to tell you life goes on. Whether you ever remarry is irrelevant—though I do sincerely hope you will again know love. What is relevant, dearest brother of mine, is your children. And I'm persuaded your indifference toward them and your immature, selfish ways have to stop. We've said nothing to you up to this point because of your overwhelming grief, but I can no longer stand by and see your children so neglected."

"My children are not neglected! They have a very fine nurse who sees to all their needs."

"But they're already so handicapped, having no mother," Felicity said. "They need a father. And they need the influence of a woman of good birth. Though she's only four, it's time Georgette had a governess. She needs intercourse with a well-bred lady. As does little Sam."

Now Glee stepped forward, her green eyes flashing. "Are you even aware of the fact your son cannot speak? He's such a sad little fellow, with virtually no parents to love him."

George *was* unaware of the fact. "At what age do most children speak?" he asked.

"Your own daughter had an extensive vocabulary when she was two," Glee said, "and my daughter is already speaking in sentences though she is a week younger than Sam."

"For Christ's sake, the lad's not yet two. What do you expect?" George said.

Felicity interceded. "He'll be two next week. I'll grant you, boys speak later than girls. My sons did not speak as early as my nieces. Still, I'm concerned for little Sam."

"I'll thank you not to pity *my* son. His nurse tells me he's quite intelligent."

"I don't for a moment doubt his intelligence," Glee said. "It's his well-being I doubt."

"He's much larger than Georgette was at the same age," George countered.

"We're not saying Sam is *physically* neglected," Felicity said. "It's his emotional battering that worries us."

"My son is not battered!" These demmed sisters of his had no right to tell him how to raise his children! There was nothing wrong with his son. The boy was just shy. That was all. The lad's mother was shy, too. God, but he missed her. What had George ever done in his life to cause such unbearable sorrow to be heaped upon him?

"You're wrong," Glee said. "He's been raised as an orphan."

"So, if I hire a governess, you expect that woman to become a mother to my children?"

"'Twould be better than things are now," Felicity said. "Though best of all would be for you to remarry."

"That's out of the question," he said.

Felicity's voice gentled. "Believe me, I perfectly understand your feelings."

"No one's been in my shoes," George said bitterly.

An idea—a wonderful, brilliant idea—seized Glee. "George! Felicity! I have a solution to the dilemma."

"To what dilemma?" George asked.

"The dilemma of your children having no mother," Glee answered. "Sally could be their governess! She is already perfectly devoted to your children, and just yesterday she told me she wished to find a position as a teacher. This is infinitely bet-

ter because she's so excessively fond of little Sam—
and of Georgette, too."

"Sally Spenser?" George asked.

Glee put hands to hips. "Of course! What other
Sally dotes on your children?"

He shrugged. "Never thought of the niece of an
earl being a governess. Doesn't sound right."

"She's merely Lord Bankston's grandniece,"
Glee said.

Felicity walked up to George and settled a gentle arm around him. "Think on it, George. In the
meantime, Glee can make inquiries to see if Miss
Spenser would even consider being your children's governess."

Glee's thoughts were flitting through her brain
at a miraculous rate of speed. Not only would Sally
be perfect for the children, she would be good for
George, too. Not in the romantic sense, of course.
They weren't at all suited. In fact, they argued all
the time. But Sally, with her honest tongue, was
probably the only woman on earth who could handle George. If anyone could turn him around, it
would be Sally Spenser.

"I should wish for both of you to dine with
Blanks and me tonight. Miss Spenser is presently
my houseguest, George, and you will have the opportunity to see for yourself if you think she will
do."

Chapter 2

"You weren't gone very long," Sally said as Glee flew into the room without removing her hat.

"Though Winston Hall seems as if it's in the country, it's but three miles from Bath."

"Is everything all right there?" Sally asked.

Glee seemed distracted, then glanced up at Sally. "We—Felicity and I—are quite naturally concerned about George."

As was Sally. He was blazing a path of self-destruction. Just hearing his name mentioned in concerned sighs caused Sally's stomach to drop. Then it occurred to her that something might have happened to George, something even worse than losing his wife. Her heart began to thud in her chest. "Has anything happened to him?" Her voice croaked.

Glee spun around. "Oh no."

Sally inhaled. Why had Glee still not removed her hat?

"It's really quite lovely out today," Glee said. "Shall we stroll over to Crescent Fields?"

"Allow me to fetch my hat," Sally said.

A few minutes later the two ladies were strolling along Gay Street, hurried shoppers speeding past them.

"Felicity is especially concerned about George's children," Glee began. "She feels they need the influence of a genteel woman."

"I agree completely with her. Just yesterday it struck me how sad Georgette's face was when she asked you to plait her hair. It's not fair that those children don't have their own mother."

Glee pressed a gloved hand to her quivering mouth. "Oh, you shall break my heart."

"Every time I see George's children, it breaks my heart," Sally said solemnly.

"I told George how attached you are to his children." Glee slowed her pace and hesitated before she continued. "I also told him you were contemplating taking a position as a teacher."

Sally's heart sped up. "And what did he say?"

"He asked if I was speaking of Sally Spenser, for he could not believe the niece of an earl would go into service. You see, I suggested you for the position with his children."

Sally whirled around to face Glee, her eyes flashing in anger. "You did what?"

"I said you would be perfect for his children."

Sally could never consent to live under George's roof! Especially since she was so thoroughly in love with him. Besides, George would never have her. He was well aware of the abrasiveness of her personality. He ought to be. He had been the brunt of her criticism all too many times. No, she thought, shaking her head, George would never consent to have such a sharp-tongued she-devil under his roof. He preferred gentle souls like Dianna, who had never issued a disparaging remark in her entire life.

"The idea of being employed in your brother's household is absurd," Sally said. She stepped down off the pavement to cross the street but had to wait for a sedan chair carrying a frail, white-haired invalid to pass.

"Why is it so absurd?" Glee asked. "You've never hidden the fact of how attached you are to his children."

Sally hustled across the street. "I adore his children."

"You'd be good for them, too. Poor little Sam loves you above everyone, I do believe."

Tears began to prick at Sally's eyelids. She *did* love the precious little creature so! But living under his obstinate father's roof was out of the question. "You're making this very difficult for me," Sally said.

"Then why won't you consider it? For Sam's sake?"

"Because Lord Sedgewick would never have me. You know how we seem to collide with one another." It seemed funny to Sally that Glee had never guessed Sally's affection for her brother in all these years. Sally had been enamored of him since she had first visited Hornsby Manor when she was twelve. It was already obvious to Sally at that time that Glee worshipped her brother's best friend, Blanks. The corners of Sally's mouth turned down. Though both crushes had stood the test of time, only one of them had been reciprocated.

"That's why you'd be so very good for George. You're the only person who can unflinchingly tell him the error of his ways."

Sally gave a bitter laugh. "No man wishes to hear of his shortcomings."

"George will come around."

Come around? Then he had already nixed the idea of engaging her for his children? Though not surprised, Sally was hurt. She had her pride. She would *never* live under George's roof, even were he to fall on his knees and beg her.

Even if it meant losing the opportunity to swaddle Sam and Georgette in her love.

She had every assurance George would succeed in engaging a capable lady of genteel birth. The thought of it caused Sally's heart to sink. She hated the woman already. The woman would not only be able to spoil Georgette and Sam, she would also be able to see George every day. Sally swallowed hard. Would that it could have been she.

What if the lady George engaged was meanspirited? What if she did not love Sam and Georgette as Sally did? The thought was crushing.

But Sally had her pride. 'Twas all she had.

At dinner that night, all was amiable. Sally made it through every course without provoking George one single time. After dinner, when the men drank their port, the ladies retired to the drawing room and sat in a row on the silk brocade sofa, Sally in the middle.

"So, have you mentioned the post to Sally?" Felicity asked Glee.

Glee sighed. "I did. She's not interested."

Felicity turned to Sally, disappointment on her face. "But I know you are excessively fond of my brother's children."

Sally met her gaze. "That I cannot deny."

"She objects to their father, I believe," Glee interjected.

"I don't object to George, I mean, Lord Sedgewick, at all! I'll own that it appears I'm at daggers drawn with him more often than not, but I'm really quite fond of him." Her voice lowered. "In fact,

I've grown concerned for his welfare, as I know you two have."

Felicity took Sally's hand in hers. "Won't you please consider taking the position in George's household?"

Sally averted her gaze from Felicity's clear blue eyes. "There's the fact your brother does not want me. In fact, he does not even like me, I'll wager."

"How could he not love you?" Glee said.

Sally giggled. "Believe me. To Lord Sedgewick I'm nothing more than an opinionated shrew."

"I do believe you could influence him as no one else," Felicity said.

"She's right," Glee chimed in.

The door creaked open, and, her heart in her throat, Sally watched the gentlemen enter the drawing room. Though George was the shortest of the three men, he was still above average height. And there was no question in Sally's mind he was the most blatantly masculine of the three. There was a ruggedness about him that belied his privileged station in life. With his powerful chest and broad shoulders and bronzed skin, he looked as if he heaved heavy crates into the bow of a ship day in and day out.

Yet no man as impeccably dressed as the Viscount Sedgewick could know such labors. Sally's eyes ran from his stockings up the length of him, lingering over his powerful legs, which showed to advantage in dove-colored superfine breeches. And she swallowed hard. Despite that he was nine and twenty, his waist was as small as it was before he married. Her gaze came to rest on his square face and his casually styled golden hair. His teeth were as white as his highly starched cravat. She noticed, too, the alluring cleft that pinched his strong chin. His was a face she never tired of.

"Glee said we could play whist tonight," George said, "and I'm claiming Miss Spenser for my partner."

Glee shot an impatient look at her brother. "That's hardly fair to claim the best female player here for your partner, since you're already so skilled at whist."

"Moreland's skill is equal to mine," George said as he cast an apologetic glance at Blanks. "Sorry, old boy, but whist has never been your game."

Glee came to her husband's side and hooked her arm through his. "But, you must admit, Blanks is far better than you at billiards."

"And at riding, and at any number of pursuits," George said.

"You do shoot better," Blanks conceded.

"You and Sally just go ahead and play with Felicity and Thomas," Glee said. She looked up at her husband. "Blanks and I shall set up the chessboard. I'm so very happy to have him home tonight, I shall hoard him to myself."

George felt guilty for taking Blanks away from Glee so often. Both men had changed vastly since Dianna had died. Before her death, he and Blanks were the two most happily domesticated men in the kingdom. Now George couldn't bear to be at any of his residences, for all of them evoked memories of the happiness he and Dianna had shared there.

George suspected poor Blanks accompanied him everywhere for two reasons. The first was to keep George from killing himself. The second was to deny himself Glee's torturing presence. For Blanks, when in his cups, had confessed that he had vowed not to bed Glee for fear of losing her on childbed as George had lost Dianna.

As wretched as he felt for Glee, George didn't

want Blanks to impregnate her, either. He feared losing one more woman he loved.

He pulled out the chair for Miss Spenser, then sat down across from her. While they were waiting for Moreland, who was pouring himself a snifter of brandy, George felt compelled to make conversation with Miss Spenser.

"How long do you plan to stay in Bath?"

"Only for a few weeks," Sally answered. "What about you? Do you not have any plans to return to Hornsby Manor?"

He stiffened. He couldn't go back there. It was where he and Dianna had been happiest. Besides, he would go mad without the amusements of Bath. When he had Dianna, he had had no need of amusements. "Not in the foreseeable future."

"A pity."

There she goes again! What was the opinionated Miss Spenser going to chastise him about this time? "Why do you say that?"

"It is my belief that you conducted yourself with great maturity during the time you resided at Hornsby and turned the estate back to prosperity."

Why was the chit always right? Damn her. The superior Miss Spenser. Since he had left Hornsby, the coffers had begun to dry up again. Of course, it did not help that he had squandered a considerable amount of money on his recent hedonistic pursuits.

"Also, I think country life would be more agreeable for your children."

She *did* have opinions on everything! "A pity your life is so dull you have time to contemplate my actions so thoroughly."

A great sadness came over Miss Spenser's face. Really, he had overstepped the bounds of propriety. "Forgive me, Miss Spenser, 'twas a most unkind thing for me to say. I should be flattered that you care at all about my children and me." A moment later, he added, "Daresay my children need all the care they can get, or so my sisters tell me."

"Forgive me, my lord, for being quite unable to hold my tongue, but your children—especially your son—could use more caring from you. I only tell you this because I am so devoted to them. They both are extraordinary children."

Conflicting emotions of anger and pride surged through him. Anger at the outspoken Miss Spenser and pride in the children Dianna had borne him. He decided to ignore Miss Spenser's impertinence. "I suppose I should thank you for the pretty words about my offspring."

"I do not desire your thanks. I only spoke the truth."

That was the woman's problem! She was constantly blurting out the truth, no matter how offensive the truth was. Really, he did not know why Glee suffered the chit's company. Of course, Miss Spenser never chided Glee. Perhaps that was why his sister tolerated the brazen maid.

The Morelands joined them at the whist table, and George dealt the cards. After evaluating his hand, he watched his partner. She looked different tonight. Actually better than she usually looked. It was the hair. He always pictured the spinster with hair as thick and straight as a brush used to paint a barn. But tonight her blond hair smoothly waved. He had to admit it a vast improvement. Though he didn't know why she bothered attempting to make herself attractive. No man would ever have her. Too demmed disagreeable.

Out of the blue he remembered Glee's outrageous proposal to have Miss Spenser come to a position in his household. How bloody awkward that would be. Not as much because they clashed, but because of the difficulty of having an employee who was as highborn as he. How *would* one get on under such circumstances? Would he have to dine with her every night? What about Sunday services? Would she expect to sit in the family pew? Good Lord, there was much to contemplate before he was ready to engage a well-born lady for his children.

Not one time during the ensuing game did Miss Spenser berate him. In fact, she even complimented him on his skillful play. And when a particular rule was in dispute, she agreed with his interpretation of it. Which was a novelty. When she had been his partner in the past, she had argued with him about rules. But not tonight. Tonight she was being very agreeable.

She even smiled readily, and she was in possession of a very fine smile. Deep dimples on both cheeks. With her hair curled, she actually looked rather pretty. Of course, she was much too thin. And her skin was indelicately dark for a lady, but he thought he rather liked it.

He and Miss Spenser could not seem to lose a hand all night, and he was quite pleased with himself. Tonight had been far more entertaining than sitting in the card room at the Upper Assembly Rooms and losing his ass. Perhaps he really should listen to his sisters. What would it hurt if he stayed in, say, one or two nights a week?

"Oh, George," Felicity said, "this has been so exceedingly fun. We must do it again soon."

"At Winston Hall?" Thomas asked, his glance darting to George.

"I should love to." George stood up and bowed at his partner. "And, Miss Spenser, I should be honored if you would do me the goodness of being my partner again next time."

"I am the one who would be honored, my lord," she said.

To Blanks's dismay, George opted not to go out later that night. "I believe I'll go on home and get a good night's sleep for a change," George announced.

"You can't be serious," Blanks said, his brows drawn.

"Oh, but I am."

George did go home and go to bed. But he was unable to sleep. He kept thinking of how difficult it would be to find a more qualified woman than Miss Spenser to help with his children.

Chapter 3

Both of his children turned sharply when George opened the door to the nursery. Georgette dropped her cat and flew toward her father. "Papa! Papa! What are you doing here?" she asked as he swept her up into his arms.

"I've come to give you a piggyback ride." He gave her fair cheek a loud kiss, then hoisted her on top of his shoulders. Georgette began to giggle as her father carried her from one end of the vast nursery to the other. Even the children's nurse, Hortense, giggled at the sight of Lord Sedgewick behaving the buffoon.

On their second trip to the window, where they turned around, George's glance connected with his son's pensive little face. Sam was the only one in the room who was not giggling. The boy backed into the wall as if he were afraid of the large man who was playing the nadcock.

George set down his daughter, then turned to Sam. "Should you like a ride on my shoulders, too?" He felt as if he were addressing a stranger. In fact, George was not sure if he *had* ever spoken directly to the boy before.

George was still reeling from yesterday's unexpected news that his son did not speak. It had come as a complete surprise. More than that, such a piece of information was most alarming. Was something the matter with the boy? He eyed his son, who was reluctant to give a response.

The lad's lower lip quivered, and his green eyes widened. Finally, Sam nodded.

George bent down and picked up the boy. He had never before held his son in his arms. George was surprised that Sam felt a great deal heavier than Georgette even though he was much shorter and much younger than she. The lad was rock solid. George hoisted him on top of his shoulders, careful to keep a tight hold—not that he needed to; Sam's chubby little hands clutched his father's hands with a death grip. That the boy had enough sense to be afraid of heights indicated to George that he was possessed of intelligence.

As soon as George began to charge across the nursery floor, Sam began to giggle. Relief spread over George. At least there was nothing wrong with the boy's ability to make noise. Felicity was most likely right, then, about boys talking later than girls. That's all there was to it.

When he finished and put the boy back down, Sam continued to smile. George found such an expression completely uncharacteristic for his somber son.

Now that George had brightened the day for his children, he could leave. But, oddly, he found he did not wish to leave. His thoughts flashed back to his own nursery days and the infrequent times when his father would visit George and his sisters in the Hornsby nursery. George had especially loved it when his father read *The Life and Perambulation of a Mouse* to him. George strolled across the wooden floors to the little cabinet on the nursery's west wall to see if the book might have made the trip from Hornsby Manor. He thumbed through a handful of moral tales before he came to the familiar, dog-eared book that was narrated by a mouse. He picked it up, then turned back to face his children.

"Should you wish for me to read you the mouse's story?" he asked.

Georgette's eyes lit up. "Oh yes, Papa, that would be ever so nice!"

George went to sit on the big rocking chair and patted his knee for Georgette. She hopped up and sat on his right thigh, snuggling her face into her father's chest.

Then George looked at Sam's solemn face and patted his other knee.

Sam looked from the knee back to his father for a moment before slowly mounting the proffered leg. George hauled him up and hooked a hand around Sam's waist, then began to read. He held the book in his right hand and requested his daughter to turn the pages for him.

As he read, George could not see Georgette's face, but he clearly saw that Sam was mesmerized by the story and was unable to tear his eyes away from the illustrations.

When George finished the story, the nursery door eased opened. George looked up and into the face of Miss Spenser. She looked considerably different than she had the night before when her hair had hung in blond ringlets. Today it once again looked like a paintbrush. In fact, she looked like the Sally Spenser he had known nearly half his life.

To George's astonishment, Sam jumped down off his knee and rushed over to Miss Spenser, holding his little arms up to her. Could that be his shy son? In his almost two years of life, Sam had never before displayed so much excitement. At least, not in front of his father. It rather disappointed George to admit to himself that Hortense had never been able to elicit such an enthusiastic response in the children who had been in her charge their entire lives.

George was equally astonished at the look of utter delight that washed across Miss Spenser's face as she lifted Sam into her arms and nudged her face into his golden curls, where she dropped a kiss.

Then she looked up at George. "Hullo, my lord. I hadn't expected to see you here."

"I'm not often here. But I can see that you're no stranger to my children's nursery."

Sam bounced in her arms, pointing to his father.

"Yes, I see your papa," Miss Spenser cooed at Sam.

But the babe vigorously shook his head.

Apparently, it was not his father Sam was pointing at. "Oh, I understand, you little scamp. You want me to rock you." Miss Spenser gave George an apologetic glance. "I'm afraid you've got the chair where Sam and I always rock."

George chuckled as he vacated the chair for Miss Spenser. "I can see my son has no need to learn how to speak, for he communicates exceedingly well without words. Tell me, is he accustomed to getting his way so easily?"

It was Hortense, not Miss Spenser, who answered. "No, yer lordship. Far be it from me than to coddle the children. 'Tis strict discipline that

children need." She set her hands to her hips and
gave a reproachful glance in Sam's direction. "And
I've told Master Sam a thousand times he has to
speak in order to get what he wants from me. I'll
have none of that wretched pointing."

George nodded at the nurse. How could it be
that he had never noticed how stern the middle-
aged woman was with his children?

Georgette picked up her cat and she, too, walked
up to Miss Spenser. "Papa read us the mouse story
you always read to us."

Miss Spenser slid a glance at George. "I first
read it at Hornsby, you know."

Then she must have known it had been a great
favorite with him and his siblings. How thoughtful
of Miss Spenser to introduce it to his children. A
pity their own father had failed to do so.

Miss Spenser stroked Georgette's dark hair. "How
pretty you look today, pet."

Georgette's face brightened. Did Hortense ever
say pretty things to his precious daughter? Most
likely not. The plain nurse was probably of the
opinion that such comments were far too indulgent.

Next Miss Spenser addressed Fluffy. "And how
very well fed you look today, Mister Fluff." She
looked at Georgette with twinkling eyes. "I expect
your kitty cat cleaned his bowl today."

Georgette giggled. "Just like Mr. Whiskers in the
story you made up for us."

Sam had removed one of his shoes. Now, why
had his son gone and done that? George wondered.

He was soon to find out.

Miss Spenser grabbed Sam's big toe and began
to recite the *This Little Piggy* game.

And Sam squealed with delight. As soon as Miss Spenser finished, Sam once more offered her his foot, this time with a commanding grunt. "You must say 'please,' " Miss Spenser said firmly.

George watched intently. Would this slip of a woman succeed with Sam where no one else had?

Sam shook his head and pointed his little foot at her with another commanding grunt.

Miss Spenser lifted his foot to her lips and kissed the top of it. "I will not do the piggy game until you say 'please.' " Though her words were stern, her voice was kind.

Surely the lad could say one little word. It was clever of Miss Spenser to know that single words had to come before sentences. And wasn't it clever of her to bribe his son into speaking? A pity Hortense was not as clever as Miss Spenser. But, then, few people were. Glee had often remarked on her friend's intelligence. Why, Miss Spenser could even read and write Greek!

Finally, Sam issued a sound. It wasn't the word *please*, but it was a single syllable with a strong E sound.

"Very good, sweetheart," Miss Spenser said to Sam as she proceeded to repeat the piggy game.

As George stood there watching his children gathered close to Miss Spenser, he realized Glee and Felicity were right. Miss Spenser was the perfect person for his children.

But how was it his sisters already knew what George had never even guessed? For how long had the spinster been paying such visits to his children? And why would a young lady of excellent birth prefer to be in his nursery instead of parading around the Pump Room on some buck's arm? It all seemed very peculiar to him.

"Miss Spenser," he said, "could I persuade you to join me and the children for a romp in the park?"

"Today?"

He nodded.

"What park, my lord?"

"Sydney Gardens, I think."

"The children do love it there," she answered.

How in the bloody hell did she know more about *his* children than he did?

She moved to get up. "I should be honored to accompany you. 'Tis quite lovely out today."

He nodded at Hortense. "You're dismissed."

Before she left the room, Hortense peered at Miss Spenser through narrowed eyes.

The two adults and two little ones set out on foot from the Sedgewick town house. All except for Sam, who was carried in Miss Spenser's arms. George had attempted to carry the lad, but Sam clutched Miss Spenser frantically and buried his face into her shoulder.

George held Georgette's hand, and whenever they happened upon an acquaintance of his, he was rather proud to display his lovely daughter. How he loved to gaze upon her! It was like having a piece of Dianna back.

By the time they reached Pulteney Bridge, George insisted on taking Sam from Miss Spenser. The poor lady's arms must be aching from the heavy load.

He was rather embarrassed that the lad not only clung to Miss Spenser but also seemed afraid of his own father. The boy would have to learn not to thwart him. With a stern reprimand, he yanked Sam from Miss Spenser. He was about to chastise the boy when a strange feeling came over him. It was he, not the boy, who should be chastised. For he had been an absent father. Naturally the lad would be more comfortable with Miss Spenser than with him.

George met Miss Spenser's disapproving gaze. And it humbled him. "I'm afraid I've been a wretched father. The poor lad is likely terrified of me."

Any well-bred young lady would have attempted to allay his words. Any well-bred lady except the authoritarian Miss Spenser. "Then you must rectify your absences," she said in a tone a schoolmistress would use with one of her pupils.

No woman—save his bloody sisters—had ever spoken to him in so didactic a manner. Why, there were more than a dozen women in Bath this very week who would address him with pure adoration. Not even Dianna had ever thought to chastise him, even though she could have used him as wet clay in her hands. Yet this skinny spinster with straggly hair spoke to him as if *she* were his elder sister. He had a mind to put her in her place, to tell her not to poke her nose where it was not wanted.

But he could not. For she *was* wanted here. His children obviously adored her. Even if he did not.

They crossed Pulteney Bridge and soon found themselves at Sydney Gardens, where a dozen nurses in starched aprons oversaw their young charges who were running and playing and making believe on the green lawns.

George set Sam down, and the toddler immediately began to run as fast as his little legs would carry him, his squeals of delight trailing behind him.

Miss Spenser smiled up at George. Those dimples of hers were frightfully attractive. He found he could no longer be angry with her.

Georgette ran after her brother and easily overtook him. "You can't catch me," she taunted.

George chuckled to himself, then offered Miss Spenser his crooked arm. "Shall we take a stroll while the children play?"

She hesitated a moment before slipping her arm through his. "This has really been such fun," she said as they began to walk the paths close to the children. "I shall come to admire you dreadfully."

"And that would be bad?"

She tossed back her head and laughed. "Oh no, my lord, 'twould be quite good, actually. You see, I've lamented ever since . . . since her ladyship died, that you've not been closer to your children. They need you much more now that they don't have a mother."

So Miss Spenser's intelligence extended to matters other than knowledge found in books. She was a keen observer of human nature. Demmed female. She made him feel most inferior. And no woman had ever done that before. He swallowed hard. "I've had other . . . things occupying me since my wife died."

"Everyone knows how devastated you were, my lord," she said in a sympathetic voice. "I certainly do not fault you for your grief. I only pray that time has lessened it so that now you will be able to address your children's needs more than your own."

Demmed impertinent female! So she thought him a selfish lout of a father! Like hell she didn't fault him for his grief! If that sanctimonious spinster had ever possessed the capacity to love as he had loved Dianna, she would have some idea of the pain he had endured, because no man would ever have reciprocated her affection. No man could be attracted to such an opinionated, outspoken woman who didn't even have the promise of a dowry.

"Forgive me," she said softly. "I had no right. I'm

sorry I implied . . . I'm sorry for what I said. Please know that any offensive remarks were the result of my excessive fondness for your children."

He patted her hand. "I understand. It's rather as if you're one of my sisters. After all, we've been acquainted half our lives."

She looked pensively at him. "Though I hold you in great affection, I've never thought of you as a brother, my lord."

Great affection, my foot! Of course she did not feel toward him as she did toward her brothers. She loved her brothers, and George was quite convinced she despised him.

He drew in a deep breath. As much as it pained him to admit it, he had come to decide his children did indeed need Miss Spenser. And he was determined to have her. Even if he could barely tolerate the young lady, and even if he had no idea how to go about hiring her or keeping her under his roof. He again patted her hand that rested on his arm. "I have a proposition I wish to put before you, Miss Spenser."

She gazed up at him with an arched brow.

"My sister tells me you may be seeking employment."

She did not answer for a moment. Then, in a cracking voice, she said, "Yes, I shall."

"I shan't beat about the bush, Miss Spenser. I wish for you to come into my household and take charge of my children. They obviously adore you. I have no experience in such matters, but I'm prepared to do whatever it takes to entice you to come."

His stomach jumped nervously as he awaited her reply.

It was a long time in coming. "My lord, I cannot give you a response today. Your offer was completely unexpected. I must have time to think about it. There's no question of my affection for your children, but I must come to a decision which is beneficial to my own future."

"Of course." She wouldn't come. She hated him too much. She wanted no part of a future fraught with bickering between herself and her employer. He sighed again. "If you were to come into my employment"—he could not bring himself to say *service* for she was, after all, the niece of an earl—"I should attempt to make myself more agreeable to you."

She laughed. "That's a very kind thing to say, my lord. Especially since I well realize how difficult that would be for you. Because of my abrasiveness."

Now he laughed, too.

Chapter 4

Sally was touched that Lord Sedgewick insisted on walking her back to Blankenship House. He really must have a strong desire for her to come into his service, a prospect she found as flattering as it was perplexing.

When she arrived at Blankenship House, Glee was entertaining callers, and since Sally had no desire to make pleasantries while still trembling from Lord Sedgewick's proposal, she cried off, saying she had letters to write.

In the lovely room Glee and Blanks had provided for her, Sally flung her pelisse on the satin counterpane, stormed to the gilded vanity, and gazed into her mirror. Just as she suspected, she looked wretched. She should have curled her hair this morning. Had she known she would see *him* today, she would have.

But, she reminded herself, she could rest easy that he had no interest in her as a woman. Most likely, he had no interest in any woman. Any living woman.

Therein lay her dilemma. Though the viscount would never think of her as anything but a sister, she was not immune to his virile attractiveness. She could never be with him and not have the fact of his undeniable masculinity slammed into her. She turned away from the mirror and strolled to the window. In a town house, a window either looked out over a street or over an alley. A pity her window looked over the empty alley.

She turned away and came to sit on the edge of her bed. Closing her eyes, she visualized Lord Sedgewick as he had looked when he offered her the position in his household. The square cut of his jaw, the deep cleft in his chin, the masculinity in his deep voice, all these things had the power to reduce her to an adoring idiot.

She tried to remember the exact words he had used. The chief enticement Lord Sedgewick had dangled in front of her—having charge of both his children—was tempting, to be sure. She had not been able to bear the idea that another woman would supplant her, and she had worried that the other woman would not love the children as dearly as she loved them.

Sally also reveled in the notion of turning out that grim-faced old stick, Hortense. The children had enough to overcome without having such an overbearing curmudgeon lording herself over them.

Sally smiled as she thought about the many fun things she could do with the children. She should put aside her feelings toward their father and tell Lord Sedgewick she would be honored to be given the responsibility of his children's care. After all, they needed her, and they loved her. As she loved them.

That she could even hesitate over the decision made her feel wretchedly guilty.

But she must make a rational decision, not one based on emotion. If she were not acquainted with Georgette and Sam, what would she do? No question about it, being a governess was far more flexible than teaching in Miss Worth's School for Young Ladies. Her exposure to society and her choice in clothes alone would be much broader were she to accept his lordship's offer. She had no doubts that Glee would continue to treat her as a cherished friend, rather than as her brother's servant. In his household, too, Sally would be treated with the respect due to one of her station—except, of course, when she was embroiled in one of her arguments with Lord Sedgewick. For despite his promise to get along better with her, she knew she was vinegar and he was water, and the two could never mix.

She was in an utter quandary. Were she to follow her heart, it would only be trampled on by the man she had always loved. She was not sure she could stand to be close to him, knowing a love between them could never be. At least if she went to Miss Worth's she could attempt to put memories of Lord Sedgewick behind her. If that were possible. Even during the three years of his marriage, she had never been able to gaze upon his golden good looks without suffering pain. Pain for that which could never be.

Then a most alarming notion crowded into her brain as she sat there on the bed, kicking off her satin slippers. Were she to turn him down and he engaged another genteel woman . . . what if the *other* woman had designs on George, er, Lord Sedgewick? What if the other woman seduced him?

Sally's heart drummed madly. How she detested that woman who did not even exist! She could not allow such a circumstance to occur.

Of course, there were no assurances that when his heart mended, George would not remarry. A woman of good birth who possessed both beauty and a hefty purse might well capture his heart. Sally needed to face this likely possibility.

Now, though, she would put up her hair in curl papers because she would be going to the Upper Assembly Rooms tonight. And even though Lord Sedgewick no longer danced, he did come there to try his luck at hazard and cards, and he did partake of refreshments. And she wished to look her best in case he happened to glance upon her.

Since her husband now preferred the card room with George over dancing with his wife, Glee no longer cared for dancing. But for Sally's sake, she suffered stepped-on toes from her husband's chums, Appleton and the twins, who made certain neither she nor Sally lacked for partners at the Assembly Rooms that night.

Sally was well aware that Glee had hopes Sally could live happily ever after with one of Blanks's bachelor friends. They were all perfectly amiable, but thankfully none of them had yet to become enamored of her. Which was a very good thing, since she would never have been able to return their ardor.

After the tea break, Sally saw Lord Sedgewick. He strode past the card room, which was quite a departure from his usual habits. Her gaze riveted on him, she continued to watch his progress. He was coming to the ballroom! Her heart began to beat erratically, her hand flying to smooth her hair. Not that she expected him to give her a glance.

But to her complete surprise, he walked straight to her and bowed. "Would you do me the goodness of standing up with me this set, Miss Spenser?"

Her eyes round, she nodded. Lord Sedgewick was undoubtedly foxed. She could smell the port on him, and she could see the glassiness in his reddened eyes. And it hurt her dreadfully whenever she discovered he was back soaking, soaking to mend his wounded heart.

Her stomach flipped when he took her hand and possessively led her to the dance floor. When they faced each other in the longway, he nodded. "May I say you look lovely tonight, Miss Spenser? I rather prefer your hair curled."

She vowed to curl it the rest of her days. Even if his drinking upset her, she could not deny that the effect it had upon him left her very merry indeed.

When the set was finished, he put a hand to her waist and whispered into her ear. "Oblige me by strolling the octagon with me."

Too nervous to find her voice, she nodded and let him lead her to the adjoining chamber. When they reached the octagon, he offered her his arm, and she placed her hand upon it, fervently hoping he would not notice its trembling.

"I am prepared to do whatever it takes to secure you for my children," he began.

She had not known he valued his children so highly he would stoop to beg the outspoken Miss Spenser to come and live in his home. "Surely, my lord, you have not given your proposal significant reflection. Have you not considered how . . . how forthright I am in my . . . my criticism of you? I am persuaded you could not above half tolerate my tart tongue."

He threw his head back and laughed.

Which once again reminded her of his inebriated condition. "Even tonight," she said, "I am powerless to prevent myself from chiding you."

He gazed at her with dancing eyes and a crooked smile. "Chiding me for what?"

"For drinking so heartily when the evening is still so young."

He came to an abrupt stop and gave her an icy glare. "My drinking is none of your concern, ma'am."

Despite that her breath grew ragged, she forced a retort. "As your children's champion, I should be concerned over anything that would lessen your ability to be an exemplary father."

He continued to glare at her. "Am I given to believe that if you came into my service you would intend to govern me in the same manner you would the children?"

She couldn't answer him. For neither as his children's governess—nor as his sisters' friend—had she the right to berate Lord Sedgewick. But, as his children's governess, she knew she would never be able to hold her scathing tongue.

"Answer me, Miss Spenser," he said harshly.

"I have no right to reprimand your behavior, my lord."

He laughed a bitter laugh. "But you would wish to do so, would you not, Miss Spenser?" He gazed at her with watery, red eyes.

She slowly nodded.

"Then I suppose you are right," he snapped. "Such an arrangement would never work."

Her heart sank. The matter was now out of her hands, and she wished it were not. She instantly regretted she would never have the pleasure of being governess to his children, that she would never have the opportunity to live under his roof, to be able to see his face that she loved so dearly every day.

He offered her a stiff arm. Her eyes became watery as he walked her back to Glee and took his leave.

Immediately, she worried that in his rage—and in his cups—he would storm to the card room and play foolishly and lose everything he possessed. And it would all be her fault.

She almost went after him, to try to change his mind, but she realized it was for the best that she not come into his service.

When the Assembly Rooms closed at eleven, Glee went to the card room to find Blanks but was told he and George had left. "Oh dear," Glee said to Sally, "I suppose the stakes weren't high enough here for them. I do hope my brother doesn't lose his head."

Sally set a gentle hand on Glee's arm. Glee had no fears Blanks would lose his fortune, for her husband's pockets were enormously deep, but Sally knew Glee was upset that Blanks was spiraling downward with George. There was little doubt that the two men would drink heavily and game heavily well into the morning. A pity. Both men had been such happy homebodies . . . before Dianna died.

Neither Sally nor Glee talked during the carriage ride back to Blankenship House. Glee was as morose as Sally, who took little consolation in the fact she and George had come to the right decision. Why could she not have taken the position and kept her mouth closed? Her wretched tongue had ruined everything.

The following morning Sally wrote her letter of application to Miss Worth's and, with heavy heart, posted it. Since she knew from Glee that Blanks— and therefore George—had not come home until very late, Sally decided to go see the babies. She had no fears of having to face their father.

On the way to their town house she stopped and bought a comfit for each child. When she arrived in the nursery, the children flew into her arms. She

bent down and hugged each of them, then gave
them their sweet. From the corner of her eye she
saw Hortense's disapproving glare.

" 'Twill make 'em sick," the sourpuss said.

Sally turned to her and smiled graciously. "Should
you wish to take off an hour or so, I would be happy
to mind the children." A pity The Curmudgeon
could not permanently leave, Sally thought, though
surely Hortense must hold the children in deep affection. After all, they had been in her care since
the day they were born.

"I believe I shall. I've plenty to occupy me," Hortense said as she made her way toward the door.

Once Sam finished his comfit—leaving fudgy
smudges around his mouth—he came to the rocker
and in his wordless way demanded Sally sit there
and hold him.

She laughed as she sat down and hauled him on
her lap, dabbing his face with her handkerchief,
then kissing his clean cheek.

The first thing he did was pull off his shoe.

"You're such a goose," she said good-naturedly.
She kissed the top of his head before she began to
play the piggy game.

In the meantime, Georgette came to giggle at
Sally's side. "Remember when I was little, and you
played piggies with me?" the girl said when Sally
finished. "You're my very favorite aunt, even if you
aren't truly my aunt."

Sally leaned over and kissed Georgette's little al-
abaster cheek. "I declare, that's the nicest thing
anyone has ever said to me. And now I shall tell
you a secret." She lowered her voice to a whisper.
"You are my very favorite little girl, and I think
your papa is the luckiest man on earth to have you
for his daughter."

Georgette beamed. "We had such fun yesterday

with Papa. I wish we could go to Syndy Gardens again today."

Sally smiled at the girl's mispronunciation. "I don't think I can manage taking you all the way to Sydney Gardens today—since your brother is too little to walk that far—but I daresay we can walk to Crescent Fields."

Georgette clapped her hands. "Can we go now?"

"You're to say *may we go now,* love," Sally gently reprimanded. "And yes, my pet, we'll go now." With Sam still in her arms, Sally stood up and bent her face to his. "Would you like to go bye-bye?"

He vigorously nodded his little head and pointed toward the door.

Just before they reached the Royal Crescent of like-fronted Georgian town houses, Sally thought a woman walking in her direction looked remarkably like the pretty Miss Johnson who had gone to school with Sally and Glee. As the well-dressed young lady drew closer, Sally was certain she was Miss Johnson, who had not been in Bath in a good while. Sally drew in her breath. The self-centered Miss Johnson had never been a great favorite of Sally's.

As they came face to face, Miss Johnson's brows lowered. "I did not know you had children! Indeed, I did not even know you had married!"

"Oh, these are not my children," Sally said with a laugh. "They're Lord Sedgewick's."

At the mention of George's name, a look of sympathy swept over Miss Johnson's lovely face. "Oh, the poor little motherless children."

Sally wished people would not speak so in front of Sam and Georgette.

Miss Johnson fell into step with them. "Where are you going?"

"I'm taking the children to Crescent Fields."

"A lovely day for an outing."

It looked as if, invited or not, Miss Johnson intended to accompany them. "How long have you been in Bath?" Sally asked her.

"Mama and I arrived quite late last night. Papa will join us next week. We've taken the Corrianders' town house. Do you know it?"

Of course Sally knew it. It was one of the finest houses in Bath. Miss Johnson's family was flush with riches but poor in pedigree, a situation that Miss Johnson had been encouraged to rectify by marriage. Sally had always thought the young lady clung to Glee because the Sedgewicks were an old, aristocratic family—exactly what Miss Johnson wished to marry into. She had thrown herself at George for as long as Sally could remember.

"Actually, I was on my way to pay a call on Glee," Miss Johnson said.

"I'm her guest."

Miss Johnson lowered her voice. "Tell me, what of poor Lord Sedgewick? I expect a man as handsome and as titled as he has remarried by now."

"Lord Sedgewick appears no better than he did two years ago when he lost his wife."

"Oh, the poor dear."

Glee was not convinced of Miss Johnson's sincerity.

"What the poor man needs," Miss Johnson continued brightly, "is a woman to make him forget."

And Sally perceived that the attractive, wealthy Miss Johnson fancied herself just the woman to snare him! Sally would dearly love to scratch out her eyes. "No woman could ever replace the late Lady Sedgewick," Sally said. Which, unfortunately, was true.

Miss Johnson affected a thoughtful expression.

"No, I suppose not. It would take a completely different type of woman to . . . to take Lord Sedgewick's mind off his departed wife. Since the first Lady Sedgewick was possessed of dark hair, I believe his next wife shall be blond!"

And, it just so happened Miss Johnson was possessed of *curly* blond hair. Sally fought an overwhelming urge to stuff her handkerchief into Miss Johnson's mouth. A more scheming, calloused, selfish female she had never known. "And since Dianna was gentle," Sally said, "I suppose the next Lady Sedgewick will have to be . . . loud?" Sally smiled slyly at her former friend.

Miss Johnson directed a haughty "harrumph" at Sally.

When they reached the park, Sally set Sam down, and he and Georgette began to play tag. Poor little Sam, Sally observed, still had not figured out that he could never catch up with his sister.

Sally and Miss Johnson went to sit upon a bench and discovered another old friend of theirs there. The bookish Miss Arbuckle sat reading a periodical.

"I declare, it's Miss Arbuckle," Sally said with genuine friendliness. For she had always admired the meek Miss Arbuckle.

The young lady, who wore spectacles, greeted them shyly.

"What are you reading?" Sally asked.

A smile came over her face. "It's the newest treatise by Jonathan Blankenship."

"Oh, Glee hasn't told me of it," Sally said. Poor Glee had too much unpleasantness on her mind of late to think of her brother-in-law's newest work in the *Edinburgh Review.*

"I didn't know you were in town, Miss Johnson," Miss Arbuckle said.

"We've only just arrived. I do hope we can all get

together at the Assembly Rooms. Tell me, how is company in Bath at the present?"

Miss Arbuckle shrugged.

"A bit thin, I should say," Sally answered.

The women chatted for half an hour before Sally stood up. "I really must get the children back. Their nurse will be worried."

"I'll come along with you," Miss Johnson said.

She just wants to see Lord Sedgewick, Sally mused. Where Sally's adoration of him had always been hidden, Miss Johnson's had always been overt.

When they reached the town house, Sally turned to say farewell, but Miss Johnson would not be denied a chance to see Lord Sedgewick.

"I believe I'll just come on in with you, then we can walk together to Blankenship House," Miss Johnson said.

They returned the children to the nursery. With great sadness, Sally kissed them good-bye. Would this be her last visit with them? She could be summoned to Miss Worth's any day now. She squeezed the children a bit tighter than usual. "Be good, little darlings," she said as she left the room, a tear slipping from the corner of her eye.

She and Miss Johnson quietly descended the stairs. When they reached the bottom, Sally heard the closing of an upstairs door and glanced up and into the sullen face of Lord Sedgewick, who had not seen her. His haggard looks fairly took her breath away. He had not shaved, and dark shadows hung under his eyes. He looked wretched. No doubt Miss Johnson had mistaken him for a servant for she was already out the door.

Not wanting him to know she saw him, Sally quickly turned away and left the house, her heart heavier than ever.

Chapter 5

Good lord, but he had behaved abominably at the Assembly Rooms the night before. George winced as he drew open the velvet library draperies and came to sit in front of his desk. His plan was to look over the ever increasing stack of tradesmen's bills, but the tumult raging within him pulled his thoughts elsewhere.

As much as he hated to admit it, the sanctimonious spinster had been right. Being three sheets to the wind before the clock struck nine was appallingly bad form for a man of his years.

'Twas one thing to get bosky when one was with one's fun-loving friends. 'Twas quite another to drink oneself into oblivion in the middle of the afternoon in the privacy of one's own library. But that is just what he had done. And his wretched head was paying dearly today.

As satisfying as it had been to take the children to Sydney Gardens the day before, it had also painfully reminded him of how much his children had missed by not having a mother. They clearly adored Sally Spenser, and, more importantly, they needed the genteel young woman.

If being reminded of his—and his children's—unbearable loss wasn't enough to send him to the liquor cabinet, the discovery that the nurse he had long trusted so implicitly was nothing more than an unfeeling, dogmatic dragon inundated him with feelings of guilt. So, like a cad still at Oxford, he had drowned himself in drink.

A lot of good that would do his children. He thought of his sweet little Georgette, and his heart physically ached for love of her. She deserved a better father.

She especially deserved Miss Spenser. He could search the kingdom high and low and never find a lady better qualified than Miss Spenser. Not only was she of impeccable lineage, but she was possessed of a keen mind, too. Most importantly, she truly loved Georgette—and the boy, too.

Now George had gone and offended Miss Spenser. No sooner had he told her he would do whatever it took to secure her for his children than he had told her what a bloody bad idea it was. A fine lout he must have appeared. Was he so weak a man that he was threatened by the well-meaning mouth of a spinster of but two and twenty years?

There was nothing to do but to swallow his diminishing pride and beg the lady's forgiveness. He should be prepared to do whatever it took to secure her for his children.

At the very least, he should be able to tolerate her didactic ways. After all, she only spouted off so because of her affection for the children. And for him, he admitted reluctantly. He knew she was truthful when she told him she had always held him in great affection. Why else would she beg that he change his wayward ways? A simpleton could see that he was doing his best to follow Dianna into the grave. And what would that do to his children? He ought to admire Miss Spenser for caring at all for him. Truth be told, he could not understand why she—or anyone—would.

For the sake of his motherless children, he would have to swallow humble pie.

He reached across the oak desk and took up his plume in order to enumerate a list of concessions he would grant Miss Spenser. He had to leave no consideration unaddressed. The lady must be given to understand how desperately he needed her and how important it was to him and the children that she come to live with them.

First, he had to assure Miss Spenser of his sincerity in wanting her. He began to write. Miss Spenser's opinions would always be solicited. She would have to be assured she would never be treated as a servant but as a treasured member of the family. She would not be given the title of governess, because that is not what he wished her to be. She would be a *companion* to his children, a mother figure, so to speak. She would be given her own chamber in the family wing. She would, he paused as he wrote, take her meals with the master of the family.

With regards to the children . . . Miss Spenser would have complete authority over them. That authority would extend to the hiring and dismissing of any employees who would interface with his children. A nurse. A future governess. Even a drawing master.

What of financial compensation? He set down his pen as he thought. Miss Spenser would be expected to dress as the well-connected lady she was, and would be at liberty to make purchases to assure that she dressed as a member of a viscount's family. The bills for her wardrobe, of course, would be sent to him. In addition, he was prepared to settle her with one hundred fifty pounds a year. He swallowed hard as he took up the pen and continued to write. An exorbitant sum, to be sure—as much as all his servants put together got and then some.

Then an idea struck him, and he put down his plume, a frown on his face. He got up from his desk and began to pace the library's Turkey rug, shaking his head. What a bloody idiot he had been! Indeed, even his usually wise sisters had been exceptionally foolish to encourage him to engage Miss Spenser for his children.

Miss Spenser could not be allowed to live under his roof! Think of what the gossips would say. She was an unmarried lady. The niece of an earl. And he, the Viscount Sedgewick, was an unmarried man. No proper lady would ever give consideration to a position of such perceptible intimacy. Especially in light of the reputation he had earned in his bachelor days before his marriage to Dianna. Indeed, he thought with shame, even in his grief, he had not been without the physical comforts offered by women of loose morals.

He shook his head ruefully. No respectable lady would ever consent to his proposal.

What was he to do? Except for Dianna's hand in marriage, he had never wanted anything more than he wanted Miss Spenser. For his children. It was imperative that he secure her. If his children could not have their own mother, then Miss Spenser was the next best thing.

A sobering thought struck him like a slap in the face. There was something he could do! Of course, he had no guarantees that Miss Spenser would look favorably upon this new, bizarre proposal. The girl, after all, ran rather contrary to what was expected of a young lady. Fact was, there was nothing she could do that would surprise him.

His heart beating erratically, he settled on this novel scheme. 'Twas, after all, the only logical thing to do to secure Miss Spenser for his children for the rest of their lives.

He would simply have to marry her!

As distasteful as was the idea of anyone replacing Dianna, George was willing to go through with it. After all, there was no hope for another love match for him, for he would never again meet the likes of Dianna. No matter what the cost to himself, he owed it to his children to secure Miss Spenser for their mother.

Surely the chit would look favorably upon the prospect of becoming Lady Sedgewick. A woman of neither beauty nor fortune could never hope for a better offer.

And it wasn't as if he would be robbing her of a love match. It was doubtful any man would ever desire the outspoken, opinionated Miss Spenser for a wife. He would actually be rescuing her from spinsterhood.

Of course, he would have to make it clear to her that it wouldn't be a *real* marriage. Dianna was the wife of his heart, and no woman could ever supplant her. Then, too, the prospect of bedding Miss Spenser held no allure whatsoever. In every other way, though, Miss Spenser would be treated with the honor and respect due his wife and due a woman of Miss Spenser's station.

Quite satisfied with himself, George decided to visit Blankenship House that very afternoon and present his proposal to Miss Spenser.

* * *

When he arrived at his sister's house, it was assumed he was calling for Blanks.

"No," George said to his sister, "it's Miss Spenser whom I should wish to see."

Glee glanced from him, past that dreadful young woman whose father was a sausage merchant or some such, to Sally Spenser. Miss Spenser, who was not as pretty as the sausage merchant's daughter but infinitely more gracious, stepped forward.

"Would you do me the goodness of accompanying me to the Pump Room?" he asked her. No sooner were the words out of his mouth when he realized the impropriety of being unescorted with an unmarried lady. He had been away from the Marriage Mart for so long his brain had turned to porridge.

That odious sausage-maker's daughter, whatever her name was, came to stand beside Miss Spenser. "What a very good plan, my lord," she said.

A frown on his face, he realized he had to settle for escorting both women. Then Blanks decreed that he and his wife would accompany them. Therefore, five of them set off for the Pump Room, which was just blocks from Queen Square. George found himself in the ridiculous position of having a spinster on each arm. He also found himself being gushingly addressed by that upstart gel, Miss Johnson, he believed her name was.

"I had the pleasure of seeing your beautiful children not one hour past," the gel told him.

"Where, may I ask, did this meeting take place?" he asked.

"Miss Spenser was taking them for a walk to the Royal Crescent, and I had the good fortune to run into her."

He cast a grateful glance at Miss Spenser. He was touched that, despite his own abominable behavior the night before, she had still sought out his children and indulged them. How fortunate they were to have her. He smiled smugly. Thanks to him, his children would be indulged by Miss Spenser for the rest of their days. For surely she would accept his suit. "How kind of you, Miss Spenser, to offer the children another treat so soon after yesterday's trip to Sydney Gardens."

"They did so enjoy playing at Crescent Fields," Miss Johnson said. "They are such absolute darlings! And what a handsome fellow your little son is. I declare, you must have looked exactly the same when you were a lad of his age."

"So I've been told," George said, a look of distaste on his face. He had always been disappointed the boy did not favor his mother more. Like Georgette. Just thinking of his daughter warmed George's heart.

"I was just remarking to Miss Spenser," Miss Johnson said, "that it was time you married again, my lord."

"My feelings exactly," he answered.

A smile spread across Miss Johnson's fair face.

He cast a quick glance at Miss Spenser, and it seemed her usually tanned face had gone white. How very odd.

George hoped that when they reached the Pump Room his friends, Appleton and the twins, would be there. He would persuade one of them to relieve him of the Johnson chit so he could speak privately with Miss Spenser. More likely than not, though, they would not be there. They were far more comfortable with bloods than with young ladies. A most unsociable lot, to be sure. He tried to think of what amusements would compete for their attention today. No boxing matches. No cockfights. No horse racing. Perhaps in their boredom the threesome would be at the Pump Room.

"My Papa will arrive in Bath next week," Miss Johnson was babbling. Babbling to him, George realized. Why did the young lady suffer under the delusion he was remotely interested in anything she had to say? "He has expressed a profound interest in renewing his acquaintance with you, my lord," the sausage-maker's daughter continued.

So nervous was he over his impending interview with Miss Spenser, he could scarcely attend to Miss Johnson's words. As she spoke uninterrupted, he slid a glance at Miss Spenser. Her hair was curled today, and he thought she looked almost pretty. There was a grace about her that made her outshine a woman like Miss Johnson. And when he smiled at Miss Spenser, she favored him with a soft smile that revealed her deep dimples. When she smiled like that, she really was pretty.

Once they arrived at the Pump Room, his sister ordered her husband to escort her on a turn about the room. That left George with one woman too many. A quick glance around the lofty chamber confirmed that his bachelor friends were not there. Which assured George of being stuck with the obnoxious Miss Johnson. "Ladies, allow me to fetch you the water," he said.

He left them and went to the attendant to procure the cups of the nasty-tasting water. From the corner of his eye, he saw Appleton and the twins stroll into the room. This was even better! Taking the cups from the attendant and balancing them, George went straight to his friends and spoke to Appleton. "Do me the goodness of relieving me of Miss Johnson."

Appleton glanced toward the two ladies. "You are referring to the pretty blonde standing with the plain Miss Spenser?"

If he did not have these cups of water in his hand,

George might have sent a fist into Appleton's face. How dare he call Miss Spenser plain! How could anyone with such delectable dimples be plain? And how could one actually prefer Miss Johnson over Miss Spenser? "I am," George said curtly.

"Then it shall be my pleasure," Appleton said as he walked directly to Miss Johnson and begged to be allowed to escort her around the perimeter of the chamber. George held his breath as he watched her set a hand on Appleton's forearm, then he came up to Miss Spenser and offered her the cup of water. "I seem to have an extra," he said, offering it to one of the twins, who declined it.

"Didn't know Miss Johnson was in town," Melvin said.

"She arrived only last night," Miss Spenser answered.

The other twin, Elvin, was following Blanks and Glee with his eyes. "Pix must be delighted to have Blanks at the ready today," he said.

"Pix?" George asked.

"Your sister. We call her Pix 'cause she's so little."

"Oh, so you do," George conceded. He knew Blanks detested the familiar practice.

Although it was impolite to leave the twins, George looked into Miss Spenser's chocolate-colored eyes, and said, "May I have the pleasure of walking with you, Miss Spenser?" as he offered her his crooked arm.

He sighed when she finally set a gentle hand on his forearm. The two of them began to stroll the chamber. With every step he took, his heartbeat accelerated. Good lord, what if the chit laughed at him! Or refused him? He reminded himself that he was prepared to shed his pride for the sake of his children's happiness. He had only to think of the bitter Hortense, knowing his children deserved better, to resolve anew to offer for Miss Spenser.

"It was most considerate of you to seek out my children today," he began.

"I did not seek them out to be considerate. I sought them because they bring me joy."

It was the same with him! At least with his precious Georgette. Every time he laid eyes on his sweet daughter, it brought him happiness. Oh yes, he had made an excellent decision. There was no better woman than Miss Spenser to be stepmother to his children. He rather swelled with pride when he thought of making her the new viscountess. His children had suffered long enough. "I am gratified that you feel as you do."

They walked in silence for a moment when he said, "Miss Spenser, I wish to apologize for my appalling behavior last night. I've come to realize the wisdom of your words when you chided me. In fact, I deserved a better tongue-lashing than I received."

Her slim hand tightened upon his arm, and she turned to gaze upon him with those great brown eyes of hers. "I care too deeply for you to receive any gratification from your words, my lord."

His stomach vaulted. She made him extremely uncomfortable. Why did it hurt her when he showed poor judgment as he had last night? It would be so much easier for him if she did not care for him, yet he had to admit she would make a fine wife. A loyal wife, too, he'd wager.

Whether she realized it or not, she did care for him as one would for a brother. And, come to think of it, he cared for her in the same way he cared for Felicity and Glee.

"I am flattered, my lord, that you are most likely

speaking so prettily to me in order to secure me for your children."

His pulse accelerated, and he swallowed hard. He placed a firm hand on top of hers. "Yes, I do want you, Miss Spenser. But I want you for my wife."

Chapter 6

Her heart leapt in her chest and pounded in her ears. At first she *had* thought that in her love for George she had imagined that he said he wanted her for *his wife*. She could not trust her ears. Lord George Sedgewick would never wish to make her his wife.

She was aware that he was looking down upon her, but she could not bring herself to make eye contact with him, nor was she able to speak. She was too embarrassed to speak, actually. For to respond to him was to admit she was deserving of being the Viscountess Sedgewick. She, Sally Spenser, who was on the threshold of becoming a schoolmistress at Miss Worth's School for Young Ladies.

Just as she was about to ask him to repeat himself, she realized that the Viscount Sedgewick had indeed asked for her hand in marriage. And she completely understood why.

Quite simply put, he wanted her for his children's stepmother. With his simple declaration, Sally held him in higher regard than she had in the twelve years she had known him. She had been previously unaware of the depths of his love for his children. For his children, he was willing to sacrifice himself on the altar. 'Twas the noblest thing he had ever done.

Her first inclination was to emphatically turn him down. She had always vowed to die a spinster rather than marry where there was no love. But just because Lord Sedgewick did not love her did not mean there was no love. She possessed enough for both of them.

How sweet that he would even contemplate allowing her—skinny, plain, dowryless, outspoken Sally Spenser—to attempt to fill his beloved Dianna's shoes. All for the love of his children. For Sally had no delusions that he had any love or desire for her.

She respected him even more in view of the fact that if he merely wanted a stepmother for his children, he could have secured the hand of a lady in possession of far more beauty and fortune than she. But he was not seeking the best wife for himself but rather the best mother for his children. How completely unselfish he was being!

She looked at his hand covering hers. In her whole life she had never felt closer to another being. His very touch sent her heart soaring. She knew he would never love her. At least not as a man loves a woman. But she loved him so thoroughly, she could not deny herself this fleeting chance to grasp the next best thing to possessing his heart: to possess his respect and his name. It was more than she had ever thought to secure in a lifetime.

There were so many reasons to accept his suit, not the least of which was the intoxicating prospect of being mother to Georgette and Sam. How she would love spoiling them! By marrying their father she could also ensure that they would never have to suffer a mean-spirited nurse or an unfeeling stepmother.

Also, there was the heady vision of a future in which she and George could intertwine their lives in a common purpose. From his apology, she realized that she might even wield some influence over him. Would that she could put a stop to his self-destruction.

Already, the bond of the children was a stronger one than that with which most married couples began their marriages.

Oh yes, even without a chance of owning his heart, she would be happy to be George's wife. She gently squeezed his arm. It was the most intimate gesture toward an unrelated man of her entire two and twenty years. "You honor me, my lord," she finally managed.

"What? No tart words, Miss Spenser?"

She wondered that she could even hear him for her heart was pounding so furiously. "No, my lord. I confess you've left me speechless—for once."

"Then am I given to believe you will honor me by becoming my viscountess?"

My viscountess! The very thought robbed her of breath. "I care for your children—and for you, my lord—far too much to deny you." Oh goodness, why had she made herself seem such a foolish, adoring featherbrain?

"And I care for you too much to mislead you, Miss Spenser. You realize the marriage will be . . ."

"Unconsummated," she answered.

"Exactly, though I'm surprised a maiden such as yourself understands the meaning of the word."

The liquid warmth that had filled her since hearing his proposal spread to center between her thighs. Oh, she understood much more than that.

Lord Sedgewick had a most disturbing effect upon her! "Actually, I learned that word in *Romeo and Juliet* when I was twelve. Because it was then unfamiliar to me, I had to look it up. One can learn a great deal from reading, my lord, and I read a great deal."

He burst out laughing as he continued to pat her hand. "You know, Miss Spenser, I believe we will deal very well together."

She smiled up at him. "I believe we shall. First, though, you must call me Sally."

He lowered his voice. "And you are to call me George."

She took a deep breath, then slowly exhaled. "Do we tell the others now?"

He clasped her hand within his. "If you wish."

Even though George did not love her, Sally felt like shouting her joy from the steeple of the Bath Cathedral. She and George were to be partners for life! Together, with her cherished Sam and Georgette, they would be a family. "I suppose we should first iron out details." She turned and offered him her broadest smile. "When should you like to marry?"

"I could get a special license, and we could marry by next week."

She would like that ever so much. The sooner the better, for she feared George might change his mind. "You do know I have no dowry to speak of."

He nodded. "You have other . . . attributes that entice me."

She laughed. "I never realized my love for children would come to bear so importantly in my life's plan. Oh, George," she said wistfully as she gazed into his eyes, "we will have such great fun with the children!" As he looked warmly down at her, a smile playing at his lips, she thought he seemed happier than he had in these two years past.

"I shall have to inform Mama—and I suppose Edmund."

"You are out of charity with your brother?" he asked.

"Of course I'm out of charity with him! He did his best to have me marry Mr. Higginbottom, who is no less than eight and sixty years of age."

"The Mr. Higginbottom who owns the brewery?"

She sighed. "The same."

"Then I should be grateful that a large fortune is not important to you."

She squeezed his hand. "I could not marry a person for whom I held no affection." Oh dear, she had unintentionally blurted out her feelings.

"Then I should also be grateful that your concern for my children has transferred to their father."

"I can scarcely remember back to a time when I did not know you, George. You've always been . . . like family to me."

"Now we will be family," he said contentedly. "Bath Cathedral next Thursday?"

Her eyes moist, her dimples piercing happy cheeks, she nodded. "But let's wait to tell the others when only family is present." She disliked being scrutinized by an obviously jealous Miss Johnson, and she did not think she could bear the pitying glances Appleton and the twins would likely give George. He *could* have done so much better.

They had now circled the room twice, which was already once more than Miss Johnson had allowed

Appleton to escort her. The poor fellow. Mr. Appleton was but the younger son of a baronet. A pity he was not the elder Appleton.

"I believe I shall ride to Surrey tomorrow and speak to your brother. Whether you are close to him or not, it's my duty to do so."

It had been a long time since George was so in tune to what his duties were.

Mission accomplished, her betrothed was now anxious to be away from the Pump Room. He walked again with both ladies back to Blankenship House, where he said farewell at the door. Then he turned to his sister. "I shall arrive early tonight because there is a matter I wish to discuss with you. I'll ask Felicity and Thomas to meet here as well."

"How ominous-sounding you are," Glee said.

Miss Johnson moved closer to George, looked up at him and fluttered her lashes, then spoke. "You will be at the Pump Room tonight, will you not, Lord Sedgewick?" Miss Johnson asked.

It was to Sally he replied. "Indeed I shall."

George hurried back to Westgate Street, hoping to arrive before Georgette went down for her afternoon nap. He scurried up the two flights of stairs and opened the door to the nursery. His daughter was in the process of affixing a bonnet upon the head of that huge cat of hers when she looked up and saw him.

Her large brown eyes widened in mirth. "Papa!" She ran to him. "Have you come to read us the story you read yesterday?"

"If you like, love. But I've come to tell you something I believe will make you even happier." He scooped her into his arms and carried her to the big rocker. From the corner of his eye he watched Sam, who stayed several feet away, his thumb shoved into his mouth. Never mind the lad, George thought. He was too young to understand the importance of what was occurring, anyway. The importance of the sacrifice his father was making for his children.

"Oh, tell me the surprise!" Georgette said as she slid her little arm around her father's neck.

His heart began to flutter. Good Lord, but he really had come too far to back out now. 'Twas a grave step he was taking.

"What is it, Papa?" Georgette asked again.

"I have decided to marry Miss Spenser so you can have her for your mother." There! It was out, never to be retracted. Now, to watch his daughter's reaction.

It was all he could have hoped for. Georgette's face brightened, and both her arms looped around his neck. "My wish! It did come true!"

He held her to him. "What wish, love?"

"Every time I see a star I wish for Miss Spenser to be my mother. That is what I wished above everything. It's what I told Aunt Glee I should like last Christmas, but Aunt Glee said that was not a proper present."

He held her tightly to him, contentment and joy filling his heart. Then Georgette scooted off his lap and ran to her brother. "We are to have a mother, Sam!"

The boy obviously did not understand what his sister was saying. She dropped to her knees and spoke sweetly to him: "Would you like Miss Spenser to come live here?"

His thumb still in his mouth, Sam nodded, and he turned hopefully toward the door.

* * *

That night they all gathered in the drawing room of Blankenship House. Felicity had been late, which was not uncommon for his eldest sister. George had spent the past few hours deciding how he was going to inform his family of his decision to marry Sally Spenser.

He was keenly aware that the announcement would come as a great surprise to them, especially in light of his avowal to never remarry, to never allow anyone to replace Dianna in his heart.

He was also sensitive to Miss Spencer's feelings. He could not very well treat her as if she were a prize mare he had purchased for his children. Nor could he allow others to think he would marry where there were no feelings of love. It would not be fair to Miss Spenser to have others think she had no worth to him as a woman.

For her sake, he would allow others to believe that he was, indeed, ready to remarry. With heavy heart, he vowed to keep his love for Dianna buried within the deepest chambers of his heart. For Sally's sake, he would no longer speak of Dianna.

Even though Sally knew he could never love her, he could never humiliate her. She was too important to the children—and to him.

"Do tell us the great secret," Glee urged once they were all seated in the firelit room.

He came to stand beside Sally, who looked her best with her hair in golden ringlets and dressed prettily in a saffron gown. He drew her hand into his.

The only sound heard was the crackling in the grate.

"Miss Spenser and I wanted those of you in this room to be the first to know." He lifted her hand to his lips and kissed it. "Miss Spenser has done me the goodness of agreeing to be my wife."

For several seconds, the only sound heard was the fire. Then Glee sprang to her feet and flew across the room to throw her arms around Sally. "We are to be sisters! I declare, this is the best news I've had in years."

Then she turned to her brother and embraced him. "I'm so very proud of you," she said, not without emotion. "I was not aware you were possessed of such very good sense."

Now Felicity was queued behind Glee to hug her brother. "I, too, am so proud of you, George. You could not have found a finer woman in all the kingdom."

George beamed. "You ladies are not telling me anything I am not already aware of."

Blanks and Thomas followed with congratulations.

"When is the wedding to be?" Felicity asked.

"I've begun steps to procure a special license, with the intention of marrying Thursday next. Tomorrow I will speak to Mr. Spenser."

"Oh, George dearest!" Glee said, "This is such wonderful news!"

"Actually, you are not the first to know," George said to his sisters. "The first to hear of the nuptials was my daughter." He looked somberly at Glee. "Why did you never tell me what she wished for before?"

A fleeting look of sorrow swept across Glee's face. "I . . . I feared such a wish would never be granted."

Sally stood up beside her betrothed and possessively set her hand on his arm. Then they all gathered up their wraps and set off for the Upper Assembly Rooms.

Chapter 7

After draping Sally's serviceable black cloak a-round her slender shoulders, George assisted her into Moreland's waiting carriage for the short ride to the Assembly Rooms. It really seemed decidedly odd to be sitting so close to his younger sister's best friend. Had this been but a single day earlier, Miss Spenser would have been sitting beside Felicity, and he would be sitting next to Moreland.

What a profound difference a day made. Now Miss Spenser was not just his sister's best friend, she was his betrothed, the woman he had chosen to spend the rest of his life with.

Without him consciously summoning such mor-bid reflection, he winced as he remembered the woman he *had* thought to spend his life with. And he grew solemn. *Oh, Dianna, I don't mean to forsake you. I shall never love anyone except you.*

Once again he vowed to bury his deep and un-dying love for Dianna. Outwardly, he would honor Sally as if she were the wife of his heart. Only Sally and he would ever know differently.

He pressed her slim hand within his own. How

very fortunate he was to have secured her. And how unselfish she was to consent to marry where there no carnal love, only a pure love for the children borne by another woman. He squeezed Sally's hand tighter.

As they drew up to the Upper Assembly Rooms, his chest grew tight. He would have to make the announcement tonight. Tonight he would give the best performance of his life.

The six of them congregated together on the row of chairs reserved for peers and were soon joined by Appleton and the twins. George's friends' puzzled glances at the way he hovered solicitously over Sally throughout the evening did not escape his notice. He only hoped Sally was unaware of their scrutiny. Shielding Sally from his friends' thoughtlessness mattered more to him than feeling he was betraying Dianna by his affectionate manner.

When Blanks publicly announced his and Sally's forthcoming nuptials, George could have sent his fist crashing into Melvin's shocked face. Had the man no sensitivity for Miss Spenser's feelings? George flicked a glance at Sally. A pink flush had crept up her face.

George quickly took her hand and feigned the role of a devoted suitor. The girl deserved at least that much.

"I know how heartily you detest losing another of your bachelor friends to matrimony," George said to Melvin, "but I shall be extremely offended if you do not perceive how fortunate I am to have persuaded the lovely Miss Spenser to become my bride."

George held his breath as Melvin's gaze flitted from George to Sally and back to George.

Fortunately, Melvin was a gentleman. He gathered his composure, turned to Sally, a gentle smile on his face, and bowed. "May I offer felicitations upon your nuptials? It goes without saying Lord Sedgewick is a most fortunate man."

"I should be a complete imbecile if I did not acknowledge that it is I who am the fortunate one," she said, tossing a smiling glance up to George.

"Forgive me if I seem surprised," Melvin added in a low voice. "It's just that with Sedgewick's fortunes being somewhat reduced, I looked for him to marry an heiress."

The devil take him! George thought. What a crass remark for Melvin to make. Did the fellow not remember George had once married an heiress? An heiress he had dearly loved.

"Truth be told, I too thought his lordship could have married better," Sally said. "I only pray he does not come to regret not having done so."

George sucked in his breath. "Never, my love," he said to Sally.

A look of pity on his face, Melvin took Sally's hand and patted it. "Never concern yourself with such thoughts, ma'am. If Sedgewick is determined to wed you, he'll do everything in his power to make it a successful marriage. He can be rather driven that way."

George frowned. He *had* been driven—with Dianna's money—to restore Hornsby Manor. Now he was drinking and gambling away all he had once amassed. Miss Spenser deserved better.

The orchestra began to play, and George turned to his betrothed. "May I have the pleasure?"

She answered him with twinkling eyes and an outstretched hand.

The dance was a waltz. He could close his eyes as he drew her near and almost imagine he was once again waltzing with Dianna. Until now, he had never noticed that Sally's tall, lithe body was almost exactly like Dianna's. Such a resemblance had been completely hidden by the facts that Dianna was dark while Miss Spenser was fair, and Dianna was beautiful while Miss Spenser was plain. He decided he had better keep his eyes open.

Sally felt rather stiff—even shaky, he'd say—at first, but as the two of them talked and he teased her about her shyness, she grew more comfortable in his embrace. She really was a rather graceful dancer, which surprised him. Since she refused to sing, he had always assumed she had no musical talent whatsoever, and dancing did, after all, require some musical talent.

She smelled good, too. Not with an overpowering scent but a light floral one that suited her well. His face came into contact with her golden ringlets, and he had to smile. She wore her hair in curls to please him. Not because she had even the slightest romantic interest in him, of course, but because she aspired to make him a good wife.

In every way but one.

After that first set, George was pleased when Appleton asked Sally to stand up with him. Just as George fell back to drop into a chair, Miss Johnson came up to him, her eyes rounded. "I have just arrived, my lord, and cannot believe what I've been told. Surely you cannot be serious about wanting to marry Miss Spenser! I must have heard wrong."

Were she a man, George would have struck her. "I've never been more serious in my life, Miss Johnson. With the exception of fortune, Miss Spenser is possessed of everything any man could ever hope to gain in a wife."

Her brows lowered. "How could you settle for . . . that when you were married to such a beautiful woman?"

His anger boiled within him. "I fail to see how

Miss Spencer's loveliness could have escaped you."
He glanced across the dance floor until he caught
sight of Sally's saffron dress as she faced Appleton
in the middle of the longway, and George feigned
a look of pure adoration. "When her hair is curled
as it is tonight, there could not be anyone lovelier
than Miss Spenser."

George turned his back to Miss Johnson. A
rather direct cut for a rather rude woman.

Though George refused to dance with anyone
but Sally that night, he took pleasure in watching
her being treated with respect by his friends. Each
of the twins dutifully took turns dancing with the
future viscountess.

The evening grew tediously long. George did
detest these affairs. He would much rather be in the
card room. Actually, he looked forward to being
safely wed so he could return to his ways of de-
bauchery.

After what seemed an interminable length of
time, the activities drew to a close. Instead of departing in Moreland's carriage, George said, "I prefer to walk the short distance back to Blankenship
House. I wish to be alone with my betrothed."

At George's announcement, Felicity's eyes flashed
with mirth, and a sly smile lifted a corner of Moreland's mouth.

George offered Sally his arm, and they began to
stroll along the well-lighted pavement, something
he never would have done at night in London. But
Bath was a most safe city. A pity it did not compare
as favorably to London in other respects. After all
this time in Bath, George still was not used to seeing the twisted, misshapen, infirm masses of suffering humanity that found their way to the city,
eager to be cured of their afflictions, though seldom satisfied with the results.

"I go to Surrey tomorrow to speak with your brother," he said.

"It's really not necessary. I'm of age."

"I wish to do what's right, Sally, and your brother is the head of your household. Do you think he'll favor my suit?"

She laughed. "Can you doubt it? You're a viscount. What brother—or father—would not be delighted?"

"But my fortune in no way compares to Mr. Higginbottom's."

Sally giggled. "Trust me. You have many more attributes than does Mr. Higginbottom."

"But you said your brother was particularly anxious for you to marry money."

She laughed again. "My brother is a most parsimonious man and has, therefore, done very well for himself—partly by marrying a woman possessed of some property. He doesn't need money. And I don't require money. I believe Edmund wished me to marry Mr. Higginbottom because he thought it would increase his own consequence to say, 'My sister, who married into the Higginbottom beer fortune, you know.' "

George could not help but laugh. His Sally was most acute in her perception of human behavior. He had never actually met the pompous Edmund Spenser, but Blanks had, and Blanks mimicked the man's pretentious airs in a most humorous manner. If the man's own sister—who was a most amiable lady—could barely tolerate her brother, the man's behavior must be quite obnoxious.

"Should you wish me to impart any information to your brother or mother?"

She puckered his lips in thought. "Only tell them I'm in favor of the match."

"Should you like me to carry a letter?"

She shook her head. "That won't be necessary. As I told you, I'm rather out of charity with Edmund—and somewhat out of charity with my mother for always siding with her firstborn. I vow, when I have children—" Her lips clamped shut. After taking several strides while contemplating the pavement with great interest, she said, "How silly of me. I shall never have children of my own, though I assure you I shall count yours as my own."

George winced. "Forgive me, Sally. I feel wretched for depriving you of children of your own."

"Don't spare another thought on it. I'm perfectly happy. Besides, I could never love any other children as much as I love Georgette and Sam."

For the second time in the same day, he was indirectly speaking of the most intimate blending known to man, yet it was a blending Miss Spenser would never come to know. He felt guilty for depriving her of it.

And depriving her of so much more.

They covered the next two blocks in silence.

"After I visit your brother I shall obtain the special license, and I plan to visit with my London solicitor to make the marriage settlements. I shan't return until Monday."

"May I see the children while you are gone?"

"Please do." He covered her hand. "My daughter never told me until today that each time she saw a star, she made a wish on it. Do you know what she wished for?"

Sally looked up at him with a puzzled expression on her face. "What?"

"She wished she had you for her mother."

He watched Sally and was utterly touched to see her eyes moisten and a single tear roll down her tawny cheek. He stopped under the street lantern and gazed into her solemn face. He thought she had never been lovelier. He gently brushed the tear away. Then he did a most peculiar thing. He lowered his face to hers and settled his lips on hers.

He would have wagered she had never been kissed before, but in no way did her kiss feel like that of a befuddled first kiss. Her lips were soft and pliant, and she melted into his chest as if she were long familiar with such intimacy.

Good lord! What was he doing? He snapped away from her. "Forgive me," he said in a shaky voice. "I don't know what came over me. The tear . . . it was so pure . . . such a betrayal of affection for those I hold most dear."

She placed a steady hand on each of his shoulders. "As dear as I hold them. The darlings."

He chuckled and set off walking again. He felt deuced awkward over that kissing business. It was best that he not mention it again.

Or repeat it. Ever. After all, Sally wasn't his Dianna.

"While I'm in London I should like to get you a wedding present," he said. "Is there something you desire?"

She shook her head. "What I should love above everything is a piece of jewelry that has been passed down for generations of Sedgewicks. Only upon receiving something like that will I ever truly believe I'm to be a member of the family!"

"All the Sedgewick jewels, quite naturally, will come to you, Sally."

She smiled and curled her hand around his arm. "There is something I should like for a wedding present."

His pulse quickened. Surely Sally was not marrying him for his money, not that there was a lot of it. He raised a quizzing brow.

"I should like you to save your money. I don't want you to spend it on me. Nothing would make me happier than to see you once more restore your fortune as you did upon your first marriage. And I know that it was you, and not your wife's wealth, that brought Hornsby back to its glory."

Though he should have been pleased with her praise, he was not. Her words ignited his anger. Did the chit think to order his life just because he was honoring her by marrying her? Did she plan to nag him over every penny he chose to waste? Would she constantly be chastising him?

Dear God, what had he gotten himself into? And it was far too late to back out now.

He spoke coolly to her. "Don't think because you're my wife you will have the right to tell me how I can and cannot spend *my* money."

"It's not the money I care about, George. It's you."

He shrugged and lifted his defiant face to the dark night skies. "You'll not be changing me, Sally. I am what I am, and you're going to have to settle for it."

"I know what you're capable of being, George. I don't have to like you settling for less."

He removed his hand from hers. "I see that marriage will not rein in your forthrightness. How reassuring that being my wife will not lubricate your abrasiveness."

"At least we both know what we're getting into," she snapped.

Chapter 8

Sally lay in her bed a long time that night, her disturbed thoughts preventing sleep. Though her words had made George angry, she did not regret uttering them. Had she to do it over again, she still would not have held her tongue. For she only spoke her heart. George's self-destructive ways *did* trouble her, and just because George was honoring her with his name did not mean she would ever cower before him.

One of the reasons she was marrying him was hopefully to be in a position of influence over him, to encourage him to mend his destructive ways. Truth would be the foundation of their marriage.

If, indeed, the marriage occurred.

What if George rethought his decision to marry her? What if he decided to risk censure for crying off rather than endure for a lifetime her shrewish ways? She really could not blame him were he to desire to break the brief engagement. Why would any man wish to shackle himself to the likes of her? Not only was she bereft of fortune, but she was also exceedingly plain. She kicked at her coverlet as she lay in the dark.

Straight hair. Straight body. Flat purse. Abrasive tongue. There was absolutely nothing about herself to attract a man. Especially a man as handsome and privileged as the Viscount Sedgewick.

He was sure to cry off. As she lay in the darkness of her room, she pictured him at his desk, a candle illuminating the paper upon which he was drafting a letter of retraction to her. And for the second time that night, tears seeped from her moist eyes.

Amid her deepest gloom, hope bubbled within her when she remembered the magical moment when George's eyes wistfully held her and he dipped down to taste her lips. The very memory of it sent her heart racing. For a few seconds she had allowed herself to believe George felt her beautiful. Loved. For a few seconds she had known the bliss she had only dreamed of. Even if she was never kissed again, she would remember this first kiss from the only man she could ever love.

As Glee's guest, Sally was used to being awakened each morning by Glee's own maid rapping at her door and cheerfully entering the room with a pot of steaming brew and rack of toast.

But this morning it was Glee herself who flew into Sally's room carrying a tray bearing a teapot and two cups. "Did you sleep well, dear sister?"

The thought of being sister to her dearest friend on earth sent a wave of contentment over Sally. Then she remembered that Glee's brother was quite likely regretting his unwise, hasty decision to make her his wife. Sally sat up in bed. "To be truthful, no."

Glee plopped on the bed. "It's no wonder. Yesterday was a most momentous day for you. I'm surprised you slept a single moment."

"There was much to consider. Lord—George's declaration, as you must know, was completely unexpected."

"I'm so glad you did not choose to behave coyly and beg more time to consider his proposal." Glee reached for the teapot and poured out two cups, giving one to Sally.

"Truth be told, I was rather afraid he would retract the offer if I did not pounce upon it." Sally sighed. "I daresay, he's quite liable to cry off today. I fear I was rather brutal in my criticism of him last night as we walked home. He wasn't at all pleased with me when we said good night." Sally's hand flew to her mouth. "Please don't think I criticized your brother for any reason other than my concern for his well-being."

Glee took Sally's hand and squeezed it. "I know how much you care for George's well-being. That's why you're the perfect wife for him. I'm exceedingly delighted my foolish brother has displayed such extraordinary good sense in begging for your hand."

"I'm afraid you're much in the minority," Sally said. "I daresay there was not another present at the Assembly Rooms last night who shared your excitement over the match—except, of course, Felicity. Did you see the outraged Miss Johnson storm for the chambers after confronting George?" While dancing with Mr. Appleton, Sally had kept George within her line of vision. Her heart had beat erratically as she watched the lovely heiress stroll up to George and speak. Then Sally's lips curled into a smile as she took great pleasure in watching George give Miss Johnson the cut direct. Sally had actually giggled when Miss Johnson angrily stomped off.

"I'd give a lief to know what my brother told her. I've never seen a woman in such a rage."

"Oh, I have a very good idea the nature of the conversation which occurred between them," Sally said, placing her cup back in the dainty saucer. "No doubt, Miss Johnson demanded to know if there was any truth to the *disgusting* rumor that he had asked the completely unsuitable Miss Spenser to become his wife. Then when George confirmed it, she no doubt heaped a pile of criticism upon me, and George—gentleman that he is—defended me. I can picture him saying something like *Miss Spenser is a most worthy young woman.*"

Sally and Glee began to giggle.

"Surely it did not escape your attention that Miss Johnson has coveted your brother for many years." Sally felt guilty for not admitting she had been obsessively attracted to George for half her life, too.

Glee giggled again. "I thought I was the only one aware of it."

"And I thought I was the only one!"

"Dear me, the entire town must have observed her pursuing ways." Glee replenished their empty cups.

Sally shrugged. "I'm being very uncharitable toward Miss Johnson."

"Don't fret, pet. She's probably far more uncharitable toward you than ever you could be toward her. In fact, I can just hear her. She's probably saying you'll embarrass my brother in your unstylish clothes."

Sally's brows lowered. "Do you think I'll be an embarrassment to him?"

"You know George doesn't give a fig about fashion! However, as the Viscountess Sedgewick, you *will* have a certain image to uphold. That's why

I've burst in on you this morning. We must go buy you a trousseau today!"

Sally's eyes flashed, and she clutched at her bodice. What if George had already delivered his letter of rejection? "Have you seen or heard from your brother today?"

"No. Wasn't he to leave early this morning to visit your brother?"

"He was. If I didn't scare him off."

Glee issued a melodious little laugh. "Don't worry, you goose. George would never do that."

"Are you sure? Perhaps he had a letter delivered for me?"

Glee's brows lowered. "Actually . . ." Her words waned. "There *is* a letter for you in George's hand." Glee went to the bell rope and rang for a servant.

Sally's heart sank, and a sickness coiled in her stomach.

When the servant answered Glee's call, she met him at the door and sent him to get Miss Spenser's letter. As soon as the door closed, Sally leaped from the bed and began to search for her clothing for the day.

By the time the butler returned a moment later, Sally was completely dressed and took the letter herself. Her heart drumming madly, she lowered herself into a chair near the window and began to read the hastily scratched note.

> *Dearest Sally,*
> *Forgive me for my beastly ways. I shouldn't like to go off with such ill-feelings between us.*
> *Yours, G.*

Sally looked up at Glee through misty eyes. "He apologizes for our harsh words, though I daresay they were entirely at my instigation."

Glee strolled to her and set a gentle hand on her shoulder. "You will be ever so good for George."

Sally bent over the bed and began to smooth out the sheets and counterpane.

"Leave that for the servants, you goose!"

Sally sighed. "You know I cannot. I detest anything that's untidy."

"My poor niece and nephew. As their stepmother, you will no doubt demand they be as tidy as you."

Sally smiled. "I find it much easier to pick up for them than to teach them to pick up, but I'm trying to learn to teach them. I daresay I must be rather lazy."

"Never that! Now allow Patty to help with your toilette so we can go shopping."

Sally plumped up the feather pillow. "I don't see how I can go shopping when I have no money."

"Silly, you don't need to buy anything. I shall. Remember, you will have a certain image to uphold as the Viscountess Sedgewick. And you want George to be proud of you, don't you?"

Sally's stomach fluttered. She hated to think of being an embarrassment to her future husband. "But . . ."

"Don't spare a thought for the money. You know I have married a very wealthy man, and it will give me great pleasure to see my sister dressed as her new station will demand."

Sally felt utterly humiliated. Humiliated that she dressed so poorly. Humiliated that she might embarrass poor George. Humiliated that she had almost no money of her own.

"I'm sending Patty in to do up your hair," Glee said, "though I think 'twill take a great long time to render it curly again."

"It doesn't need to be curly today. I only curled it to please George. While he is gone, Pattty can have a break from the tedious curl papers."

Glee gave her friend a peculiar glance before leaving the room.

That afternoon, courtesy of Gregory Blankenship's deep pockets, Sally was fitted for a half a dozen ball gowns and a similar number of morning dresses and promenade gowns. Glee took pleasure in helping her friend select new hats and gloves and shoes.

Though the shopping was exhilarating to Sally, who had never been indulged in such a manner in her entire life, it was also tiring. Late in the afternoon, the two ladies settled in a tea shop, where Glee had arranged to meet her husband.

Blanks came in, bearing a letter for his wife. She took it and glanced at the handwriting as her husband sat down next to her. "It's from George," she said, her puzzled glance sliding to Sally.

Sally's insides clinched. Was George going to use his sister to break off the engagement? Then why, she chided herself, would he be traveling to Surrey to speak with her brother?

Glee opened the letter and quickly ran her eyes over it, a smile hiking across her face. "What a dear!"

Sally heaved a sigh of relief.

"Are you speaking of your brother?" Blanks demanded with jest.

"I am." Glee set down the letter and shifted her vision to Sally. "He wanted me to see to it you got a new trousseau befitting your new station. He wished to have all the bills sent to him."

Sally flushed. She did not at all like feeling so much a charity case. Despite her embarrassment, she glowed over George's thoughtful gesture. He must have had many duties to attend to this morning in his haste to be gone on his journey, yet he thought of her.

He really was a very fine man. His sacrifice demonstrated it most assuredly. What great love he must hold for his children.

Then Sally's brows drew together. *For one of his children,* she amended. For though he always spoke of *his children,* only one of them held his heart.

Sally vowed to change that.

For the remainder of their repast, she watched Glee and her husband and the strange distance that had grown between them. Each of them bore the signs of heavy sorrow, and complete, tortured love for one another.

Even though she was much fatigued, Sally left Glee and Blanks at the tea room and went to see the children. Just thinking of them becoming her own brought sweet fulfillment.

She entered their house and marched up the narrow stairway to the top-floor nursery. It wasn't until this very moment that she considered she would actually be mistress of this house by next week. But being the Viscountess Sedgewick was not what was important to her. The children were. And their father.

When she opened the nursery door, Georgette came running to her. "Mama!" she called, her arms uplifted. Tears moistening her eyes, Sally gathered the child into her arms. "I'm so happy, darling, that you're to become my very own little girl."

Georgette's arms tightly encircled Sally's neck. "I'm happy, too. Now I shall have a mama like the other girls—and like Joy."

92 *Cheryl Bolen*

Sally stroked the little girl's thick mahogany-colored hair. Then she looked down at her own skirts and saw Sam standing there, his thumb shoved into his mouth. "I wonder if your brother knows what is about to happen?" Sally asked as she kissed Georgette's cheek, set her down, and drew Sam into her arms.

"I told him," Georgette said. "I do wish he would talk."

"He will," Sally assured. "You and I will teach him, beginning next week."

"Which room will be yours?" Georgette asked. "I hope it's next to mine."

Sally's stomach fluttered. Because town houses were a great deal smaller than country houses, the husband and wife generally shared a bedchamber at their town house. But, of course, George would not wish to share a chamber with her. "It doesn't matter where my room is, love. Nothing can ever take away the fact that we will be a family. I shall be your mother, and you shall be my beloved children." She nuzzled her mouth into Sam's golden curls, and he gave a hearty baby laugh.

Then Sam pointed toward the rocking chair.

"Say 'chair,' Sam," Sally said sternly.

He shook his head.

The little imp! He knew very well every word she uttered. "Say 'chair,' sweetheart," she repeated soothingly.

He made the A sound, though the consonants weren't right.

She kissed his chubby cheek. "Good boy!" She drew him to her breast and squeezed him tightly before she sat down in the rocking chair and began to play the piggy game with him.

Chapter 9

George was supposed to return on Monday. Because of that, Sally refused to leave Blankenship House all day Monday for fear of missing him. She thought perhaps he would come by the afternoon. But he did not. All through dinner, she looked for him, but he did not come then, either. She was heartily glad that Glee and Blanks did not wish to go to the Assembly Rooms that night, for she was far too worried to leave the house.

She and Glee took their needlework to the drawing room, but with every stitch of her needle Sally's thoughts stayed on George. Was he all right? Had something happened to him? Had he drunk too much and been unable to travel? Or, heaven forbid, had he changed his mind about marrying her?

By nine o'clock she began to worry she had done the wrong thing by not going to the Assembly Rooms. George must have gone there looking for them.

Moments after she entertained that thought, she heard voices, then footsteps, in the marble hall. She whipped her gaze to the door and saw George come strolling into the Blankenship drawing room. He wore evening attire and gave no sign that he had been traveling for several hours.

Sally's heart leapt as she gazed upon his manly countenance, upon that rugged face she loved so dearly. She wanted to run to him and throw her arms around him, but of course she could not do that. He would surely cry off then.

He glanced first at her, then came and took her hand, brushing his lips across it. "You have been well, my dear?"

"Oh yes," she replied. "And you? You must be greatly fatigued from the journey."

He nodded greetings to his sister before sinking into the soft silk of the settee Sally sat upon. "Glad I am that you're *not* at the Assembly Rooms tonight."

A timid smile brightened her face. Exactly why she had not desired to go there. "Pray, my lord, was your journey successful?"

"Indeed it was. You were correct about your brother. He was delighted to bless our union. In fact, he and your mother will be here Thursday for the wedding."

Thursday! It really was going to happen. Sally still could not believe George was going to marry her. She fully expected to awaken from the dream any minute. Though she was not close to either her brother or her mercenary parent—not as she was to her younger brother and her late papa—Sally was nevertheless pleased to learn they would attend the wedding. For some peculiar reason, their presence would make the ceremony more sacred. More binding. More irrevocable. A sense of well-being bubbled within her. "You have the special license?"

He patted his pocket. "I do." He gazed upon her, his eyes running the length of the ivory gown she wore. "A new dress?"

Sally swallowed. "Yes. Your sister has done me the goodness of indulging me at half the shops in Bath. The new Viscountess Sedgewick will be very well turned out indeed." It felt exceedingly odd to call herself by so lofty a name. It was especially strange since she still thought of the lovely Dianna as Lady Sedgewick.

He closed his hand over hers. "As it should be."

On Thursday morning they wed at Bath Cathedral. Despite the groom's high social standing, it was a small wedding attended only by family and a handful of close friends.

When George stood on the precipice of the sanctuary and gazed at Sally walking down the nave toward him, he swallowed hard. For a fleeting second he had expected to see Dianna in Sally's place. But it was only Sally. Sally, whose face was grim and whose steps were unsure. In her unadorned white silk gown, she looked more like a frightened child than a woman about to become a viscountess. Sally Spenser certainly was no great beauty, but she would make him a good wife. A pity she was not Dianna. A dark cloud fell over him as he linked Sally's arm to his own. Such an utterly symbolic gesture. Their whole lives would henceforth forever be intertwined. Irrevocably joined together. His stomach dropped.

As they stood with their hands clasped before the bishop, George once again smelled Sally's distinctive light fragrance. And it seemed as if huge shafts of sunlight began to fill the cathedral, dispelling the gloom he had experienced a moment before.

Following the ceremony, a lavish wedding breakfast was held at Moreland's Winston Hall, where the enormous dining room was spread with meats of every sort and a vast array of pastries from Moreland's talented French chef. Moreland insisted George sit at the head of the table. Felicity insisted Sally sit at her new husband's side.

It felt deuced awkward to be calling Sally Lady Sedgewick, yet he could never begrudge her the title. She was also assuming the loving care of the children from whom Dianna had been taken. He would have to quit thinking of Dianna. She was dead. Two long years he had mourned her. He had even wished to follow her to the grave, but no longer. He must live now. For their children.

Throughout breakfast he found his bride exceptionally quiet. He also noticed that she barely touched her food, though Miss—blast it all, he must learn to call his new wife by her Christian name! Sally. He had long been aware that Sally was not possessed of a large appetite. No wonder she was so skinny. He vowed to help fatten her up. "Come, my sweet, you must eat," he said gently.

Her head bent toward his. "I fear doing so, my lord, for my stomach is not at all settled today."

By Jove! She had the jitters! He'd never thought the singularly strong Sally Spenser could have anything weak about her, but she was possessed of a weak stomach. He chuckled and brought her hand to his lips. "Surely you will toast our union with champagne."

She nodded. "It will be my pleasure."

A moment later they lifted their glasses for the wedding toast. Then George rose from the table and offered Sally his arm. "Lady Sedgewick and I plan to share the day with our children," he announced. Then he nodded at Appleton. "Bring the twins around about seven."

"But surely, Sedgewick—" Appleton began to protest.

George cut him off. "Just because I'm getting married doesn't mean I wish to become a recluse."

"Are you sure?" Appleton asked, his puzzled glance darting from George to Sally.

"I'm sure," George snapped.

At the town house George had been letting in Bath these past two years he escorted his bride from room to room, introducing her to the staff as they went. With her arm linked through her husband's, Sally glowed as she moved through her new home, George thoughtfully referring to her as "the new mistress" or "Lady Sedgewick."

On the second floor, they came to his room. Her heart stampeded as he led her within its chamber. She looked around at the masculine trappings and deep jewel colors. "I've had a new linen press brought here for you," he said as if he were commenting on the weather.

Sally was stunned. Hadn't George insisted there was to be no physical intimacy between them? Her probing eyes met his.

He closed the door behind them, bent his head toward her, and spoke softly. "I wish others—including the servants—to believe you are my wife in every way." Then he straightened up and walked to the window that looked out over the street, and he drew the red velvet draperies open. "Don't fear, Sally dear, I shan't be robbing you of your virginity."

Her heart fell. But she did so wish for him to rob her of her virginity! She wished to become his wife in every way, but of course, that could never happen. Not when he would always be in love with a woman cold in her grave. And Sally knew she could never measure up to the woman she was attempting to replace. A deep flush crept up her face.

The scarlet did not escape George's notice. He grabbed her by her shoulders and peered at her face. "By Jove! You're blushing! I did not think Sally Spenser—I beg your pardon, Sally Sedgewick—ever blushed. Surely my mentioning your virginity is not the source of your embarrassment?"

No one had ever mentioned the word *virginity* before in front of Sally. Oddly, the description embarrassed her. She would far rather be a well-pleasured lady than a pure virgin. Well-pleasured by George, that is. "I've . . . It's just that I've never heard that word spoken before."

He dropped his hands and chuckled. "But of course you've seen it in print and are acquainted with its meaning?"

"Of course." How she wished the blasted color would leave her hot cheeks!

"Do you object to the sleeping arrangements?"

"You mean to sharing your bed, albeit in a most chaste manner?"

"That is what I was referring to."

"I have no objections. I, too, wish everyone to believe us truly married." The words sounded hollow. As would be their marriage. How could it be a marriage when that one, all-important component was missing? How could she hope to be a part of him when they did not share that most intimate bond? She felt bereft. She would never be truly married to the man she loved with all her heart.

From the second floor, they made their way up to the nursery.

Georgette flew to Sally. "Are you truly my mother now?"

George answered. "She truly is." He stooped to pick up his daughter, and Sally bent to lift Sam. She glowed as George gathered the four of them together and spoke throatily. "A family at last."

Georgette bent to her brother and spoke in a voice like that used with babies. She pointed to her father and said, "Papa." Then she pointed to Sally and said, "Mama."

Sally watched the toddler for a reaction. Smiling, he clutched his arms around her and said, "Mama."

A gush of tears rushed from her as she gathered Sam closer and wept. All the while, a smile arched across her wet face. She tried to brush away the tears, but more kept coming. She looked up at George to assure him of her happiness and found that he, too, was crying.

At seven that night, Appleton and twins called for George. It was just as well, Sally decided. Every minute she spent with her groom would only result in making her wish this were a true wedding night. It was best he go off with his bachelor friends.

"We're going to meet Blanks for cards," Melvin informed George.

Poor Glee, Sally thought. Her husband had forsaken her, too.

That Appleton and the twins had no obvious compunction over robbing her of her husband on her wedding night sent the scarlet to Sally's cheeks once again. They had no compunction because they assumed George had already taken his conjugal rights. Her thoughts flitted back to this afternoon as she had stood with George within their bedchamber. All of the servants were conspicuously absent from the entire second floor. It was as if they expected Lord and Lady Sedgewick to consummate their marriage in that very bed that very afternoon. She felt a deep and gnawing void.

The gentlemen each drank a glass of Madeira and commented on the wedding before departing for a night of whatever it was fun-loving bachelors did.

Only her husband was not a bachelor. Nor was Gregory Blankenship.

The men had barely left when Sally, sitting in the drawing room with her embroidery, heard the sound of a carriage coming to a stop in front of the town house. She peered from the window and watched as Glee, an emerald cloak covering her blazing hair, disembarked. Still another person who had no compunction about disturbing one of the freshly married Sedgewicks on their wedding night.

A moment later Glee joined Sally in the drawing room. Tossing her cloak to the butler, she scurried into the room and dropped onto the settee, which matched the one on which Sally sat. "This reminds me terribly of my own wedding night."

That her wedding night was so widely discussed was painful to Sally. "How could this possibly remind you of your wedding night?"

"I'm going to tell you something I've never told anyone before. Not even Felicity," Glee said.

Sally arched a brow.

"I trapped Blanks into marrying me. He had wanted no part of being married and no part of me."

Sally shook her head. "I don't believe you. One has only to be around you two to know how deeply you're in love."

"We are. Now."

"But I know you loved him when you married."

"I did. He didn't."

Sally threw down her sewing. "Surely you're jesting." That was it. Glee was telling Sally this to make her feel better on her fruitless wedding night. "Blanks is completely besotted over you."

Glee's rosy lips lifted into a smile. "I believe you're right, pet, but it wasn't always so."

Sally's back sank into the settee. "Pray, you must tell me the whole story."

"As you know, I've always been madly in love with Blanks."

Sally nodded. *As have I with George.*

"And when I found out he would lose his fortune if he wasn't wed on the day he became five and twenty, I simply proposed marriage to him. I told him it wouldn't be a real marriage, but a marriage of convenience."

Exactly as ours is. "Go on," Sally said, unable to remove her gaze from Glee.

"He turned me down. Even though it meant losing his fortune, he hated the idea of marriage so thoroughly, he rejected my offer."

"Then how—"

"I forced him to compromise me."

"Surely you didn't—"

"Knowing George was coming to find Blanks and me, I pulled down the bodice of my dress so George would think Blanks had been taking his pleasure on my body, and my brother would force Blanks to offer marriage."

"Glee! How positively wicked!"

"Yes, it was rather, was it not?"

"Did your plan work?"

"Oh yes. Dear Blanks was too much the gentle-

man to tell George of my wickedness. I do believe
Blanks actually hated me for a short while, but I
knew what I did was for his own good."

"How well you knew your husband—better than
he knew himself."

"As you know George," Glee said, shooting Sally
a concerned glance. "I have finally come to realize
something you've managed to hide from me for a
great many years."

"What is that?" Sally asked.

"Your love for my brother."

'Twas rather like having the wind knocked from
her, Sally reflected. Hadn't she carefully tried to
conceal her feelings for George, especially after he
married the flawless Dianna?

Glee continued. "I've only just now come to realize you've adored George since your first visit to
Hornsby when you were . . . what? Thirteen years
of age?"

Sally hung her head and nodded. "Twelve, actually."

"And for ten years there has never been anyone
for you except George?"

"I'm so wicked, I still loved him even after he
married Dianna."

Glee's face grew solemn. "You're not wicked.
Quite the contrary. You love my brother and his
children selflessly."

Sally feigned a laugh. "Those who think I'm selfless have no idea how much pleasure I derive from
Georgette and Sam."

"My niece and nephew are indeed fortunate to
have you—as is their father." Glee's voice softened.
"I give you six months."

Sally's brows hiked up. "Six months for what?"

"To win George's heart, of course."

"That has never been my expectation."

"Then why did you marry him? I know you don't give a fig for rank."

"We—George and I both—thought it would be good for the children—and as the viscountess I can dismiss that old dragon of a nurse."

Glee's eyes widened. "You married in order to dismiss a nurse?"

"Oh, there were other reasons. I don't at all approve of how George is destroying himself, and I mean to be a thorn in his side."

Glee laughed. "My dearest Sally, trust me when I tell you, you will come to mean much more than a thorn to my brother."

Dare she allow herself to hope for more? It seemed unfathomable that George could ever love another woman than Dianna. And even more unfathomable that she could ever be that woman.

Chapter 10

Sally was unable to stay awake until George got home. With her maid's help, she had spent rather a long time on her toilette before going to bed. She felt terribly awkward commanding her own lady's maid. Would she ever become accustomed to having a personal maid? George, dear man, had engaged the young lady only the day before their wedding. With Hettie's help, Sally had attempted to preserve her wedding-day curls. The young maid also helped remove the fine gown Sally had worn that night and assisted her into a thin ivory linen night shift Sally had never before worn.

After Hettie left the bedchamber, Sally applied the perfume that was her own mother's blend. As she had slipped between the soft, cool linen sheets, she grew nervous. After all, she had never before slept with a man. Though this wasn't really like sleeping with a man. Still . . .

She woke the following morning to a darkened room. For a few befuddled seconds she had forgotten where she was. Then she remembered. She spun around to face the sleeping man who was her husband. He had never before seemed so big. Indeed, his sprawl covered well over half the bed. She propped herself up on one elbow and observed him. Her breath quickened at what she saw: golden skin covering supple muscles. From one well-formed shoulder to the other his body covered an expanse as long as four books stretched end to end. Though the hair on his head was the color of burnished gold, a thatch of thick, dark hair trailed from his chest to below the rumpled sheets. Even the strong smell of port about him was pure, intoxicating masculinity.

Her heart expanding to fill her chest, she continued to peruse her sleeping husband. When had he come in the night before? What had he and his friends done? Obviously, he had imbibed great amounts of liquor. Had he also lost great amounts of money at the tables?

It suddenly occurred to her that he could wake at any moment and find her—nearly naked—staring longingly at him. Were she possessed of a large bosom she thought she would rather like the idea of George seeing her in her night shift. But the vision of her boniness would not be one to ignite desire. Better that she cover herself.

Reluctantly, she left their bed, thinking to dress for the day, but how could she strip bare, knowing that he could awaken at any moment and behold her? Oh dear, what was she to do? A screen was what was needed for this shared chamber.

But were she to request a screen, it would seem she was a most unnatural wife. Even though she was a most unnatural wife, she hardly wished to announce that fact to the servants—and hence to all of Bath. She would simply have to learn to dress while at the same time keeping her private parts covered.

She tiptoed to her linen press and selected a muslin morning dress. With one hand holding it out to cover her, she attempted to strip off her night shift. When the night shift fell to the ground, Sally hurriedly stepped into the morning gown. Then she sighed.

It was her sigh that woke him.

He bolted upright in the bed and turned in her direction. Raising a mischievous eyebrow, he said, "Need help with your buttons, my lady?"

Her heart raced. Actually, she did need the help, but she was too embarrassed to ask him. In fact, she was too embarrassed to have two consecutive cognizant thoughts. All she could think of was her husband's brazen masculinity as he sat up in their bed, devilishly handsome without a shirt.

She began to move, unaware of what she was doing but vaguely thinking that for some inexplicable reason she wished to be near him. She reached the bed, then turned her back to him. "I beg that you fasten my buttons, my lord."

"I will—when you call me George. I'm your husband, Sally, not your lord and master."

He was her husband. How she loved to hear him say it! It made their marriage seem more real. "Yes, George."

She felt the warmth of his rough hands brushing against the bare skin of her back, and a ripple of delight shuddered through her. Once he had completed his task, he placed his hands on her shoulders and spun her around to face him.

Having glimpsed a view of herself in the looking glass, she knew how wretched she looked. Like the fleeting glory of a beautiful flower, the curls she had longed to preserve had vanished during the night and were replaced by coarse straight strands that resembled freshly shorn straw. "Hettie will curl my hair soon," she uttered self-consciously. "I know how wretched I look now."

"You don't look wretched at all," he said in a gentle voice. His glance lowered. "A most becoming dress you're wearing. Is it new?"

She nodded. "I daresay everything I wear from here onward is new. Glee said none of my old clothing was fit for the Viscountess Sedgewick, and I don't wish to be an embarrassment to you, George." As if the very fact of his marrying her was not an embarrassment. He could have done so much better.

As he sat there, the lower part of his body beneath the tangled sheets, his handsome face fell into a frown.

"What's the matter?" she asked.

"We'll have to think of a way to ensure more modesty within the walls of this room. I regret there's no dressing room here." His glance darted to the part of his body that was covered by the sheets.

Surely he was not naked! Her heartbeat accelerated. "Should you desire that I turn my back as you remove yourself from the bed, my lord?"

"Perhaps you'd better," he said in a voice like the one he used with Georgette. She and Georgette were both virginal, after all, she reasoned with bitterness. She twirled around and faced the door. "I will be asking the same of you. 'Tis a bit awkward."

"I daresay we'll grow accustomed to it."

Had he and Dianna known—and enjoyed—each other's bodies thoroughly? Her heart plummeted. She must not allow herself to think about her predecessor. It was most unfair to compare herself to Dianna's perfection. She would never know a moment's happiness if she continued to torture herself with questions about Dianna.

She heard him come down off the bed, landing hard on one foot as he struggled putting the other into his breeches. From the corner of her eye, she saw his bronzed arm reach across the top of a nearby chair to retrieve the white shirt that had been tossed there the night before. She turned to him, her eyes narrow. "I don't think your nakedness above the waist will offend me." She fully intended to greedily watch as he buttoned the shirt. Would she ever tire of drinking in his physical perfection? She tried to picture George old and portly, but the vision would not come.

"Did you have an enjoyable evening last night?" she asked.

He started to button his shirt. "I always enjoy it when I'm with my friends. They make me laugh, and they make me happy."

If only she could. "Glee tells me Blanks, too, is rather enamored of the fast life with Appleton and the twins. For the life of me, I fail to see how three such mundane men could be the source of such levity."

"I admit when taken one by one, none of them is particularly plucky, but together we have a great deal of fun."

"I think it's time they got married. None of them are spring chickens any longer. They're all past thirty, are they not?"

"They are, but they're exceedingly shy with well-bred ladies."

Her eyes twinkled mischievously. "Does that mean they are not shy with women who are not well bred?"

"I can't discuss that with you, Sally." He dragged up his limp cravat and circled his neck with it. "You're a lady. A virgin. Such is not fit for your delicate ears."

She came up to him and brushed a stray lock of

tumbled golden curls from his brow. "You forget, my dear husband, that I have two brothers."

"I never shared with my sisters information of such a . . . personal nature."

"Edmund didn't, either, but my younger brother and I are very close—and he does happen to be in His Majesty's Navy!" Her eyes glistened.

"I'll wager he's had his share of women."

"Even when he was up at university, he tells me." George chuckled as he sat in the chair and began to put on his boots. "We had a girl at Oxford . . . what am I doing telling you about things that should remain unspeakable between us?"

She came up to set a hand on his shoulder. "Please, George, don't treat me like I'm a virgin. I'd as lief people thought me otherwise." If she couldn't be a thoroughly bedded wife, she would at least like to be thought of as one.

"That will be deuced difficult, my dear. You are so very . . . decent."

"I'll wager you won't find me so decent when next we are at daggers drawn against one another—a circumstance I anticipate to occur within the next few days."

He nodded. "Yes, we don't seem to be able to go more than a few days without a disagreement." He finished putting on his boots.

"George?"

His head snapped up at the forlorn note in voice. "What, Sally?"

"Promise you won't ever hate me. I vow I shall never hate you."

He stood up and came to lower his forehead to bump against hers. "I promise I shall never hate you." His voice was especially low and unintentionally provocative.

He pulled away and moved toward the door. "You and Hettie or Lettie or whatever the gel's name is can commence to curl your hair now. I'm going to see if there's a breakfast to be had this morning."

By the time Hettie had curled Sally's hair, George was nowhere to be found. She should have expected him to be gone. After all, 'twas the season for horse racing in Bath, and George did love to wager on the horses.

It was just as good he was gone, for she had many duties to dispatch today. Just because she was young and from a lesser family than her husband did not mean that Sally would allow herself to become meek and complacent in her husband's home.

It was now her home, and there was much that needed attending to. The lack of a woman's hand showed greatly within the walls of this town house. She would start by removing the clutter. Everywhere she looked were papers and periodicals that no one had ever seen fit—or been qualified—to throw out. On the worktable in the drawing room, for instance, she shuffled through a heap of papers, some of which had been there for the past two years, as evidenced by the date on a yellowed copy of the *Edinburgh Review*.

With the housekeeper, Mrs. MacMannis, on her heels, Sally swept through each room, barking instructions for tidying each chamber. The tidiness issue taken care of downstairs, except for George's library, Sally grimly marched upstairs to the nursery. As usual, both children ran to Sally when she entered the room. She quickly kissed each of them, then explained she would be back shortly. "I have business with Hortense." Sally turned to the nurse. "I beg a private word with you, Hortense."

The stone-faced woman followed her from the room and down two flights of stairs to the first-floor library. Sally winced at its untidiness. She would have to assist her husband in going through his hoards of paperwork. Sally closed the door behind her and ordered Hortense to be seated.

Sally's heart began to race. As much as she disliked Hortense, she disliked more the task she was about to perform. "I must tell you, Hortense," Sally began, "that while I find you a most competent nurse, I do not find you suitable for my step-children."

Hortense's sour face became even more sour, and her mouth dropped open in shock. "How is that, my lady?"

"Because our children have been denied their mother's love, I believe they crave to be cared for by a woman of a far more affectionate nature than that which you possess."

"I can't help it if my disposition is not so lovey-dovey. I've never been mean to the children, nor have I ever neglected them."

"No, you haven't, but it's been my observation that you're too inflexible."

"But—"

Sally cut her off. "There's really nothing you can say that will persuade me not to turn you out."

"Turn me out?" The woman's eyes narrowed. "Does his lordship know of yer wicked actions against me?"

"My husband has given me the authority to make all the decisions concerning his—our—children for he knows how precious they are to me."

"I'll not leave before I have my say with the master."

"I have no objections to your speaking with Lord Sedgewick. I believe he will agree with me." In a dismissive voice, she added, "We will, of course, give you a good recommendation and are prepared to settle you with half a year's wages to tide you over until you find new employment. You are competent, and I am certain you will find a satisfactory post in another household. Perhaps you'll be the right person for other children. But not for mine." Sally strolled to the door. "You may pack your things now, Hortense. We have no further need for your services."

The following morning, George found himself in his library face to face with The Curmudgeon. Not only was the woman possessed of a sour disposition, she was also cursed with a face perpetually set in a frown. He fleetingly thought of the frightening effect the woman must have had on his children. How fortunate that Sally was tossing her out. A pity he had heretofore been blind to Hortense's shortcomings. "Sit down, please, Hortense."

He was never comfortable when turning out a servant. Deuced unpleasant. Sally—during their bedchamber chat this morning—had apprised him of her conversation with Hortense the day before; so he had a good idea of why Hortense had sought this interview with him. "You wished to speak with me?" he asked, meeting the woman's icy glare as he lowered himself into a chair behind his massive desk.

"I did," she said, her face tightly contorted into a scowl. "I thought you—as the person who hired me—should be aware that the new Lady Sedgewick has dismissed me."

"I am aware of that fact, ma'am, and I must tell you the decision to do so was mutually agreed upon by my wife and me."

Hortense's jaw lowered, and her eyes slitted even more narrowly. "But my lord! For these past four years my only concern has been for your children, and not once in that time has one word been leveled against my competence."

"You are most competent, Hortense, but my wife and I desire someone who is possessed of a less stern nature to deal with our children."

Her dark eyes seemed to shoot off sparks. "Just because I'm not all lovey-dovey, that upstart new wife of yours holds me in dislike."

"The decision was as much mine as it was Lady Sedgewick's," George defended. He still had not become accustomed to the idea of Sally Spenser claiming Dianna's title, even though she had already glided smoothly into the role of mother to Dianna's babes. "And I'll not have you speak disrespectfully of my wife," he added.

Hortense rose to her feet and glared at him. "I can see there's no further need to continue this conversation."

"No need at all," George said, standing and escorting the dissatisfied woman to the door.

After she was gone, a lightness buoyed George. Good riddance to horse-faced Hortense! He experienced another emotion, too, though it took him a moment to realize that it was a swelling pride over Sally. He only wished he could have seen her when she unflinchingly berated the heartless nurse. His Sally was doing a fine job. A most fine job indeed.

Chapter 11

In the days that followed, their lives fell into a routine. It was not a routine that was particularly to Sally's liking. She went to bed alone every night yet woke up each morning with George, smelling of cigars and port, beside her. Their private time each morning was the only part of the day when she was really able to talk to him, for he was always off to a horse race or a boxing mill, and at night he much preferred carousing with his male companions over dancing attendance upon the plain woman he had married.

Sally's heart flinched whenever it crossed her mind that George and his friends might be keeping company with whores. She knew George to be a virile man, and she often found herself wondering if he ever desired sexual relations with anyone other than the wife he had lost. Her brother David had told her men had a biological need to bed women, whether they loved the woman or not. Though she had long been accustomed to the idea of her virile younger brother keeping company with women of that sort, Sally was completely unable to picture George with that kind of woman.

Since she had little influence over her husband's behavior, Sally decided to concentrate her efforts on those matters she could control. The condition of their house was shaping up. Her firing of Hortense must have put fear into all the other servants for they never seemed to stop working. Indeed, every chandelier sparkled, all the books in the library were free of dust, and every piece of furniture in the house had been moved so the floors beneath could be thoroughly cleaned. She rather fancied it was the most thorough work the servants had ever been required to do.

In regard to the now vacant position of nurse, Sally had notified the agency that she was in need of a gentle, kindhearted woman to serve as nurse to her children, and she was soon besieged with applications that she divided into two stacks: one for rejections, the other for consideration. Of course, she would not make so important a decision without consulting her husband.

Each day she made time from her schedule to take the children to one of Bath's parks. As much as she and Georgette tried to get Sam to speak, their efforts were fruitless. Other than "Mama," he refused to say anything. Not a single night did she lay her head on her pillow and not worry about the little boy who was now her son.

Though she had not been successful at getting Sam to talk, she had been extremely successful at teaching him and his sister to put their things away in the proper place. It became a joke between her and Georgette that the children must not turn out to be as sloppy as their papa. "What are we to do with him?" Sally would lament, her eyes sparkling as much as the children's.

She and George had now been married for three weeks and had not had even one of their famous disagreements yet. A decidedly unusual occurrence.

That was to change.

Once Sally had read a stack of over two hundred applications for the nurse position, she narrowed it down to two and twenty. Then she informed her husband over breakfast one morning that she expected him to assist her in selecting a new nurse.

"I trust you completely," he said, not deigning to look up from his morning newspaper. "After all, I heartily approved of dismissing The Old Curmudgeon." Both of them had ascribed that moniker to Hortense.

"It's not that I'm incapable of making a good decision," Sally countered, "it's that it's a decision you and I should make together. They are *your* children."

He glanced up from his paper briefly. "Ours, and I'm certain you'll do a far better job than I in selecting the new nurse. After all, I'm the one responsible for saddling the children with The Curmudgeon."

She smiled. "Even were I their blood mother, I would seek your guidance in this decision."

Mildly irritated with her, he tossed his newspaper aside. "You will not let up until I accommodate you, will you?"

"No, I won't," she said, her eyes shooting daggers at him.

He had to admit his slim wife could be a rather formidable opponent. Again, he wished he could have heard her when she dismissed The Curmudgeon. He'd wager that she'd minced no words. She certainly never had with him. He could count on her to be completely truthful, though he had to admit she was never offensive. He drew in his breath and tossed her an impatient glance as he threw down his newspaper. "Very well, dearest nag. Where shall we undertake this momentous task you insist on involving me in?"

"In your library, I think. Besides, we haven't finished tidying that chamber."

He mumbled an oath about her incessant tidying. Despite his impatience with her constant efforts to physically unclutter his life, he had to admit the house was far more enjoyable now that she had become its mistress. Not even Dianna had known how to eliminate the clutter from their life. And he rather fancied neat rooms now that he possessed them.

He removed himself from the breakfast table and followed Sally to the library. She gathered up a stack of letters and went to sit upon the sofa. She patted the spot next to her. "Come sit here, George."

He sat beside her and watched as she read a letter that was neatly printed. It was the only application that was not in handwriting—and printing seemed more masculine than feminine trait, George thought.

"This one," Sally began, "states her age as eighteen. Though she has no experience, she is quick to point out that she was responsible for the care of two younger sisters and four younger brothers."

"You'd think she'd want a rest from children," George quipped.

"It's probably the only thing she knows. I'm not in favor of hiring this one."

"Because she lacks formal experience?"

"Oh no," Sally said. "Because her abundance of experience has likely rendered her too inured to children. I should like someone who is enchanted with children—quite possibly someone with no experience with children, who will, therefore, find their every action delightful."

He found himself smiling down at her. Every word she said, though impossible to prove empirically, seemed so wise. No wonder she was at the top of her class at Miss Worth's School for Young Ladies. "Then it is to be hoped one of the applicants will be imbued with those qualities you seek."

"I *did* demand a sweet nature in the job announcement."

He laughed. "I'm sure you did. I can't picture you leaving anything to chance."

She looked up at him wondrously. "You've entrusted me with the most important task on earth, that of raising your precious children. I mean to be successful. I don't just want them to be well taken care of and well educated, I want them to be happy. I want them to be compassionate and caring . . ." Her voice trailed off.

He felt all choked up. Her tender heart for his children seemed to do that to him. Without being aware of what he was doing, he lifted her hand and kissed it. "Each day of our marriage, I'm more convinced of what an excellent wife I've chosen."

She gave him a wistful look and spoke with a shaky voice. "That's a very sweet thing for you to say."

"Men don't wish to be sweet, Sally."

She returned her attention to the stack of applicants. "Is that why men never smile in their portraits?"

"I suppose it is."

She continued to summarize each applicant's letter. One was from a woman who had been nurse in homes of The Quality for the past three and thirty years. Another was from a woman who lamented that her little lambs had gone off to Eton, and she was no longer needed. George wished to see what Sally would think of that lady. He thought she would be favorably impressed.

She was. With that application, she started a new pile for the letters from applicants who were under serious consideration.

"She sounds like a softie," he said. "Just like you."

She laughed. "I'm afraid there's not a servant in the house who thinks of me as a softie."

"Don't ever belittle yourself on account of being a natural-born mistress. You're fair and generous and offer praise to your servants when they have earned it. I heard you the other day when you insisted the servants rest for a spell while they were cleaning windows. And by your example in working beside them, you've earned their undying respect—and loyalty."

"I do so hope you're right. I worry that I'm too demanding."

"I think we're all aware the house was in a shambles when you took over its running."

"I wouldn't say it was in a shambles—"

"It was," he interrupted.

"Well, it is to be hoped the servants don't begin referring to me as The Curmudgeon behind my back."

"They won't. You're still a softie. They've only to see you with the children."

"A softie is precisely what I would like for the children." Her glance fell on the next application.

"Then you've found your woman. This one who laments that her lambs have grown."

She set aside the stack of letters. "I believe you're

right, George! Can you ever in your wildest dreams imagine The Curmudgeon referring to our babes as lambs?"

Our babes. God, but it felt good to share responsibility—and love—for his children with another living, breathing, compatible soul. Since joining his life to Sally, it had become so much richer. Though still it was tormented. Because of Dianna's loss.

Sally glanced back at the woman's letter. "Her name is Miss Primble. There's another thing I like about her."

He lifted a quizzing brow.

"Her lambs were little boys. It has been my observation that far too many governesses and nurses have a preference for prim, ladylike little girls. I want someone who likes boys." Tossing him an apologetic glance, she quickly explained herself. "We never have need to worry that Georgette will not be a great favorite because of her sweet nature, pretty manners, and cooperative ways. But boys, as you must know, are totally different from little girls."

He swelled with pride at Sally's mention of Georgette's attributes. He knew her praise was genuine, that she loved Georgette as he did.

He also swelled with pride that the woman whom he had selected for his children's mother had an appreciation for boys. His own nurse had certainly not. She had been the original Curmudgeon. Even though he was not as close to the boy as he was to his daughter, George appreciated the fact his wife would never neglect the son Dianna had died bearing. "I suggest you put aside that stack of letters and draft a letter immediately to Miss Thimble."

"Miss Primble."

"Should you like to use my desk?"

"You mean our desk, do you not, my dearest husband? I mean to share everything in this house equally with you," she said with a little laugh.

What a paradox his wife was! She made it sound as if she married him for mercenary reasons, when he knew that to be as far from the truth as possible. Were she possessed of even a smidgeon of pecuniary greed, she would never have turned down the marriage proposal offered by Mr. Higginbottom, who was one of the wealthiest men in the kingdom. No, George thought, shaking his head to himself, never was a less mercenary lady than Sally born.

He suspected that since he hadn't made Sally his wife in that most important way, she was adamant to express her wifely rights in all other areas. Of course, she was probably grateful not to have to engage in sex with him. Women—well-born women especially, even Dianna—did not particularly enjoy the sexual act. And he'd wager that this little bag of bones he had married was no exception. Oh, she was loving enough. But he could not imagine her ever writhing with joy beneath his naked body. She was much too proper. A vicar's daughter and all that. Her father had likely laid her mother but three times. One for each offspring. For Mrs. Spenser seemed cold as ice.

He watched as Sally moved gracefully to *their* desk. Her hair, as it was now every day, was curled, and she wore her clothes especially well. She looked rather like those drawings the women ogled over in the fashion magazines.

As she sat down and began to write, he came to stand over her, oddly curious to see his own wife's handwriting. How peculiar that he had never before had occasion to see it. Her penmanship, like herself, was neat, precise, and flawless. No doubt she was Miss Worth's prized penmanship pupil, too.

"You have a lovely hand, my dear." He hoped he did not offend her by frequently referring to her as *my dear.* It seemed a most natural thing to call this woman who had become his wife.

"Thank you, George. I regret that I cannot return the compliment. Your penmanship is rather like you are, dearest husband—a bit slothful."

"Just a bit? You wound me. I thought my penmanship was abominable. At least that's how Miss McGillicuddy referred to it."

"I take it Miss McGillicuddy was your governess."

"Mine and Felicity's and later, Glee's."

"That was a most uncharitable thing for her to say. It only reinforces my belief that the majority of governesses prefer little girls."

"Miss McGillicuddy certainly did. At least she strongly preferred Felicity. But, then, of course, Felicity was perfect in every way."

"Like Georgette," Sally said, nodding.

He beamed. "Exactly. Now, when Glee came around . . . I admit Glee led the old bag on a merry dance. She wasn't at all like Felicity."

"Poor Glee, she always did so hate being compared to her perfect sister. Even though Glee is spectacularly beautiful in her own right, do you know she doesn't believe she can ever measure up to her elder sister?"

"She certainly measures up in Blanks's eyes. He's far too besotted over her for his own good. Told me any number of times how blessed he is to have captured the loveliest lady in the three kingdoms."

Sally frowned. "I do so worry about the both of them. I don't believe I've ever seen two people more in love—or more estranged."

George nodded, frowning. "A pity. He was so deliriously happy. Before he realized his love for Glee could kill her."

In childbed. Like Dianna. Sally's heart thumped. "Blanks is far too morbid. Can't you try to convince him Glee comes from sturdy stock?"

"Ever since . . ." he had vowed to speak of Dianna no more. It was the only way to be decent to the very decent woman who had consented to become his wife. He cleared his throat. "Blanks has lost two women whose lives were intertwined with his. His own mother's and that of his wife's sister-in-law. How can I assure him he won't lose Glee?"

"George! Surely you know how robust the women in your own family are. It took a nasty fall from a horse to kill your mother. Felicity has borne two children with not a single ill effect, and Glee's borne one. Let us hope Joy's not their last."

"I honestly don't know what to hope for." His voice cracked as he spoke.

"I believe Glee would rather die in Blanks's arms than to live to old age not in his arms."

The devil take it! Die in Blanks's arms. 'Twas a most evocative thing for a virgin to say. There was a great deal more passion in the woman he had married than he would ever have believed.

He had to remove himself from this room. All this talk of love and passion and dead wives was more than he intended to bear. "I really must be gone, my dear," he said as he swept from the chamber. "Get Peters to post the letter to Miss Thimble today."

"Miss Primble," Sally called after him.

Chapter 12

There were more people than normal at the Pump Room this day, Sally reflected as she and Glee swept into the crowded chamber and began to search for Felicity, who had promised to meet them there. Sally's glance met that of Miss Johnson, whose glare alighted on her for a moment, then flicked away with no acknowledgement. To Sally's astonishment, Miss Johnson stormed to the water attendants without even taking leave of her companion, the nearsighted Miss Arbuckle.

The horrid Miss Johnson must be furious indeed that the unworthy Sally had snagged the prime prize on the Marriage Mart. As the victor, Sally could afford to be gracious. She had no plan to cut off her acquaintance with Miss Johnson nor to criticize the young lady in any way.

The bespectacled Miss Arbuckle glanced up and saw Sally and Glee, nodded brightly, and began to make her way to them, only just this moment realizing her companion had left her without a word of farewell.

"I trust you're doing well this afternoon, Miss Arbuckle," Sally said to the young lady.

She nodded to Sally, then turned her attention to Glee. "Tell me, my dear Mrs. Blankenship, is it true the younger Mr. Blankenship is coming soon to Bath?"

Sally's heart went out to poor Miss Arbuckle, who was hopelessly in love with Blanks's younger brother. The young man also appeared to hold Miss Arbuckle in deepest affection, but since he was a younger son and not possessed of large financial prospects, he chose to stay a bachelor. Glee said he had a most generous settlement but was far too parsimonious to ever desire a wife.

"Dear me," Glee answered, "I don't know. Blanks may have received a communication from him which he has failed to impart to me."

Miss Arbuckle's face fell. Then she returned her attention to Sally. "I know it's none of my concern, but I am curious to know the source of your falling out with Miss Johnson."

"I've had no falling out with Miss Johnson," Sally said. "I'm eager to know what makes you think Miss Johnson and I do not get on."

"I don't like to gossip," Miss Arbuckle prefaced, "but Miss Johnson's taken to saying the most vicious things about you—and about Lord Sedgewick."

Glee openly bristled at her friend's words. "It is my belief that Miss Johnson is decidedly upset that my brother offered his hand to Sally and not to her. Surely you have noticed how Miss Johnson has always pressed her company and her attention upon my impervious brother."

"I have noticed but wasn't sure others perceived things as I perceived them," Miss Arbuckle said.

"You know how spoiled she is," Glee added. "She

always gets what she wants and cannot bear to be thwarted in anything."

"I daresay she did have her sights set on becoming Lady Sedgewick," Miss Arbuckle lamented.

"I'd really prefer not to be having this conversation," Sally said, raising her eyes to the balcony where the musicians played.

"Well, I'm not ready to let it drop!" Glee protested. "I must know what kind of things Miss Johnson is saying about my brother and dear sister."

The blood rushed to Miss Arbuckle's face. Then she moved closer and began to whisper. "She said Lord Sedgewick has compromised Miss Spenser— I mean the new Lady Sedgewick—and was forced to marry her."

Sally's eyes widened, and her temper flared.

But not as much as Glee's. "That's outrageous! Sally is a lady, and my brother is a gentleman. I know for a fact he would never compromise a young lady of good birth."

Sally was utterly humiliated. Did all of Bath think the only reason George married her was because she had freely offered him her sexual favors? No doubt most would be quick to believe such a lie. It made far more sense than the truth. Who would ever believe Lord Sedgewick would select the plain and penniless Sally Spenser for his wife? And who would think the fun-loving gallivanter capable of marrying for the sake of the children he seemed barely to tolerate? Only Sally knew how dearly he loved those children.

It was all she could do to keep from bursting into tears. Then she saw her husband and Blanks enter the chamber, and she was sure she would explode into a torrent of tears. She drew in a deep breath as George walked toward her, and she prayed that she would be able to keep her composure.

Unfortunately, George's initial glimpse at her told him something was wrong. His brows low, his voice gentle, he hastened to her side and spoke with concern. "Are you quite well, my dear?"

"No, she's not!" Glee said, stomping up to her brother. "You'll never believe what the odious Miss Johnson has gone and done."

"What?" George demanded, jerking away to face his enraged sister.

Glee put hands to hips. "She is spreading the most hideous rumors about you and Sally."

His brows dipped into a V. "Pray, what could she possibly have to say? My wife and I have nothing to be ashamed of." He flicked a smiling glance at Sally.

"She is telling everyone that the only reason you married Miss Spenser was because you had compromised her."

His eyes flared in anger. "Why would she make up such an outrageous lie?"

"Because *she* wanted be the next Lady Sedgewick," Glee said.

George was so furious, sparks seemed to shoot from his eyes. "Then I'm the reason my wife has been so maligned?"

"Don't blame yourself, George," Glee said.

"I won't have my wife so viciously slandered." He turned to face Sally and cupped her face with his big hand. "I won't allow her—or anyone—to ever hurt you."

Before she could reply, he turned with a jerk, left their circle, and stormed across the floor, past the water attendants, past Appleton and the twins without speaking, and came up to Miss Johnson, who was surrounded by young men.

* * *

A pity the wretched Miss Johnson was not a man, for George would have taken great pleasure in beating her to pulp or in challenging her to a duel. Lamentably, he could do neither.

"Bath is so dreadfully dull this season," Miss Johnson was remarking to her admirers when George drew up beside her and glared.

"A word with you, Miss Johnson," George snapped.

She tossed a startled glance at his angry face. Her laughing eyes went cold. Her glance flicked back to the circle of young men gathered around her. "Excuse me."

George gripped her arm and walked to a bank of windows.

"You're hurting my arm," she protested.

He spoke in a voice as cold as ice water. "Count yourself fortunate you're not a man for I would likely wish to kill you."

Her eyes rounded with fear. "Why would you wish to do that, my lord?"

"You cannot deny that you've been spreading lies about my wife and me all over the city."

She clutched at her breast. "Never! Why, Miss Spenser is a very dear friend of mine."

"She's not Miss Spenser!" he snapped. "She's Lady Sedgewick now, and I believe you to be jealous of her good fortune."

She gave a mock laugh. "Me? Jealous of mousy Sally? Really, my lord, do you not have eyes in your head? Am I not possessed of far more beauty than . . . your wife? Do I not possess more wealth?"

"The physical attributes you possess, I fear, are greatly offset by your vicious tongue and want of good manners."

She stomped her slippered foot. "How dare you say such things to me!"

"Unlike you, Miss Johnson, I speak the truth."

Even as they filled with tears, her eyes narrowed to slits. "You will pay for maligning me in such a manner."

She turned away from him, but he closed his hand around the top of her arm. "You will *never* again malign my wife, Miss Johnson, or I shall see to it that there is nowhere on English soil where you or your family will ever be received."

With that final, bitter retort, George stormed back to his wife. He was not unaware that half the assemblage had witnessed Lord Sedgewick administer a blistering set-down to the humiliated Miss Johnson.

That night, carrying a torch, Betsy Johnson slipped from her darkened bedroom and made her way to the mews located on the back side of their block. Her father's money ensured that their stables could be located adjacent to their impressive house.

Even though she barely eased the stable door open, the noise set the horses whinnying in their stalls. Holding up her lantern so she could see better, she located the crude wooden stairway that led up to the sleeping loft of their groom, a young man named Ebinezer who was no more than a year Miss Johnson's senior.

As she came to the top of the steps, she heard the rustle of straw from Ebinezer's mattress. Since she no longer needed stealth, she settled her boots loudly on the floor where Ebinezer's straw bed lay.

The groom, wearing a rumpled nightshirt, bolted up when he saw his lovely mistress standing not ten feet from him. "What brings ye 'ere at this 'our, miss?" he inquired, quickly covering his bare leg with the sheet.

"You," she said throatily, her hand moving to stroke her breast, making slow, sensuous circles around her nipple. Then, before his startled eyes, she began to unfasten her dress. His eyes widened as her pale blue gown slipped to the floor.

Betsy Johnson stood before him wearing only a thin linen chemise that was nearly as transparent as glass.

The freckle-faced young man's mouth dropped open and he turned his gaze to the wall. "Really, miss, you ought not to be 'ere doin' these things."

She strolled toward him, lifting off her chemise as she sank onto his straw mattress. "Look at me, Ebinezer. Turn around," she said in a harsh whisper.

He slowly turned, his eyes falling to her breasts that were the size of apples, tipped with rosy, pointed nipples. He drew in a long breath.

"Let me feel you, Ebinezer," she whispered huskily, sliding her hand beneath his nightshirt, closing her hand over his engorged shaft. "Ah, I see you're ready for me."

"But miss—"

She drew closer to him and could feel the heat of his breath as she settled her lips on his, her hand sliding possessively over his swollen member.

"Do you know where I want you to touch me, Ebinezer?"

He swallowed hard. "No, miss."

"Between my legs. Side your finger into my slickness, Ebinezer," she said throatily into his moistened ear. "I'm like hot, melted butter. Just for you." Then she drew her thighs apart as she sat to face him.

He obliged.

Her hips began to rise with his movements, and she clenched herself tightly around his finger. "Faster, Ebinezer!" she shouted.

He went faster.

In feeble increments, she lowered herself to his

mattress. "Now, Ebinezer, now! I want your big cock inside me."

Groaning now, Ebinezer rolled over on her and eased himself into her lubricated orifice.

"Harder, Ebinezer!" she urged. "Come into me harder."

Grunting hungrily, the groom began to pulse into her with frenzied thrusts until she screamed out her pleasure, her voice as ragged as his. With one final thrust, he cried out his own bestial pleasure, then collapsed over her.

She did so enjoy a good fuck. Those silly girls at Miss Worth's had never guessed what she was doing climbing from her dormitory window at night and prowling the streets of town, lifting her skirts for any man staggering from a public house.

Oh yes, she had craved these illicit unions since she gave Simms, the underfootman, her virginity at the age of twelve. Not that Simms had wanted it. He protested that she was an innocent young maiden, but his protests died out when he found her fully developed naked body squirming beneath his bedsheets one night.

She had been a most mature twelve-year-old. It was because of Papa's books. Her father, as wealthy as a nabob but blissfully ignorant, had thought to become a fine gentleman by purchasing two tons of leather-bound books for the Johnson library. Neither her fool father nor fool mother had ever opened a single book.

Ah, but Betsy allowed the books in the library to nurture her. There was one particular book . . . she would wager her own papa was unaware of how very many sexual positions there were. And her papa was a lusty man, himself. More than once she had peered through keyholes to watch him take his pleasure on buxom housemaids.

Almost always, her corpulent father was on top.

He was not nearly as adventuresome as his only offspring. There was not a position Betsy Johnson had not tried.

She ran her hand over Ebinezer's hard buttocks. He was obviously more experienced than the new footman, who had a propensity to come much too quickly. No doubt, Ebinezer's age accounted for his experience. The footman was but seventeen. She looked forward to furthering Ebinezer's experience.

They both lay there panting for a moment. Then Betsy did something that startled her groom. She sat up and lowered her face to his groin and closed her lips over his wet tip. "I thank your cock," she said as he pulled down his shirt to cover himself.

Brushing herself up against him again, she whispered huskily, "Did you enjoy me, Ebinezer?"

"Aye, Miss Johnson."

"Should you like me to come back again?"

He lowered his face to hers and kissed her. "Aye, Miss Johnson."

"I will pleasure you as you've never been pleasured before, Ebinezer." Her tongue traced her own lips. "There is, however, something I wish you to do for me."

"Anything, Miss Johnson," he said, his hands greedily stroking her bare breasts.

"There is a very vile man upon whom I should like for you to spy. Mostly at night, I'm afraid, but don't worry about missing me warming your bed. I vow you'll not go wanting for my favors."

She drew closer and sucked his tongue into her mouth. "Shall we have another go at it, love?" Her hand slid over his slick shaft.

Chapter 13

Miss Primble did not look at all as Sally had pictured her. For one thing, she was much younger. The new nurse was no older than Sally's own two and twenty years. Which meant that she must have come to her "lambs" who were now at Eton when she was little more than a girl, fourteen at the most. Awfully young to take on such responsibilities, Sally thought. Even though she was much younger than expected, Sally immediately decided that her youth was a good thing. After all, Georgette and Sam liked Sally above all others, and she was but two and twenty. The children would likely be more comfortable with a younger woman. The Curmudgeon was forty if she was a day.

Another thing about Miss Primble that Sally had not been prepared for was her plumpness. Sally decided she must be a very good eater indeed. She only hoped Miss Primble's affinity for overindulging would not influence Georgette and Sam. They both looked absolutely perfect just the way they were.

Sally strolled up to the new nurse with a welcoming smile on her face. "I'm so happy you were able to come so quickly." She glanced at Miss Primble's valise. "First, allow me to show you to your chamber." Sally gave the butler orders to carry up Miss Primble's valise.

They walked up the stairs to the second floor. The first room they came to was Sam's, which Sally indicated to the nurse. The next was Georgette's, and next to Georgette's was a small room for Miss Primble. Sally showed her the room, which lacked a bed though it did offer a comfortable chair. "You will sleep in the children's room," Sally informed her. "Actually Georgette has taken to sleeping alone quite well since her former nurse left. But Sam's just barely two, and I prefer that someone stay in his room with him. He is frightened of the dark. He's such a baby still," Sally said in an indulgent voice.

Miss Primble nodded. "I 'ope he doesn't miss his former nurse too dreadfully."

"He doesn't."

Miss Primble shot a quizzing gaze at Sally.

"I dismissed her because she was not particularly pleasant to the children."

"How could someone be mean to God's most precious little creatures?" the outraged nurse asked.

Sally smiled. She liked Miss Primble very much indeed. "Come, let's go to the nursery."

Miss Primble followed Sally up the last flight of stairs to the children's nursery. There, Georgette was dressing up the big cat, and Sam was standing on a stool gazing out the window at the horses that perpetually passed in front of their town house. The tot had become completely fascinated with horses, and he never tired of looking at them. Sally had decided she really must speak to his father about procuring a pony for Sam. Of course, he was far too young to sit one by himself, but she saw no reason why she could not grasp on to him as he sat a gentle mount.

"Sam! Georgette!" Sally called, "Your new nurse, Miss Primble, has come. Please come and greet her."

Sam turned back to the window, but his sister dropped the discarded baby bonnet that was in her hand, walked up to her new nurse, and prettily said, "How do you do, Miss Primble?"

Despite her size, Miss Primble nimbly dropped to her knees to face Georgette. "I am doing very well now that I've come to Bath to take care of you and your brother. You must know I am depending on you to help me take care of little Sam. Do you think you can you help me, lamb?"

A smile on her face, Georgette nodded.

"Tell me, does yer brother like to rock in a rocking chair?"

Georgette nodded again. "With Miss Spencer— I mean, with Mama."

Miss Primble sent a questioning glace to Sally.

"I'm actually just the children's stepmother," Sally said with disappointment. She far preferred others to think she was the children's true mother because that's how she liked to think of herself. "I've only been Lady Sedgewick for a month."

Miss Primble rose to a standing position. "But you're . . . you're so concerned, so loving. I took you for their real mum."

Sally beamed. "I think of myself as their real mother. I've known them all their lives." She lowered her voice. "Their mother died on childbed with little Sam. I'm most likely the closest thing to a mother he's ever known. Their previous nurse was rather an ogre."

Miss Primble's eyes narrowed. "There ought to

be a special place in hell for those what are unkind to children."

"She really wasn't unkind," Sally explained. "It was more that she was never, ever kind."

Miss Primble frowned. "A pity."

"There's something I should like to tell you," Sally said. "Both the children love to be read to. They a especially like *The Life and Perambulation of a Mouse.*"

Nodding, the nurse waddled over to the rocker and dropped her considerable weight onto its seat. "Sam!" she shouted.

He spun around.

"Don't stand there, ye little goose. Come sit on Miss P's lap so as I can read to ye." She reached down and picked up the book that they loved their father to read to them.

Sam's eyes rounded as he jumped off the stool and came running to Miss Primble.

She gathered him up and set him on her wide lap. "I'll need ye to turn the pages for me, lad."

He nodded his little head.

Smiling, Sally backed out of the room, knowing at last that her children were in good hands.

Hazard was not his game, George decided. The devil take it—and the twenty quid he had already taken. George got up from the table at Mrs. Glenwick's Gaming Establishment and moved to the vingt-et-un table where Elvin, the quietest twin, sat. "Any luck?" George asked.

"A bit."

George tossed his coin on the table. "I daresay your brother wishes he could say the same. He's down rather heavily."

"Our pockets would be a great deal heavier if we

didn't feel compelled to always be in Bath with our friends."

"As would mine." George peered at the card that faced down. Not good. Another deuced seven! "But it is so deadly dull in the country. No mills. No horse races."

"No Miss Avery's."

"Blanks and I aren't as enamored of Miss Avery's girls as you fellows are."

"I should hope not. The both of you are married men, though I'm at a loss to know when either of you have a chance to bed those lovely wives of yours. You're with us lonely bachelors every night of the week."

George went rigid. His sleeping arrangements with Sally were not Elvin's affair. Of course, he would greatly dislike for anyone to know of his complete abstinence from sexual relations, and he would as lief not have others know why he had married Sally. His lack of interest in her as a woman could humiliate her. Already, she had been humiliated over the devious Betsy Johnson's accusations. "There's a lot to be said about making love in the daylight," George said.

Elvin smiled slyly. "The woman's body is a lovely thing to behold."

Quite oddly and completely unsummoned, George conjured up a vision of Sally lying in their bed, offering her slip of a body to him. Even more surprising was the profound physical effect such a vision elicited below his waist.

Elvin turned over his card. "Vingt-et-un!"

Frowning, George indicated his need for an additional card. It was a queen. He threw in his cards and watched Elvin scoop up his winnings.

When play began again, Elvin said, "I don't understand you or Blanks at all. If I were to be blessed with a lovely wife, I assure you I'd be in her bed early every night."

The fellow had to be talking about George's sister. Glee was a reputed beauty, though she was merely a pesky little sister to George. A pity Sally was not deemed attractive—except by Mr. Higginbottom. Upon reflection, George decided he would never again imbibe Higginbottom ale. Couldn't tolerate a man who would prey on innocent young women like Sally. Even if that prey included the offer of marriage.

As the dealer turned over her card, George thought of Sally's naked flesh, and he grew more rigid. Sweat beaded on his brow. The lady he had married really was not so unattractive. Though her skin was a bit darker than that acceptable by fashion mavens, he rather liked its tawniness. Her face was free of any type of blemish, and her teeth were straight and white. Her smile was actually quite nice, and he found her large chocolate-colored eyes rather sensuous, actually. A pity her hair was so deuced straight, and a pity she was so very thin. But, then, actually, she was shaped much like Dianna, who had also been slender. And Dianna's naked body had been a feast for his greedy eyes. And greedy hands.

"Will you come to the races tomorrow?" Elvin asked.

"When have I ever missed?" George said with a smile.

"I suppose Lady Sedgewick is too new a bride to complain over your many absences."

"Lady Sedgewick is not noted for her meekness. She has no problem confronting me with the error of my ways. It's my belief she does not disapprove of my nocturnal activities."

"You're not painting a very flattering picture of your own prowess in the bedchamber."

George stiffened. "I assure you Lady Sedgewick is a well-pleasured woman." He disliked lying to his lifelong friend, but he disliked more the idea that Elvin would think George did not find Sally desirable. The poor girl had given up enough to become his wife. The least he could do was allow others to think he found her desirable.

They both lost the next hand, and Elvin tossed in his cards and stood up. "I'd better rescue my brother while he still has enough money for Miss Avery's."

George chuckled as he strolled to the faro table, where Blanks was at play. "I believe I'll be on my way home now," George said. "I've been most generous to Mrs. Glenwick thus far tonight."

Blanks turned to his friend. "Wait just a moment and I'll give you a lift in my gig."

Riding was better than walking. A pity George could no longer afford to keep a gig. If his luck didn't turn, he'd have to sell the carriage and the matched bays next. Not a welcome proposal at all.

Early mornings were Sally's favorite time of the day. That was the only time she was completely alone with her husband. That they were in the intimacy of their own bedchamber made their time together even more welcome. She had grown so completely comfortable with him, she no longer blushed when he beheld her in her skimpy night shift.

During these private mornings they discussed the day that awaited, or they told each other what happened on the previous day. Sally kept him abreast of the children's activities.

It seemed to her during this brief, glorious interlude each day that she was truly married to George. Her eyes would rake over his powerful body and she would fight the urge to stroke the dark hair that formed a V on his mighty chest. She came to think of his body as belonging to her, for he presumably shared it with no one else. His well-muscled body was like her dear papa's last letter to her: something she received succor from but shared with no one else.

This morning he stirred back and forth for a moment, then opened his eyes and offered her a lazy smile.

"Miss Primble came yesterday," Sally said to him as she watched him come awake. She was lying beside him, resting her head on her hands.

He moved to his elbows, fluffed up his pillow, put it in back of him, and sat up. "Will she do, do you think?"

Sally's eyes danced. "I believe she will."

"Do the children seem to like her?"

Sally copied him, punching her pillow and fitting her back to the bed's headboard. "It's really too early to say. She was very good about enlisting Georgette's 'help' with Sam. You know how Georgette enjoys feeling needed. It seems to me Miss Primble plays to that need in your daughter."

"And Sam?"

"She's the first person—besides me—that Sam has ever willingly gone to. She hadn't been in the nursery five minutes before she had him snuggling in her ample lap."

His green eyes sparkled, and a lazy grin tugged at his mouth. "She's a large woman?"

Sally nodded, then burst out giggling. "You should have seen Sam nestled into her rolling bosom. He looked so utterly content."

George tossed his head back and gave a hearty laugh. "Then my son is not adverse to generously breasted women!"

Sally could not remember George ever before calling Sam his son. It was usually "my children" or "the boy." Never "my son." She glowed. "I shall become extremely jealous of Miss Primble for Sam is sure to prefer her bosom over mine—which is nearly nonexistent."

Color rose to Sally's cheeks when she found George's gaze sliding to the little nubs which barely stuck out beneath her night shift.

"Not all males are enamored of a large-chested woman," he said. "I never particularly fancied buxom women."

He used the past tense. Did that mean he no longer fancied women of any type? That it was Dianna or no one? Sally had no right to ask him, but . . . "George?" She gazed at the stubble on his cheeks and felt the heat of his body. She felt so utterly close to him. "Have you . . ." she cleared her throat. "Have you had a woman since Dianna?"

His eyes flared, and a look of fury came over his face. "My sexual activities are none of your business!" He lunged from the bed—completely naked—and slipped his breeches over his bare limbs.

Sally's voice cracked when she answered him. "I'm your wife, George."

He glared at her. "You're Lady Sedgewick. You're mother to my children. But you're not my wife." Then he stormed from the room.

So he had finally put to words what Sally already knew. She would never truly be George's wife.

Chapter 14

In the morning room Sally found her husband, a cup of coffee in one hand, the morning newspaper in his other. She walked to the table where the pot of coffee had been placed and poured herself a cup. Then she came to sit near him. She wanted to beg his forgiveness for daring to ask him so personal a question, but she was too embarrassed to bring up the subject again. And too humiliated over his brash—though accurate—retort. To dispel the tension between them, she inquired on the news. "I trust you will tell me if a great global upheaval is being reported upon."

He slid a warm glance to her over the top of the paper. Good—he was no longer angry.

She stood up again and went back to the table and fixed herself a plate of breakfast from the offerings there. "Should you like some cod, George?"

"No, thank you."

She had learned that he was never hungry the morning after a night of drinking. Like discarded dance cards after a ball, the lingering signs of her husband's overindulging were all too familiar to

Sally. "While you're at the races today, I thought I'd tidy your desk some more."

His newspaper dropped enough to reveal a pair of scowling eyes. "What makes you think I'm going to the races?"

She laughed. "I haven't known you half my life without learning a few things about you, George Pembroke, Viscount Sedgewick, and I know that as long as you can put weight to your feet you'll not miss a horse race." She leveled a pensive gaze at him. "Pray, how much do you have riding on today's meet?"

His mouth slid into a grin. "Fifteen quid."

Her lips puckered. "Do you know that fifteen pounds would pay the butler's and housekeeper's wages for two whole quarters? They would find fifteen pounds a veritable fortune."

"Servants' salaries are your business, my dear. I didn't marry the smartest girl from Miss Worth's School for Young Ladies for nothing. I've found you an excellent manager of my household."

"Then you don't object to me tidying your desk?"

He put down the paper. "I've nothing to hide from you, and I daresay my desk could use a good clean-out."

After he left, Sally went to the library and sat behind the large cherry desk that was nearly as masculine as the man she had married. She smiled as her glance wiped over his messy desk. She loved to do little things for him, whether it was fastening the buttons on his shirt or sorting through his heaps of mail and periodicals.

She began with the periodicals. Most of them she pitched, saving only the most recent editions. These she placed in a stack on the far left corner of his desk.

Next, she tackled the burgeoning mound of

crumpled posts. Few of these were dated, so she did not know whether it was safe to throw them out. She decided to sort them into subject matter. One section for tradesmen's bills. Another for personal letters and notes. On second thought, she deemed none of the personal correspondences worthy of saving. That they had been opened indicated George had already read them, and she knew her husband was blessed with an outstanding memory. Once he had read something, it was committed to his indelible memory. Before tossing them, though, she glanced at each to see if there was anything of importance. There was a very old note from Felicity written during her last visit to London. Another was from a school chum from York, who wrote to inform George his wife had just delivered him his first son. None of the correspondences seemed worthy of keeping. Save one.

There was a letter written by one Mr. Andrew Willingham, who described himself as George's steward at Hornsby Manor. Her brows lowered as she read it. The letter was to apply to his lordship for the sum of five and seventy pounds for a new piece of farm machinery that would increase crops, thereby increasing profits. The letter was dated some six weeks earlier.

She hastened to remove the accounts ledger from the top drawer of George's desk, and her eyes swept over the columns of figures. There was no expenditure for five and seventy pounds. In fact, no sum on the entire page surpassed four pounds.

She closed the book with disgust. Her husband apparently could not afford to pay debts in excess of four pounds, yet he would likely lose fifteen on the horse races today.

As angry as she was, she knew she had no right to judge him. He was only living in the style in which he had been raised. He spent money exactly as did his friends, none of whom had the social standing of her husband. And he really wasn't extravagant. He no longer kept a gig, and the wagers he made were not half as large as Blanks's.

Though she tried to be understanding, she was angered by her husband's failure to send Mr. Willingham the five and seventy pounds. That was money that would increase next year's income.

She got up from the desk and began to pace the room, her worried thoughts trying to find a way to get the five and seventy pounds to Mr. Willingham. Obviously, George could not spare so large a sum.

She sputtered to a stop, her face brightening. There was a way! She had almost forgotten the eighty-a-year settlement she received from her grandmother. Sally had barely touched this year's since all her needs had been taken care of by George or his family.

She went back to the desk and penned a letter to her solicitor, a self-satisfied smile on her face. As she sat there writing, Adams came in with the day's post. "An urchin just delivered this missive for you, my lady."

She reached for it and the other posts. "Thank you, Adams."

Though an urchin had delivered the note, it was written on high-quality paper. When she opened it, she was shocked to see letters cut out of newspapers forming the message. Even before she read it, it looked menacing. She trembled as she began to read it.

> *Your husband lost four and twenty pounds at Mrs. Glenwick's Gaming Establishment last night. Also, he has no desire for you. He was in another woman's bed.*

As she read the last, her stomach tumbled. Sally didn't give a fig about the lost money. It was the other woman who upset her. Greatly. Could she be the reason why George had behaved so angrily this morning when she had asked about his celibacy? Was Sally getting too close to the truth of his inconstancy?

Her head cradled in her hands, she wept bitterly. She had been better off not knowing. It was bad enough that she had fallen in love with a man whose heart was long buried. It was even more painful to learn that same husband preferred to assuage his manly needs with another woman. A woman who likely meant nothing to him.

Why not me? she asked with a convulsive sob. No woman could ever offer her husband a more willing body than the woman he had married. Sally knew that if only given the chance, she would pleasure him as no other.

She viciously tore up the menacing note and added it to the pile of periodicals and letters to throw on the fire.

As she did every morning, Sally awoke before her husband. And as she did every morning, she drank in the blatant masculinity of his bare chest and hulking shoulders. Her heart was still horribly bruised over the knowledge he found his sexual release in another woman's bed. She was better off before when she had thought he desired no one save Dianna. But now . . . now she knew of his virility. And now she knew that her physical self was so repugnant to him, he could lie beside her every night and never be tempted to slake his need with her.

She had tortured herself with speculation on the identity of the woman who had lain with her husband. For the past two days she had been unable to see a pretty woman and not wonder if she were the one.

Her heart caught as his lashes lifted, and he languidly turned toward her, his mouth hitched into a lazy smile.

"Good morning, George. Did Lady Luck smile upon you last night?"

That lazy smile hitched into a big grin. "I'm twenty pounds richer."

She fought the urge to fling her arms around him in celebration. "Speaking of riches, do you remember me telling you about the modest legacy I receive from my grandmother?" She peered into his eyes and for the first time realized they were the same color as English ivy.

His bored glance raked over the ceiling. "A hundred pounds or some such figure."

Her poor, dear husband, she thought, a smile breaking across her face. To him, one hundred pounds was much the same as eighty. "Eighty, actually."

"I don't want your eighty pounds, Sally. Do with it whatever you wish."

"I wish to send it to Mr. Willingham."

He snapped up to a sitting position and glared at her. "What do you know about Willingham?"

Clutching her thin shift to her chest, she pulled up to sit beside him, her back to the headboard. "I know he's your steward, and Glee says he's a very fine one, indeed."

"I wouldn't have him if he wasn't, but how is it you know of him and his need of money?"

She shrugged. "You said I could clean off your desk."

"You saw the letter." He did not sound happy about it.

Cheryl Bolen

"You told me you had nothing to hide."

"I don't. It's just that I don't wish to burden you with financial matters, either."

"My dear husband, it's no burden whatsoever. Since you no longer have a secretary, I propose to perform those duties. I'm rather good at ledgers."

"You're too bloody good at everything," he barked.

Her chin tilted upward. "I shall pretend you said that in flattering tones." She really hated being so overbearing, but her husband—having been born to nobility—had never learned to be practical. His secretary had always taken care of his accounting matters, but the small house in Bath was not large enough to accommodate the large staff George had once employed at Hornsby Manor. "My dearest husband," she cooed, "you have married a most practical woman, and it is my hope you will allow me to help get you out of debt."

He muttered an oath under his breath. "I don't want your grandmother's bloody money."

"It's not my grandmother's, dearest," she said sweetly. "It's ours. You've seen to it I want for nothing. Therefore, all I want is to make the lands at Hornsby more productive." She painfully recalled that a few years earlier that's what George had wanted, too. He had removed himself from the distractions of Bath and applied himself to turning around the Hornsby fortunes. And he'd been extremely successful. Until Dianna died.

He swung his legs over the side of the bed. "Very well, Sally, order my life for me."

As had become her custom, she turned so she would not see his nakedness. "If you don't care for yourself, think of the children, George. Do you not want them to be proud to bear the name of

Sedgewick? Do you not desire that Hornsby be a source of pride to them?"

He swallowed as he stepped into his breeches. "Of course you're right, Sensible Sal." He straightened up and began to put on his shirt.

She moved to him and wordlessly began to fasten his buttons, as she did each morning. Her daily thrill. She was so close she could feel his warm breath and the rise and fall of his powerful chest.

As she drew close to him, she remembered the horrid letter, and she could not bear to think of George lying with another woman. Her eyes moistened, and she quickly turned away from him as she fastened the last button. Impatient to flee their chamber, George did not notice her distress.

Chapter 15

Every day now, after her husband left the house, another of those wretched notes would be delivered, each time by a different street urchin and each time addressed to Lady Sedgewick. Every letter would be composed of words cut from the newspaper. And each time, the letter would apprise Sally of her husband's movements of the night before. Wednesday night, it was the announcement of a lost ten pounds at a cockfight. Last night, the letter confirmed her husband had won twenty pounds at Mrs. Glenwick's establishment. It seemed whoever the vicious person was who was sending the letters knew every move her husband made. Today's letter revealed that George had again bedded his lover. "Would you not wish to know who your husband's lady love is?" The letter made Sally sick.

The first few days Sally had racked her brain trying to imagine who could be so mean-spirited as to be sending her such vile letters. By the third day, though, Sally wondered no longer. She knew only one person who was that vicious. Betsy Johnson.

Sally grew to hate Bath and everything there that

was destroying her family, especially her husband. If only she could get him away from here.

Barely a day passed when he did not lose what seemed to Sally large sums of money, and never a night passed when George did not drink to excess.

By God, she was getting angry! If she had to wait up until dawn she would have it out with George.

He was gone all day and did not come home for dinner. She wondered where he was. Tomorrow's sinister letter would tell her every move her husband had made tonight. With each passing hour, she waited . . . and wondered. Was he at Mrs. Glenwick's or at the card room at the Upper Assembly Rooms? Had he and his rowdy companions found another cockfight to wager on? Her stomach clenched when she recalled the letter that told her George and his friends had enjoyed several hours at Miss Avery's. All of Bath knew Miss Avery's was a whorehouse. Sally was ever so disappointed in George. Not only was he bedding another woman, but he was also visiting establishments where he could contract unimaginably horrible diseases. Her brother David had told her about these things.

Oh, George, she lamented, *why? Why not me?*

She had barely touched her dinner and had been unable to concentrate on her embroidery. She got up and went to the piano where she banged out a passionate piece, hoping she was not waking the children or the servants who had long been in bed. When she finished, she sat and watched the ormolu clock on the mantel. It was past midnight. Early yet for George.

When he still had not come at one, she moved to the library and examined a pile of unpaid tradesmen's bills.

Because of her shuffling of papers and the crackle of the fire, she had not heard George enter the house, but she soon heard the library door open and looked up to face her glassy-eyed husband. It was rare that she actually saw him in his cups. Usually she only smelled the evidence the next morning and had come to associate the smell of stale liquor with George's unquestionable manliness.

His eyes ran over the length of her evening dress. "What are you doing up still?"

"I wanted to talk to you," she said, snagging him with a contentious gaze.

"Is something wrong with the children?"

She shook her head but continued to glare at him. "They're fine."

"Then what's the matter?" he asked in a concerned voice as he moved toward her.

"If you must know, I'm out of charity with you."

"Oh, that," he said, stopping in his stride. Then he turned and walked to the table where the wine decanter was and poured himself another drink.

"Don't, George," she said through gritted teeth.

He spun around to peruse the source of the angrily uttered words. His mouth slid into a lazy smile, and his eyes sparkled as he met her impatient gaze. "It's taken you long enough."

"Yes. I've been a fool these first seven weeks of our marriage, but not any longer. I'm heartily sick of your immature behavior and lack of concern over your children's futures."

"I am concerned over my children's futures. Why else would I have married you?"

Tears sprang to her eyes. The cat was out of the bag. She had always known why he had married her. In the past, though, he'd been too much the gentleman to tell her. But not when he was in his cups.

Seeing the pain in her face, he moved slowly toward her. "Forgive me, Sally. I didn't mean . . ."

"I'm not blind to your reasons for marrying me, George, but I am growing weary of being made a laughingstock."

"You're not a laughingstock."

"I'm just the woman whose husband avoids her company at all costs—and the costs, I might add, have been heavy. Instead of quiet dinner parties and trips to the Upper Assembly Rooms with your wife, you'd rather be throwing away your children's inheritance at gaming establishments and whorehouses."

His face grew red. She had only seen him this angry once before: the afternoon at the Pump Room when Betsy Johnson had ignited his rage. "What makes you think I've ever stepped foot in a whorehouse?"

"I have a very reliable spy." She handed him today's letter that had obviously come courtesy of Miss Johnson, whose pockets were certainly deep enough to hire a Bow Street runner to follow George every night. Sally wondered if Miss Johnson had invented another lie about George in an effort to convince the runner that George was a scoundrel of some sort.

He quickly glanced over it. "What the deuce is this?"

Sally shrugged. "I get one of those charming letters every day."

"Vile creature!" he uttered. "I'll ruin her."

"So you, too, have a good idea of who is sending these to me."

"Betsy Johnson. I'm sorry, Sally. If you'd never married me, you wouldn't have to put up with this woman's filth."

A tear trickled down her cheek.

His brows slanting into a frown, he moved to her and spoke in a gentle voice. "I swear it's a lie about Miss Avery's. I've never set foot inside the place." As he reached Sally he hung his head and spoke in a throaty voice. "Everything else is, unfortunately, true." He removed his handkerchief and dried her tears. "There now," he said gently. "How long have you been getting these wretched letters?"

"Every day since last week."

He muttered another oath. "I'd love to get my hands around her whoring neck."

Sally's mouth dropped open.

"Pardon me, my dear, but it's the truth. Betsy Johnson lifts her skirts for any man who wants her used goods. Never men of the *ton*, you understand. She likes her men—and boys—coarse. Like her father."

Sally had never been so shocked in her life. "How do you know this?"

"It's something all the men know. Was she not known to regularly climb from her window while you girls were at Miss Worth's?"

Sally's eyes widened. "How did you know about that?"

"Males have a network about that type of female."

"I can't believe it," Sally said, stunned.

"Believe it. She's no better than the women who are employed at Susan Avery's. In fact, she's a great deal worse. Those women are there because they need the money. Miss Johnson wants for nothing but a good reputation."

"You know Miss Avery's first name."

"I swear to you, Sally, that kind of woman is not for me, but I do have friends who are regular customers there."

"Is Blanks?"

"Never."

She was enormously relieved. For Glee.

He gently patted her cheek, then restored the handkerchief to his pocket. "Have you saved all the letters?"

"I burned the first, but I've kept all the others. Why, I don't know. Sort of a self-torture, I suppose."

He settled gentle hands on her shoulders. "I'm sorry for any pain I've caused you."

She couldn't face him for what she was going to say next. "The letters claim you make love to your lover nearly every night."

"So that's why you think you're a laughing-stock!" His head lowered and he brushed his lips over the limp curls on top of her head. "I give you my word, Sally, I've not been with another woman."

Wasn't this what she had longed to hear him say? Yet she did not know if she was relieved or crushed over his words. If it were true that he had not been with a woman, that meant no woman appealed to him. Especially not the woman who lay beside him nearly naked every night. Did Dianna still reach from the grave to grip his wounded heart? Oh, but Sally was beginning to wish Dianna had died in the womb. No, she didn't really wish that. For then there would be no Georgette and no Sam, and Sally loved them far too much to begrudge their birth.

But was he telling her the truth? What man would ever admit to a wife that he had been with another woman? She tilted her face to him, and their eyes met and held. For some inexplicable reason, she believed him.

"May I see the other letters?" he asked.

"They're in your desk drawer. If you were ever home, you would have had the opportunity to read them."

He angrily stalked to the desk and found them

in the second drawer he opened. Sally watched as he read the first one, cursing under his breath. He cursed even more when he read the second. When he got to the third, he uttered an oath and wadded all of them up and flung them toward the fireplace. They fell three feet short.

He slowly looked up at Sally. "Except for the references to the women, every word is true," he said, incredulously. "Someone's following me."

"Miss Johnson has a great deal of money. She's obviously hired someone to report on your activities." Sally tried to sound casual. "I daresay her goal is to hurt me."

He winced. "By all that's holy, I'm sorry, Sally."

Tears once again threatened her.

He rushed to Sally and settled his arms about her, pulling her close. "Let's see what Miss Johnson will do if I'm in my dear wife's pocket. I shall escort you to the Assembly Rooms tomorrow night and dance attendance upon you all night."

"No card room?"

"No card room."

Sally squeezed out a meek smile.

George played his role as doting husband so well the following night, Sally thought he could rival Edmund Keen. Her husband danced with no one but her, and when she was dancing with one of his friends, he stood beside Thomas or Blanks watching her. He stayed at her side as they took their tea, which was the strongest drink he consumed all night. When Appleton expressed an interest in meeting later at Mrs. Glenwick's, George declined.

Sally enjoyed herself enormously. She hadn't even had to face the odious Miss Johnson, who was absent from the activities. She was happy for Glee, who danced almost every dance with Blanks and cuddled next to him on the carriage ride home. All in all, a most pleasurable evening.

It wasn't until she and George were mounting the stairs of their town house that she realized this would be their first night to actually go to bed at the same time. The night before George had insisted upon staying in the library, ostensibly to peruse the wicked letters. Tonight her heart began to race, and she suddenly could not find her voice, and she knew that if she were to find it, it would quiver horridly.

When they got to the door of their chamber, her hand was trembling so badly she chose not to reach for the knob and give herself away to George.

He reached for it and opened the door for her. After she entered the room, he said, "Go on and change into your shift and all of that while I go down to the library." Then he leaned toward her and brushed his lips across her forehead. "Daresay I won't be back before you go to sleep. I have many papers that demand my attention."

Though she knew he was speaking the truth, she held out hope he would change his mind and return while she was still awake. She dabbed on her scent and wore her prettiest night shift to bed that night. She lay in the darkened room awake for more than two hours hoping George would come before she drifted off to sleep.

The following morning, she found him asleep in the library, the Madeira decanter empty beside him.

"George!" she shouted.

He wriggled, then slowly lifted an eyelid. When he saw her, he jerked up.

Though she was hurt that he would rather sleep

in a chair than with her, she was more angry than hurt. "What a fine picture you make, sprawled out drunk on a chair for all the servants—and even your children—to see."

His only response was to put the stopper back on the bottle and to come to a standing position. "I'll go clean up now," he mumbled.

After he had shaven and dressed, he left the house without saying a word to her.

No vicious letter came that day.

Nor did George come home until the wee hours of the following morning.

The following day urchins began delivering the notes again, and the notes became increasingly critical of George. Though Sally kept them, she chose not to share them with her husband. She was becoming completely out of charity with him and his immature behavior. Another confrontation was called for.

In the privacy of the bedchamber the following morning, she challenged him. "I think you should return to Hornsby, especially now with the new equipment being delivered. You need to be there."

George stretched his muscled arms far above his head. "Willingham is a most competent steward. I'm not needed."

"Oh, but you are," she countered.

He gave her an I'd-like-to-wring-your-skinny-neck look. "You, madame, are not my master."

"No, I'm not. A pity. Even though you don't know it yet, you need me, George."

He laughed a bitter laugh. "I credit that my children need you, but I don't need you or any woman."

"I'm not talking about sex. I'm talking about restoring your life to what it was three years ago. That's what I want for you. And for the children. I can help you rebuild. If only you'll leave Bath."

He glared at her. "I'm not leaving Bath."

"Then the children and I are."

"They're my children!"

"You said yourself they would now be mine, too. The city is no place for little ones. And they especially don't need to find their drunken father sprawled in the library with an empty wine decanter. The children need to be in the country, and I'm taking them to Hornsby tomorrow."

He threw his legs over the edge of the bed and shimmied into his breeches in front of her, even though he was stark naked. Then he shrugged on his shirt.

This time she made no move to turn away, nor did she offer to fasten his buttons. Once his shirt was buttoned, he stalked from the room, slamming the door behind him.

Appleton was not at his lodgings, but the twins were at theirs. "I beg that you will enable me to get completely foxed," he told them after their man answered his knock.

"What's the matter, fellow? Her ladyship turn you out?" Elvin asked, walking to the silver tray that held a variety of decanters of liquors and spirits. He poured George a glass of port.

"Actually, I'm glad you've come," Melvin said. "I might need you to speak to the magistrate with us."

"Whatever for?" George asked.

"Haven't we told you about the poacher?"

"What poacher?" George responded.

"The vile man who had the audacity to bag a dozen prime grouse on *our* property!" Melvin said.

"The fellow, I'm afraid, has a very large family to feed," Elvin defended.

George winced. "Can't you make allowances for the poor fellow?" George asked.

Melvin frowned. "You sound just like my bleeding-heart brother." He harrumped. "And I had hoped you'd help plead my case in front of the magistrate."

George shook his head. "Not I! I think you should give the poor blighter a job."

"Me?" Melvin asked in outrage. "Why, the bloke *stole* from me."

"It's not like he walloped you over the head and took your money," George said. "For God's sake, the man was hungry. Have a little compassion." George's gaze shot to the milder twin, whose eyes twinkled in mirth.

George wasn't altogether sure he approved of old Melvin. Oh, they'd been friends since before their voices had changed, but the man really was a bit shallow. Now, his brother was a much finer person but because of his shyness tended to be led on a merry chase by the more outgoing twin. Still, neither of them possessed an ounce of maturity. Fact was, they were a bad influence on Blanks. Blanks needed to return to Sutton Hall, to get away from his bachelor friends. He needed to sire a bevy of the healthy babes George knew Glee could present him.

George could not say anyone was a bad influence on him. He was a grown man who was able to make his own decisions. The problem was the decisions he had been making these past two years were bad. They were immature.

And, the devil take it, his sensible wife was right! *Sensible Sal.*

"I've actually come to say farewell," George said.

Four identical eyes focused on him. "Why?" two sets of voices asked at the same instant.

"I'm returning to Hornsby."

Chapter 16

The children rode in the carriage to Warwickshire with their parents. Bouncing from one seat to the other, Georgette bubbled with comments and questions. "Will my puppy be waiting for me?"

"Your puppy is now a very large dog, I've been told," George answered.

"Even though I was such a wee one, I still remember the purple flowers on the walls in my bedchamber," the little girl said.

"I expect the same wallpaper will still be there," Sally replied. "Did you like it, love?"

"Ever so much."

It suddenly struck Sally that Sam wouldn't even have a chamber at Hornsby. He had been but a few weeks old when his father fled the house that was filled with Dianna's memories. Sally glanced up at her husband. "Does the young master have his own chamber at Hornsby?"

"Actually, no," George said. "He was still with the wet nurse when we came to Bath."

"Then we'll just have to decorate a very special room for him," Sally said, trying to make it sound exciting and not really knowing how much of what she said could be understood by Sam.

"I daresay he can occupy the room that was mine when I was a lad."

As was only fitting.

The first hour of the journey through the hilly area around Bath, Sam was content to peer from the window. After that, he grew solemn, climbing upon Sally's lap and shoving his thumb into his mouth. She held him close and stroked his golden hair. She sensed that he was frightened by the strange new environment.

"Isn't the lad a bit old to still be sucking his thumb?" George asked.

"George, he's still a baby." Sally sent her husband a disapproving glance.

He sighed. "That's what you keep telling me, but I remember distinctly how very well Georgette spoke when she turned two."

Sally glared at him. "You can't compare any two children—especially when they're of a different sex."

"I'd feel a lot better if he'd only talk," George lamented.

"He may not talk, but Sam knows everything we say, and I'll not have you discussing this in front of him again," she said in a commanding voice.

George began to chuckle.

"What, pray tell, do you find so amusing?" Sally asked.

"There are those poor, unenlightened souls who think I married a meek little spinster who jumps through my hoops. Little do they know it's I who do the jumping."

Sally smiled. At least he didn't seem bitter. Sally knew she could be rather vexatious.

"Papa?" Georgette said.

"Yes, love?"

"Will my new mama sleep in my other mama's bedchamber?"

Sally's pulse quickened. She had forgotten that the vastness of Hornsby Manor allowed for separate chambers for its lord and lady, a realization that displeased her excessively. First, she had no desire to inhabit the room which would most strongly evoke the personality of its previous occupant. But even more disconcerting was the cessation of her special, intimate mornings with her husband. Were they to reside in separate chambers, they would likely never have a private minute together again. She must find a way to ensure there be a time and place where just the two of them would discuss their days.

George forced Sally to meet his gaze. "You do wish to reside in the viscountess's chambers, do you not? After all, you are the new Lady Sedgewick."

Sally knew she should be pleased that George was now able to allow her to replace the woman he had loved so desperately. She was relieved that he never mentioned Dianna by name. He was surprisingly cognizant of the fact Sally did not wish to be compared to Dianna. She was especially relieved at his perceptiveness since she was loathe to verbalizing her feelings on the matter.

Upon reflection of the matter of bedchambers, she decided she did deserve to live in the same chamber where every Viscountess Sedgewick had resided for the past one hundred and eighty years. She shouldn't have to be asked. Yet, she couldn't move into rooms the elegant Dianna's death had left empty. "Since I haven't seen how the rooms are situated, it's hard for me to say. I expect the lord and lady's chambers are adjacent?"

George nodded.

"And they're not far from the children?"

He nodded again.

"The prospect does sound desirable. However, I'm afraid my usurpal of my predecessor's chambers could make you or Georgette uncomfortable. I propose not to inhabit them until they have been completely redecorated in a style that will not bring to mind the former owner."

She could almost hear George's sigh. She knew it would have been difficult for him to see Sally occupy rooms that bore Dianna's unmistakable stamp. And she understood that.

"Papa?" Georgette said again.

"Yes, love?"

"How much longer before we're at Hornsby?"

"We'll be there long before dark."

"I was wondering . . ." Sally began.

George raised a brow.

"Would it be possible, do you think, for a pony to be procured for the children?"

Georgette's eyes widened. "That would be ever so much fun!"

"Do you not think Sam's too little?" George asked Sally.

Sam sat up straight and shook his little head.

"He is too little to just take off riding. I had in mind a gentle mount, and one of us—or Miss Primble or a groom—could walk beside him when he rides," Sally said.

"Miss P.," Georgette corrected.

Sally directed her gaze at George. "Miss Primble has instructed the children to call her Miss P. It's a great deal easier to pronounce, especially for Sam—when he starts talking."

Georgette bounced from her father's side of the carriage to Sally's and poked her face into her brother's while proceeding to speak in baby talk, "Would you like a baby horse, Sam?"

His thumb still in his mouth, Sam nodded, his wide eyes shifting to his father.

A grin eased across George's face. "Very well, we shall get a pony."

A short time later, Sam buried his little face into Sally's small bosom and went to sleep. She continued to stroke his hair even as it grew moist. She did not think she could ever grow tired of holding him in her arms. A pity he was soon to outgrow wanting to be in her arms.

She smiled as she watched Georgette climb upon her father's lap, and she experienced a deep contentment so vast she clung to a foolish wish that this journey could last forever. For she had not been this happy since the day she married.

She was as proud of George this moment as she had been when he had begged her hand in marriage. Yes, he had been immature. He had also been selfish. Yet she completely understood. Coming to Bath and engaging in the kinds of activities he had pursued there had been part of his healing process. Hopefully, he was now healed and could regain a productive life.

Betsy Johnson was not finished with Lord Sedgewick and the upstart he had married. No, not by a long shot. She had vowed that he would pay for his mistreatment of her, and, by God, he was going to pay.

When Ebinezer had informed her that Sedgewick had returned to Warwickshire, she had bleated a string of curses and raced back to her house without so much as giving Ebinezer what he surely deemed his payment should be.

But the following night she had her plan in place. She waited until her parents had gone to bed, then

padded down the stairs and slipped out the tradesmen's entrance at the back of the house. She went
straight to the mews and climbed the now familiar
wooden staircase.

This time Ebinezer, a broad smile on his rugged
face, was waiting for her. "Aye, me gal, I'd knew as
ye'd come tonight."

She set the lantern down, then, like an actress
performing on a stage, she began to shed her fur-
trimmed velvet cloak.

Ebinezer gasped as it fell to the wooden floor.
For she wore absolutely nothing beneath it. She
dipped down to remove her cloak from the floor,
careful to give him a good view of her breasts dan-
gling downward as she bent. Then she covered the
uncomfortable straw mattress with her velvet cloak
and lay on it. These stolen meetings with Ebinezer
were growing tedious. The first one had been the
best, of course. It always was. She had been eyeing
Ebinezer for several weeks and had been anxious to
learn if his considerable height was an indication of
his size below the waist. She had no complaints on
that score. He filled her well, the lad did. But she
was growing weary of him. And of the straw mattress.

Perhaps if Ebinezer were to sneak into her chamber in her father's house . . . The idea brought a
smile to her lips and sent a throbbing down deep
and low. She did so love the danger of discovery, the
danger of forbidden fruit. That's what was needed.
She would entice Ebinezer to her bedchamber. She
thought she would even fancy the idea of him groaning loudly with pleasure beside her. That might just
heighten the lure of discovery. Not that she actually wished to be found with the groom's member
inserted within her. She merely wanted to imagine
being discovered with the groom's—or the footman's
or the coachman's—member buried within her.

Just thinking on the matter caused her to become aroused. She slipped her hand beneath Ebinezer's nightshirt to see if he was, too.

Good. He was as big around as a horse's tail. "I shall be on top tonight," she informed him, rolling over on him and closing her opened mouth over his.

He came into her quick and hard, just as she had taught him to do. But she still wasn't satisfied. She rolled off him and waited for his breathing to return to normal. Then she began to pleasure him with her mouth until he grew sturdy again and she sat astride him once more and rode him as if her very life depended upon it.

This time they both cried out in ragged moans of pleasure.

When she woke just before dawn, she whispered filthy things into his ear until he awakened.

"Next time, me boy, you'll pleasure me in me own bed."

"I can't be goin' and doin' that now, miss. What about yer parents?"

She rolled to him and lifted one thigh over his leg. "It will just make it more exciting, love."

He clasped a wide hand over her bare hips.

"Ye must make love to me once more, Ebinezer, before ye go off to Warwickshire."

He bolted up. "Are ye daft? I ain't goin' to Warwickshire."

"Aye, love, ye are. 'Twill only be for a little while, and I'll see to it me father increases yer wages when ye return." It wasn't uncommon for Betsy to begin slipping into the lower classes' vernacular when she was having one of her affairs with an underling.

They went at it once more, and by the time she slipped away from the mews at dawn, Ebinezer was making plans for his trip to Warwickshire.

Chapter 17

As they drew closer to George's ancestral home, a smile settled on Sally's face. Hornsby Manor had been her favorite place on earth when she was growing up. In addition to her infatuation with George and her idolization of Glee's elder sister, Sally had loved the rolling Warwickshire countryside here. The vast Sedgewick estates were so completely different from the rectory where she had grown up.

She fondly recalled rowing across the deep green waters of Hornsby's private lake and the many long horseback rides she and Glee had taken around the estate. Hornsby was the largest house Sally had ever been in until Felicity married the wealthy Mr. Moreland and settled in at Winston Hall. Though unlike Winston Hall, with its rooms of marble and miles of gilt trim, Hornsby was rich with mellowed wood and was as cozy as her grandmother's firelit cottage.

When the carriage rattled over the familiar wooden bridge, Sally's heart fluttered. They had crossed into Sedgewick property. Her chest seemed too small to contain her swelling heart. She peered from the window at the parkland in front of Hornsby, and her eye traveled along the velvety grass up to Hornsby itself. Neither palatial nor pretentious, Hornsby was a big, comfortable family home in the Tudor style with as much timber on the facade as bricks and mortar. Her heart clenched. It would now be her home.

As the carriage rolled to a stop in front of the door, Sally's glance fell on George. Not waiting for the coachman to put down the steps, he sprang from the carriage and turned back to assist Sally, who held Sam in her arms as she disembarked. Then George dipped down and scooped Georgette into his arms.

"You must be fatigued from the journey," he said to Sally as they entered the house through Hornsby's front door. "No doubt you'll want to go to your chambers."

Her pulse accelerated. "Not until they have been redecorated, I think. Until then, I plan to stay in Sam's room with him. I daresay the new house could possibly upset him."

As if to assure himself of the lad's well-being, George threw a quick glance at his son. "Then allow me to show you to the young master's room."

Sally shook her head. "No, first we must take Georgette to her chamber. You know nothing of your daughter if you do not know how impatient she is to see her well remembered room."

Still holding his daughter, George looked down into her face. "So you're impatient to see your chamber, love?"

"Ever so much, Papa."

The family's bedchambers were all located upon the second floor, Georgette's midway down the dark corridor. As George went to open its door, Sally grew anxious. What if the servants had not prepared it for the young mistress? After all, they had not been notified until yesterday that the family was returning today.

She was relieved when they entered the lilac chamber and found that it was free of dust, tidy, and quite lovely with its wallpaper of lilacs. Draperies of a solid lilac color had been opened to flood the chamber with sunlight. Sally glanced at the half-tester bed, which also was covered in velvet that was of the same shade of lilac as the draperies.

"Is it as you remembered, pet?" George asked his daughter.

Her glance lit on every corner of the room, then she looked up at her father and shrugged. "It's . . . it's the same, but it's different. It seems smaller."

"That's because you've grown bigger," George said gently.

"Then, too," Sally added, "none of your dolls and things are here yet. It will look more as you remember when your things get here."

Georgette's glance darted to the unadorned little bed in the corner of the room. "I remember that's where Hortense used to sleep."

Sally went to put Sam down, but he clung to her neck and gave a grumble of protest. "Very well, sweetheart," she cooed to him, "I shan't put you down if you don't like."

George gazed from Sally to Sam and back to Sally. "Should you care to see what will be Sam's room?"

"Certainly," Sally said as she followed her husband from the room. "Has anyone occupied it since you married, my lord?"

He walked directly across the hall to it, shaking his head.

"What if it's not been made ready?" Sally asked.

"It will be. That was in my instructions." He opened the door and swept into the blue chamber.

Though it had been cleaned, and fresh linens had been put on the bed, the room's long years of disuse were evident in the sun-faded draperies. Sally thought the draperies and bedcoverings once must have been a royal blue to complement the gold walls. But now the royal blue was so badly faded it looked almost as if it had been whitewashed. Her eye traveled to the wooden floors that were covered in worn, though serviceable, Turkey carpets. Sally attempted to calculate how long it had been since the chamber had been redecorated. George had married when he was three and twenty, so it had been seven years since he had occupied this chamber. Judging by what she saw, Sally would guess the room must have been decorated when George was the age Sam was now.

She directed her gaze at her husband. "I believe there are two rooms that will require redecorating."

He nodded. "I hadn't realized this chamber would look so . . . so tawdry."

She laughed. "I wouldn't say tawdry. It's most likely been thirty years since it was decorated."

"I dare say you're correct," George said.

Georgette came to stand at Sally's feet and looked up at her little brother. "This is going to be your room, Sam," she said sweetly.

He held Sally's neck tighter. She was not sure if he understood or not. "Mama's going to sleep in here with you tonight, sweetheart." Sally kissed his fat little cheek.

Then Sally met Georgette's gaze and smiled smugly. "I dare say you're ready to go find your pup."

A broad smile on her face, Georgette's head bobbed up and down.

George picked her up again. "Remember what I told you. He's not a puppy any more. He's going to be rather large."

They went back downstairs and through the rear door and began to walk through the parterre garden toward the mews. They had not been outside for long when they heard a bark and saw a black and white dog running toward them. If that were Georgette's dog, Sally thought, then her father had been right. He was a large dog, as large as a collie.

"It's Champs!" Georgette cried, running toward the dog.

"George? Will she be all right, do you think?"

Worry flashed across his face, and George began to sprint after his daughter.

But he had no need to worry. The harmless dog stopped right in front of Georgette and began to lick her.

She giggled and flicked a glance at her father. "He remembers me!"

"I believe he does, pet."

Dropping to her knees, Georgette flung her arms around the dog's coat. Then she gazed up at her brother and said, "Doggie. Do you want to pet the doggie, Sam?"

He shook his head. Though fascinated by the dog and unable to remove his gaze from it, Sam was frightened just enough to keep a safe distance.

Assured of his daughter's safety, George began to stroll toward the mews, his wife and son beside him and Georgette and her dog lagging some distance behind.

Sliding a glance to Sally, George came to a stop. "Here, let me take him. Your arms must be aching."

To Sally's surprise, Sam did not protest but went readily to his father. Sally slipped her arm through George's free arm. "Do you know what Sam would love ever so much?" she asked.

George hitched a brow. "What?"

"For you to take him for a ride upon your mount."

"But I have no horse for you."

"I don't require one. I can watch you."

"You don't mind?"

"I shall be most happy if Sam is happy."

Within five minutes, George's bay was saddled, and Sally handed Sam up into his father's arms. A fleeting look of terror wiped across Sam's face as he clutched at his father, but as George's arm came around him and George spoke gently to him when the bay began a slow trot, the look of terror was replaced with unquestionable mirth. Sally had never seen Sam so happy.

Once assured that Sam was no longer frightened, George dug in his heels, and the bay bolted into a gallop. Happiness on her own face, Sally watched as they streaked forward, the wind blowing Sam's blond curls, his giggling face lifted into the heavens.

Having suddenly lost interest in her dog, a solemn Georgette asked, "Can Papa take me, too?"

Sally gathered the little girl's hand into her own. "I'm sure he means to."

When George circled back to where Sally and Georgette stood, Georgette shouted, "Can you take me now, Papa?"

"Very well," he said. "Will you get Sam?" he asked Sally.

She walked up, arms outstretched.

Sam whirled his face away and grunted his disapproval, but his father was stern. He grabbed the boy with both hands and handed him, kicking and screaming, to Sally. "Be a good lad," George said, "and we'll do this again. It's Georgette's turn now."

Sam continued to kick at Sally as she plopped him on the grass. Then she took up his sister, handing her to George.

The entire time George and his daughter rode, Sam cried. Sally swept up her skirts and sat down beside him on the grass, holding out her arms for him. For the first time ever, he refused to come to Sally. His face red, great rivers of tears washing down his cheeks, he shook his head vigorously.

"I can see this arrangement needs to be improved," she said, shaking her head.

When George returned, Sam stood up and ran toward the horse, his arms held over his head, silently begging for another ride.

George shook his head. "Not now, lad. You had your turn."

Sally came and took Georgette down while George dismounted. Meeting Sally's gaze, George said, "The boy certainly does love horses."

"Poor lamb," Sally lamented, "I've never seen him so upset."

"Tomorrow we'll have to make sure there are two horses, and each of us can take one of the children."

Sally nodded. She would take Georgette. Sam and his father needed to establish a bond, and what better way to do so than for Sam to associate his father with his favorite thing?

Before darkness fell, George, with his family at his side, sought out the steward.

When they came upon Mr. Willingham riding his horse through the orchard, the two men greeted each other affably. "May I present you to the new Lady Sedgewick?" George said.

The man, who was much the same age as George,

quickly dismounted, handed his reins to George, and swept into a bow. Then he drew Sally's hand to his lips. "Your servant, milady."

"I'm very pleased to make your acquaintance," Sally said. "My husband speaks most highly of you. Tell me, have you been able to implement the new machinery?"

His brown eyes sparkled. "I have indeed." Turning to George, he said, "Should you like to see it?"

"Certainly," George said.

Sally hoped Mr. Willingham did not detect the insincerity in her husband's voice, evident though it was to her.

Mr. Willingham took two steps, then stopped and scratched at his head. "Actually, tomorrow will be better. By the time we get to the fields this afternoon, it will be growing dark."

George clapped a hand around the man's shoulder. "I plan to devote most of the day tomorrow to having you update me on the estates."

They all began to walk back toward the house, Mr. Willingham leading his horse behind them.

"Should you care to eat dinner with us tonight, Mr. Willingham?" Sally asked.

"I would be honored to do so."

By the time they reached Hornsby, the servants' chaise had arrived, and all the servants were attempting to perform their usual duties.

Miss Primble took the children to the nursery while Sally and George mounted the stairway to dress for dinner. Her trembling hand grasped the bannister as they climbed the old oak staircase. "There is something I beg to ask of you, my lord."

George put a gentle hand to her waist. "What, my dear?"

"I would rather that you not go into the viscountess's chambers until they are redecorated."

She drew in her breath. Since the day she had become betrothed to George, neither of them had ever mentioned Dianna by name. And Sally was exceedingly grateful to him for that. "I should like for you to continue forward, not backward."

His mouth a grim line, he nodded.

At the top of the stairs, he turned to the left and walked almost to the end of the long hallway. He came to a stop and turned to Sally. "If you care to see them, these are the viscountess's chambers."

She nodded solemnly and watched as he walked to the next door and entered.

Then she opened the door and walked into a bedchamber that was done completely in scarlet. Scarlet walls. Scarlet draperies. Scarlet bedcoverings. Sally's heart thumped as she pictured Dianna sitting before the gilded dressing table. The room would have been the perfect backdrop for the raven-haired beauty. If being here sent Sally's heart thumping, she knew George would have broken down completely. It was best that he not come in here while the room still bore Dianna's distinctive stamp.

Sally would have changed the decor even if it had not evoked memories of the lovely Dianna. Scarlet simply was not her. Of all the colors in the spectrum, red would likely have been Sally's last choice for her bedchamber.

She walked up to the silk moire draperies and fingered them. Unlike those in Sam's chamber, these looked as fresh as the day they had been installed. A pity to waste them. Silk was so very dear.

Then it occurred to her that red would nicely complement the royal blue in Sam's chamber. Even with the scarlet draperies, Sam's room would be far too masculine to ever evoke Dianna. Sally decided she would order these draperies be moved to Sam's room on the morrow, the same day she would send for painters for her new chambers.

Her glance fell on Dianna's bed with its gilded canopy. And her heart quickened. That George and Dianna had made love there made her profoundly sad. When it became her room, Sally would have the bed moved to the window wall. Anything to obliterate memories of her predecessor.

And since the room was so bold and dark now, she would select something completely different. Ivory, she thought, even if it would take several coats for it to cover the red.

To the left of the bedchamber she located the dressing chamber, a small room that was completely empty, save for the red velvet curtain that covered its sole window. She saw that the room could be entered from two sides. She swallowed. The next room would be George's.

She stood there in the eerie silence imagining George and Dianna freely accessing each other's chambers. Would that she would ever be so comfortable with the man she had married.

She strode back into the bedchamber and across it, coming to another scarlet room, this one the viscountess's study. It was furnished with a French escritoire, also of gilt, and a pair of red silk brocade settees. She would love to recover those in ivory, too. A pity she would be shackled—because of scarcity of funds—with the gilded furniture. Walnut was much more to Sally's liking.

Sally took pains with her toilette to look her best for dinner. She was pleased that the curls Hettie had put in early that morning still held. Hettie pressed her emerald gown, and Sally chose to wear the Sedgewick emeralds with it.

She had no need to ask where the dining room was located. From her many visits here she remembered every chamber on the first floor as well as the rooms of the rectory that had been her only home. When she glided into the dining room, George and Mr. Willingham both stood. Was she reading too much into the look of pride that glinted in her husband's eyes?

"How lovely you look, my dear," George said as he moved to her and took her hand to kiss.

Once they were seated, he said, "Despite being short-handed, the staff has done remarkably well. I believe you'll be pleasantly surprised over the fare."

Her glance scanned the dozen dishes scattered along the table's white cloth. She was rather grateful there was no footman hovering around—a casualty of her husband's reduced circumstances. She much preferred private dinners, something unobtainable at grand houses like the Moreland's Winston Hall. She recalled several dinners here at Hornsby when servants had been in attendance, but as the Sedgewick family wealth shrank and swelled, so did the number of Sedgewick servants. More often than not, the footmen had been absent.

Just being at Hornsby exhilarated her. There was no telling how productive George could become now that he was away from Bath. Her heart fluttered when she realized she would be his helpmate.

"You have enjoyed excellent weather here of late, I understand," Sally said to Mr. Willingham.

"We have indeed."

Mr. Willingham looked completely different tonight than he had this afternoon in his buff-colored clothing. Now he wore a black tailcoat of good cut, and the fresh white of his expertly tied cravat accentuated the deep tone of his olive complexion. He was an awfully good-looking man. He was perhaps a bit taller than George. And less muscular. His dark skin with his dark hair and eyes brought to mind a Spaniard or Italian. Certainly not the Englishman he was from head to foot. Sally found herself wondering why so handsome a man was still not married.

His eyes flashed with laughter as he looked at her. "I have been racking my brains, trying to remember where I have seen you before. You're Miss Glee's friend!"

He might remember her, but she could not remember ever seeing him before, which was not difficult to understand. Whenever she had been at Hornsby—even the one time she came there after George's marriage—she had been too thoroughly besotted over George to ever notice another man. "You, sir, are in possession of a remarkable memory, to be sure. Not many remember me, as I'm rather plain."

There was genuine warmth on his face when he protested. "I assure you, *plain* is not a word that would enter my mind when I think of you, my lady. If his lordship does not object to my saying so, I think you're rather lovely."

George coughed. "Of course I don't mind. Sally is much prettier now that she curls her hair."

Sally met Mr. Willingham's gaze with sparkling eyes. "What he really means is now that I'm fortunate enough to have a lady's maid to curl my wretched hair."

"I never noticed if your hair was straight or curly," Mr. Willingham said. "I was always struck by the juxtaposition."

"The juxtaposition?" Sally queried.

Mr. Willingham nodded. "You know, the blond

hair with eyes that are almost black and skin that's golden. Not the fairness one would usually expect from a blond-haired woman."

George somberly glanced from Willingham to Sally. "By Jove! You're right, Willingham. Never thought of it before. Lady Sedgewick is rather unusual-looking."

Sally was uncomfortable being the topic of conversation. She was made even more uncomfortable by the fact that her inferior appearance was the subject of said conversation. "You must tell us all about the new farm machinery, Mr. Willingham."

The steward did just that. Not that Sally understood half of what the man and George were discussing. Even though their jargon was for the most part poorly understood by her, Sally was delighted to see how animated her husband became when discussing his lands. She was more convinced than ever that the decision to come here had been the right one.

After dinner, Mr. Willingham stayed and played loo with his employer and his wife. Long before the clock struck ten, Sally began to yawn. She had risen very early that morning in order to have Hettie do her curls for the long journey. Knowing that she would spend more hours with George this day than she ever had spent with him before, she had been determined to look her best.

"You two must be most fatigued," Mr. Willingham said as he stood up. "I'll leave now."

George and Sally also rose, George slipping an arm around his wife's shoulders. "I'll meet you at ten in the morning, Willingham."

After seeing their guest to the door, Sally and George began to mount the stairs, and Sally found herself yawning on almost every step. Mention of ten in the morning had reminded her that tomorrow would be the first morning of their marriage that she and George would not be together. Her chest tightened. Would they ever again know the intimacy they had known in Bath?

He left her at the door to Sam's room, then strolled to the end of the hallway.

When Sally entered the lad's chamber, he was crying. Miss Primble tossed Sally a forlorn look. "I've never seen him like this before, milady. He won't go to bed."

Sally's face softened as she went to Sam and lifted him, holding him close and patting his back. "I believe if he could could talk, he would be imploring us to take him home. Bath is the only home he's ever known, and I suspect he's frightened to be in a new, unfamiliar place."

"I daresay you're right, milady."

"I'll sleep with the little lamb. Will you go and be with Georgette?"

"I will, milady." Miss Primble quietly slipped from the room.

Holding Sam close, Sally paced the floor, cooing to the babe. "Don't worry, sweetheart, Mama's going to stay with you." She still experienced an intoxicating thrill each time she referred to herself as *Mama*. That title was as precious to her as *Viscountess*.

There was a knock on the chamber door. "Yes?" Sally said.

Hettie entered the room. "I thought to help you dress for bed, milady."

Pleased at her maid's complete competence, Sally smiled at her. She hated to put Sam down because of the fragile state of his shredded emotions. "Thank you, Hettie, but not tonight. I'll undress myself once Master Sam has calmed down."

Hettie's fine blond brows drew together. "Is something the matter with the little master?"

"I believe he's frightened of his new surroundings. That is all."

Once Hettie left the chamber, Sam's tears ceased. Continuing to hold him close, Sally pointed to the bed. "Mama's bed. You're going to sleep with me tonight, love."

He continued to whimper. It tore at Sally's heart to think of how many hours the babe must have been sobbing out his little heart. Holding him tightly to her, she said, "It's all right now, sweetheart. Mama's here with you."

She thought he took consolation in her words.

Before long, she shed her evening dress, donned her shift, and gathered Sam into her arms. "Come on, little love, we're going to bed now." She lay down with him, careful to leave one taper burning because of his fear of the dark. He scooted close to her, shoved his thumb into his mouth, and was asleep in less than a minute.

A smile of contentment on her own face, Sally soon drifted off to sleep.

Chapter 18

Her first full day at Hornsby was a busy one for Sally. She had started the day by making the acquaintance of the staff. After that she asked Mrs. MacMannis to take her on a tour of the house, even to the linen closets and the butler's pantry.

As Sally passed dozens of portraits of long dead ancestors, she made a mental note to have George educate her on the family history. Before the year was out, she vowed to know the name of every ancestor whose portrait hung at Hornsby. She even fancied commissioning portraits of the new Lord and Lady Sedgewick. Though she was ashamed to admit it, Sally was glad there was no portrait of the beautiful Dianna. Who would have known Dianna would die at just two and twenty? The same age Sally was now. Her stomach tumbled at the thought.

There was no money to commission portraits, anyway, until Sally and George could significantly reduce their present expenditures. That would be her first priority.

She went to her husband's library and began to pore over the account ledgers. There really was not a penny to spare. She sprang from the desk and stormed from the room, this time with the intention of conducting her own tour of the house with an eye to economizing.

In the dining room, she found that four different chandeliers were ringed several times over with expensive candles. This was far too excessive an expense. She would have most of them removed to be used in the rooms where they were more necessary. That would save the expense of purchasing new candles for months.

In the household-accounts ledger, she had noticed a rather hefty expenditure to the greengrocers. Hefty when multiplied several times a week. With all the fertile land surrounding Hornsby, everything they needed should be grown right here. Why have an ornamental parterre garden when they could have a very fine vegetable garden in its place? Surely Mr. Willingham could assign a few hands to the task. She would speak to the steward.

And by ordering that no fires be built in the daylight—except during uncommonly cold freezes—she figured they could be indulgent with night fires to warm the frigid bedchambers. A pity keeping the hearth ablaze came at so dear a cost.

And though Mrs. MacMannis had begged to be allowed to replace the scullery maid who had stayed behind in Bath, Sally decided Cook could get along with one less helper. She already had one strapping young servant to assist her. And for a household the size of Hornsby, that one could suffice.

Sally's economies were not much, but they were a start. She vowed to continue to seek ways to save money. For she was about to make a few necessary expenditures.

She returned to the library and drafted a letter to send to Bath requesting painters come to Hornsby immediately. Then she summoned the butler, and asked that he be in charge of the removal of the draperies from the viscountess's chambers to the young master's. "I should like to keep the master's old draperies in order to make clothing for the poor," she told Adams.

"Very good, my lady."

She settled back in the leather desk chair, a smile on her face. At least there would be another source of revenue soon. The sheep would be ready to be sheared next month, and Mr. Willingham said he expected an excellent price this year.

At midday George came back to the manor house for a respite, and Sally joined him at the table.

"I saw the reaper demonstrated," he told her between bites of stewed eel. "Most magnificent thing you've ever seen! That one piece of machinery can do the work of a dozen men in half the time."

It had been a very long while since Sally had seen George speak about anything with such interest. His eyes flashed with enthusiasm as he gave her the details of the new reaper. Then he set down his fork and eyed her somberly. "The pity of it is, the invention is likely to replace the worker. What will my men do if they can't farm the land their families have been farming for generations?"

"You'll just have to find other means by which they can earn a living. Not everything can be automated."

His brows drew together as he stabbed at his French-cut beans. "Willingham says it may not happen in our lifetime, but society is poised to switch from an agrarian society to an industrialized one."

"I don't see how London can accommodate any more people," she said, shaking her head.

"While I live, no tenant of mine will ever have to breathe those blackened skies in the capital or have to beg for food or lack shelter."

Her brows arched quizzically. "Pray, I thought you loved London."

"When I was a younger man. And when I had the luxury of living in a fine town house in Mayfair. That was a far cry from how the lower classes there live. I'll not allow my cottagers to ever endure suffering like I've seen in London's East End."

"The coatless, shoeless children I've seen hawking in Mayfair are enough to give me a strong distaste for London." She took a long drink of milk, then quizzed her husband some more. "Were you able to renew your acquaintance with your cottagers today?"

He smiled. "Many of them. I'd forgotten how much I enjoy being at Hornsby."

"Hornsby's who you are."

Long after Sally had swept from the room to attend to household matters, George heard her words. *Hornsby's who you are.* She was so young to understand things so keenly.

His thoughts flitted back to this morning's ride over the estates with Willingham. "It's good to be back at Hornsby," he had told his steward.

"It's good having you back. I hadn't realized how long you'd been gone until I saw how much your children have grown."

George nodded solemnly. "Georgette's quite the little woman now."

"It's really remarkable. Georgette's a miniature of her mother, and little Sam looks exactly like you."

At the thought of Dianna's beauty, a stab of pain

shot through George. He should have become used to it. After all, every time he beheld his daughter, it was as if he were once again looking at Dianna. "Poor lad," George said with a laugh.

"You've done well enough with your looks, Sedgewick. In fact, you're looking especially good. When you left . . . well, I never saw a more broken man. But you appear to have healed. And it's no wonder with that lovely wife of yours."

For a second, George thought Willingham referred to Dianna, then he realized the man was talking about Sally. It was queer to think of Sally as a beauty, but he was oddly pleased that Willingham found her so.

When they had been young men at university, Willingham had enjoyed more than his fair share of females. Not that George and Willingham had been particularly close then. The fellow had much more shallow pockets than the privileged set George ran with. Blanks. Appleton. The twins. All of them had considerable financial resources. All that Willingham possessed was a propensity to study and a face that girls were attracted to, neither of which endeared him to George's chums.

But he had been a good steward, and for that George was grateful.

"You impress me with your choice of wife," Willingham said as they had cantered through the orchards. "The new Lady Sedgewick is not only lovely, she's also possessed of a keen mind."

George's mouth slid into a crooked smile. "She was at the top of her class at Miss Worth's School for Young Ladies, my sister is forever telling me."

They turned to ride back to the house, and George noticed that he had somehow become oddly disturbed over Willingham's obvious enthusiasm about Sally. She was, after all, a married woman.

His own wife, to be sure. It was almost as if Willingham knew of his and Sally's strange relationship. Did the man hope to win Sally's heart himself? George was unaccountably miffed at the man. He did not think Willingham would be invited to any more dinners at the manor house.

That night Sally and George ate together, and after dinner they retired to the drawing room, where George poured a glass of wine for Sally and another for himself, then he came to sit beside her on the tomato-colored silken sofa. There was not a more welcoming room in the kingdom than this, he thought. He watched the fire crackle in the hearth as he remembered how it was when his sisters and his parents had shared many a night here playing games with him.

It was very good to be back at Hornsby.

"Do you play chess?" he suddenly asked Sally.

"I do, though it's probably my worst game. I'm of the opinion that chess is a game much more readily grasped by the male mind."

He laughed. "I should have known you would have an opinion even on chess."

Her face settled into a frown. "Oh dear, I am so very opinionated. I fear I'm quite vexatious to you."

"After all this time, I think I'm beginning to be impervious to it, my dear."

"Then the voicing of my opinions is to you just so much water off a duck's back?"

He gave her a sheepish look. "I wouldn't say that. I'm sure all of your opinions are of importance."

"How diplomatic is the man I married."

Grinning, he got up, fetched the chessboard, and set it up on the tea table in front of the sofa.

Then he scooted a sturdy tudor arm chair up to it and sat down.

As their play progressed, he realized his wife had been correct when she told him chess was her worst game. She was far better at faro. Still, she played with more skill than half the men he knew.

Their play was not so serious that they could not converse while playing.

"Poor Sam," she told him, "had a wretched time last night. When I came to his chamber Miss Primble told me he had been crying for hours."

George arched a single brow. "Was he sick?"

"Oh no. It's my belief he wanted to go back to his home in Bath."

"So the unfamiliar frightened him?"

"I think so. He's doing much better today. He even got up the courage to pet Champs and discovered how much he liked it. Then, too, his horse ride with you made him very happy indeed."

"He does love it. I've never seen him smile and laugh so much."

"Neither have I."

George moved his knight. "How did your night pass, sharing your bed with him?"

"He was an angel. He scooted up close to me, put his little thumb in his mouth, and went fast asleep."

A smile came to his lips when he remembered how Sam had giggled on the horse ride that afternoon. "Is Miss Thimble with the lad now?"

Sally nodded as she moved her pawn. "It's Miss Primble, you goose."

He jumped her pawn and deposited it alongside his swelling bounty. "Good of her to come to Hornsby. I understand at least one of the staff did not wish to leave Bath."

Sally nodded. "I've made the decision not to replace that one. An economy measure." Those huge black eyes of Sally's looked up at him. Did she expect he would chastise her?

He shrugged. "You will recall, I gave you free rein in household matters."

She favored him with a smile.

As the two of them sat there, the fire warming him from head to toe, it occurred to George that he and Sally were continuing the intimacy they had established during their early mornings in Bath. He stole a glance at her pensive face as she studied the chessboard, and the realization swept over him of how very comfortable he had become with this woman who had consented to marry him.

And, to his complete surprise, not once all night had he given a thought to what he might have been doing in Bath tonight. He could not imagine anywhere on earth that was more enjoyable than this room tonight in the home in which he had been born. The chit he had married had once told him he needed her. He had doubted it then, but he now understood she had been right. She had made the decision to leave Bath. And it had been the right decision. He was already looking forward to the next day riding over the estate with Willingham. He had almost forgotten how much pleasure he derived from Hornsby.

His gaze met hers. "I'm glad to be back at Hornsby. Thank you."

A solemn look came over her face. "It's I who should thank you. What you just said has made me very happy."

He forced his gaze back to the chessboard and jumped her queen. "Check."

She examined the board for a full five minutes before she threw up her arms. "I must concede, my lord. There's no way to escape."

He stood up. "Let us be off to bed, then." He took a step toward the door.

"Allow me a moment," she said, "to put up these chess pieces."

He turned impatiently toward her. "The servants can do that in the morning."

"It will just take a moment. You know, I cannot leave a room untidy."

He rolled his eyes. "How different we are."

"In almost every way," she agreed.

"Then, pray, how can you tolerate me?"

She looked up at him, a smile on her face. "You have many fine qualities. A pity you hide most of them from all but me."

It suddenly occurred to him she was right. Not that he thought he had any particular qualities that could be described as fine, but that Sally did, indeed, know him better than any other human being.

As they mounted the stairs to their respective chambers, he felt a peculiar bond to her. He wanted to touch her. He casually draped an arm around her shoulders and kept it there as they walked along the second-floor corridor to Sam's room.

She stopped in front of the door and turned her face to him.

And for some unaccountable reason, he dropped a kiss on top her golden hair.

Chapter 19

George put down the book. "Time for bed, children."

As had become their custom, he and Sally had tucked the children into bed directly after dinner and read to them before the two of them went to the drawing room. In order to promote a deeper attachment between her husband and his son, Sally insisted that George be the one to read to them.

"Oh, please, Papa," Georgette said, tugging at his sleeve, "read *The Life and Perambulation of a Mouse* to us." No matter how many times they heard that same story, neither of the children ever tired of it.

He glared at his daughter from beneath lowered brows. "But I just read it last night."

"Do read it again," Sally coaxed. "You know how they love it."

Sam, looking up at his father, nodded.

George glanced at the boy's solemn face. "Very well. Come, Sam, up on my lap."

The toddler squirmed onto his father's lap as George lifted the well-worn book and began to read.

When he finished reading, George stood up. "Now, lad, into your bed."

Sam climbed up into his big bed and got beneath the covers. Sally came and kissed his cheek. "Good night, sweetheart." She stood back and watched as George bent down and tucked the blankets firmly around his son. Unlike Sally, George was not comfortable kissing the boy. "Good night, son."

They left Sam in Miss Primble's care as George carried his squealing daughter upon his shoulders to the next room, where he tucked her in and pecked her cheek. "Good night, pet," he said.

Sally moved to Georgette's bedside and kissed her forehead. "Good night, love."

Georgette's arms came around Sally. "Good night, Mama."

Stirred by the girl's response, Sally lifted her tearful, smiling face to George. He took her hand, and they left the chamber together and went downstairs, where they took up their usual place before the fire in the drawing room.

"I'm rather tired tonight," he said, stifling a yawn. "Lambing season can be exhausting. I hope I can manage a quick game of piquet."

Sally easily won the game. Her husband was, indeed, fatigued. And no wonder. He was gone long hours every day, and when he wasn't in the fields, he was ensconced in his library pouring over farming journals. Sally decided this was a good fatigue. She smiled to herself. Now George was ready for bed at the same time he would have been embarking on a night's activities back in Bath.

"Come, dearest husband, I think you have an appointment with your bed."

Chuckling, he got to his feet and directed a mock scowl at her. "Only if you do *not* insist on tidying the drawing room before we leave. I believe you're trying to deprive our servants of their livelihood."

"Whatever you say," Sally said as she slipped her arm through his and followed him up the stairs. When they reached the door to her newly decorated chambers, he stopped and unexpectedly pressed his lips to her cheek. It was the first time he had ever done so.

The very air in her lungs swooped. She attempted to gather her composure as she gently put her hand on his arm and wistfully looked up at him. "Good night, George."

He stroked her hair. "Good night, my lady."

Then he started toward his own room.

Not daring to watch him, she hurried into her room, closed the door and fell back against it, her heart beating erratically.

A broad-brimmed hat protecting her face from the bright spring sunshine, Sally happily puttered in her new garden. Not a day went by that she did not pluck out unwanted weeds and water her fledgling plants. A pity it was too soon to see the fruits—or vegetables—of her labor. Day after day she toiled away, and still nary a leaf had sprouted.

Some two weeks earlier, Mr. Willingham had appropriated a pair of laborers to remove the ornamental flowers and replant summer vegetables in their place. The interim was exceedingly frustrating. More than once she had lamented the loss of her cutting garden. She did adore lovely flowers. But until their fortunes were reversed—and she had every reason to believe they would be—she meant to direct her efforts to reducing the greengrocer's bills. Later, she would restore the flower gardens.

Even upon regaining the flower gardens, though,

Sally was far too parsimonious to ever again rely on a greengrocer if she could help it. Not when Hornsby was so rich in land. Growing up on a small parcel of land in the village of Haddington, Sally had yearned for a wealth of land. She had vowed that if she ever possessed vast amounts of land she would personally oversee gardens of every sort.

She set down her watering can and smiled. Never in her wildest dreams had she thought to one day be mistress at Hornsby, her favorite place on all the earth.

She heard the pounding hooves of a swiftly moving horse and turned to behold her husband riding toward her. He wore no hat, and his hair was flecked golden in the sunlight. Only rarely now did she ever see him during the day. He eagerly worked side by side with Mr. Willingham, overseeing the estates. She had been enormously pleased over George's transformation. The pleasure he had derived from the horse races and the cockfights paled beside the joy he received from Hornsby. He bubbled with enthusiasm over improvements at the estate, and was rejuvenated by being around those whose goals coincided with his own. Just riding for hour upon hour over his lands filled him with a deep satisfaction, one unobtainable anywhere else. Hornsby was as much a part of him as Georgette or Sam. His past and his future intertwined in Hornsby's fate—a fate he might now be able to control.

She watched as he dismounted and came toward her, his crooked smile causing his eyes to squint. "Will it be Lady Sedgewick's peas and cabbage tonight?" His glance scanned the neat rows of humus.

She put hands to hips and directed a mock scowl at him. "You know it's too early, you beast."

"Are you finished with whatever it is you do here each day?"

"I am."

"Then I propose we ride over the estate. You've seen only a fraction of the place, you know."

Her gaze flicked to the single horse. "I didn't know. I know very little about Hornsby, actually, though I vow to rectify that deficiency."

He looked at her with amusement in his eyes. "I am suitably impressed, my lady. Already you have learned the name of every ancestor who peers down at us from portraits on the second-floor gallery. An impressive accomplishment."

"I could not have done it had you not been able to enlighten me. I confess, I feared you would not be able to name them all. I thought I would have to rely on Felicity, since she's the eldest."

"I was completely surprised that I *did* know them. I have no recollection of having acquired such knowledge."

"I daresay it was not something you consciously did, as I did."

He laughed. "Certainly not."

She came toward him. "I would be most pleased to have you show me the estate."

"Since I haven't procured you a mount yet, I thought we could both ride on Thunder, that is, if you don't object."

Her heart fluttered. Nothing would give her more pleasure than being *that* close to George, to feel his arms circling her. Well, actually there was one thing that would be even better . . . "I don't object at all. I'm not a particularly adept horsewoman."

"That's because you were raised in a village. I daresay you didn't even own a horse." He gave her a leg up.

"We didn't, actually. The first time I ever rode was here at Hornsby when I was twelve, and I was far too embarrassed to tell Glee I had no idea how to ride." She looked up at him and brushed away a stray lock of moist hair from her brow.

Once she was seated on the bay, he placed the reins in her hands, then hopped up to sit behind her.

She relaxed against him, spooning her back into his chest as his arms came around her and they began to ride. Because nature had modeled her after her tall, lanky father, Sally had never before felt either feminine or helpless, but at this moment—cradled against George's muscular body—she felt both.

The sun warming them, a gentle breeze riding with them, they rode past the orchards, past the lake and the folly, and came to the rolling hills, where herds of sheep grazed. "It's lambing season," he said, pride in his voice. "Willingham says it will be the best yet."

In the westernmost pasture Willingham and a dozen or so men gathered in several pockets assisting in the birth of lambs. George rode to where Willingham and another man were tending a birthing ewe, and he and Sally dismounted.

Willingham squatted before the ewe, his sleeves rolled up. His dark eyes flashed when he gazed up at Sally, then he stood to address her. "Forgive me for not taking your hand, my lady. My hands, I fear, are not clean."

Sally, far more interested in the newborn lamb than in Mr. Willingham, only briefly met his gaze. "When was this lamb born?" she asked, her glance flitting back to the newborn.

"Not more than ten minutes ago."

"He looks so very different without a coat."

Mr. Willingham chuckled. "It's actually a she, and I daresay this time next year you'd not recognize her."

George greeted the other young man, who was near his own age. "Good day, John. I should like to present you to my wife." George turned to Sally. "My dear, I've known John all my life. His father worked for my father, and his grandfather for my grandfather, and so on and so on. We played together as children."

"How do you do, John?" Sally said, a smile lifting the corners of her mouth.

"I'm delighted to make your acquaintance, milady."

"Tell me, are you married?" she asked.

"Aye," he said, a twinkle in his amber eyes.

"And have you been blessed with children?" she asked.

He chuckled. "Six bonny lasses and one lad, who's now two."

"The age of our Sam," Sally said, smiling up at her husband. "I do wish your wife would allow your boy to visit with our son. Poor boy is seldom around other lads. I daresay he'd be decidedly thrilled to make the acquaintance of another lad. Now, our Georgette has always had the companionship of her cousin Joy, who's two years younger than she, though I know she would love to have your daughters for her playmates, too. Have you a daughter the age of Georgette?"

His sparkling eyes meeting George's, John laughed out loud. "Me first daughter's nine. We had another daughter every year thereafter until six was born. The lad's our last."

"Then all your children must come up to the manor house," she said.

He grinned at George, then back at her. "They would be honored."

"Shearing season's but six weeks away," George told Sally. "We'll be very busy then."

"Do you think I can come to watch the shearing?" Sally asked. "I'd love to see it."

Willingham smiled at her. "If Lord Sedgewick would allow, we could use an extra hand. There are never enough hands to go around."

She glanced at her husband.

George nodded. "I can't recall another Lady Sedgewick being interested in participating, but the present Lady Sedgewick would, no doubt, be a great deal of help."

Sally was uncertain if her husband had complimented her or not. For sure, she could not fathom the gracious Dianna wrestling with the uncooperative beasts. A pity Sally could not be more like Dianna. "Though I'm ignorant of farming practices, I should be interested in learning all I can."

George's eyes twinkled as he spoke to the steward. "Lady Sedgewick is an adept learner."

Mr. Willingham smiled. "She was, after all, at the top of her class at Miss Worth's School for Young Ladies."

Sally sighed. "I vow, I shall never hear the end of that! I am exceedingly embarrassed."

"Being intelligent is something to be proud of, my lady," Mr. Willingham said.

She was even more embarrassed now. Mr. Willingham seemed to do that to her. In fact, other than Mr. Higginbottom, no other man had ever been so aware of her. Especially not the man she had married. She felt uncomfortable. "Tell me, Mr. Willingham, how many lambs do we have now?" she asked.

"Last count, forty-two. I expect a hundred or so."

She smiled up at her husband. "This is so exciting!"

"Especially when one considers five years ago the herd was down to less than a hundred," he said.

"And now?" she asked, looking up at George.

"Five hundred and growing. Should come to about five hundred and fifty by this time next week."

"Then I should say you—and Mr. Willingham—have done a most admirable job."

"I'm afraid my only contribution was in selecting Willingham," George said.

"Pray, don't listen to him," Mr. Willingham said. "His lordship is far too modest. He's one of the most knowledgeable landowners in England. You've seen his library, have you not?"

Her husband's library bulged with well-worn books and journals on farming and animal husbandry. "Mr. Willingham," said Sally, "you have confirmed my own opinions about my husband."

George set a hand to her waist. "Should you like to see the cornfields?"

"I would, indeed."

They remounted and rode across the pastures for another twenty minutes before they came to colorfully gridded land where a variety of crops grew in alternating fields. Closest to them were rows of tall, green cornstalks whose elongated leaves rippled in the breeze.

"We soon shall have our first opportunity to use the reaper on the corn," George said. "After that, it will be used on the rye crop." He waved an arm toward a square of brown farmland some distance off to the northeast. "Thank you for having more sense than I—and for paying for the reaper."

"What's mine is yours and what's yours is mine. I fared far better in the marriage bargain than you."

"I disagree." He put his mouth near her ear. "Are you hungry?"

She shrugged.

"There's food in the saddlebags. I thought we could ride back to the folly and have a makeshift picnic."

It had been years since she had been to the folly. "Oh, George, that sounds wonderful!"

George had always thought the marble folly of formal Greek style completely incongruous in the woodsy rural setting. It certainly clashed with Hornsby's Tudor manor house. Nevertheless, he preferred its setting over anywhere else in the kingdom. From the folly, he could view the entire lake and the wood surrounding it as well as the little hump-backed wooden bridge that crossed it on the south end. A beautiful setting.

Just last week he had taken a respite there, but left after a mere twenty minutes, feeling bereft. It was a place to share, and he wanted to share it with Sally. Not that they were as close as he and Dianna had been, but he had come to admit that he was as close to Sally as he was with any other living soul. Closer actually. For their every hope and dream was intrinsically tied up in each other, and it was Sally—and only Sally—who loved his children as he did. And it was Sally who had brought him back to Hornsby, the only place where he ever felt complete.

Beneath the folly's domed roof, he unpacked the cold mutton, berries that had been picked only the day before, and a loaf of fresh bread. He laid the fare on a marble bench. Each of them sat on the bench on either side of the food and silently began to eat. It was as if words would spoil the serenity. He watched her as she gazed at the lake, and without words, he knew she appreciated the setting as much as he did.

When they finished eating, she gazed up at him, wonder on her slim face. "You know, George, I don't believe there can be a lovelier place on earth than this."

Her words did not surprise him. He had come to realize Sally was, in many ways, his other half. He swallowed. He could have stopped his spreading smile as easily as he could have stopped the sun from shining. It had been more than two years since he had known such happiness. This feeling of complete contentment wasn't just his pride in Hornsby, it was so much more. It was the sun and the fairness of the day. And it was having someone to share it all with. Until now he had not realized how important it was to have another person to link his life to.

"I've hired a groom," he said.

"But you know I'm trying to keep expenses down."

"The man begged for the job. All he asks for is room and board, and we already have the stables with his living quarters. You yourself have said we need to get a pony for the children, and it's my desire to acquire a gentle mount for you."

"I've been trying to cut expenses, and here you go spending more money."

He shrugged. "I'm not spending much. Willingham—when he learned I was looking for a pony—told me of a family desirous of finding a good home for theirs because the master is too old to ride it any longer. Willingham assures me we've got enough oats to comfortably feed it."

"I must admit the children will be ecstatic, and it does seem you are trying to economize."

Oddly pleased over her approval, he slid a knuckle down her tawny cheek.

He thought her voice trembled when she spoke. "The groom is a young man?"

"No less than five and twenty, I'd say. Quite a strapping fellow. His name is Ebinezer.

Chapter 20

In many ways St. Edward's Chapel in the nearby village of Tottenford was a great equalizer. For within the chapel's stone walls every Sunday morning master and servant and tenant and squire all came together to worship the same God in the same manner. The only distinction among the worshippers was that Lord Sedgewick's family sat in the Sedgewick pew, a square box in front of the other pews. A dozen or more persons could have sat in the Sedgewick pew—and did when George's sisters and their families were visiting Hornsby.

The Sedgewicks merited the prominent pew because the vicar of St. Edward's had his living from the family, as the vicar before him had, and the vicar before him, going back for at least two hundred years.

This morning Sally was going to make the acquaintance of the present vicar, one Charles Basingstoke, who had been at Oxford with George and who had served St. Edward's since shortly after George ascended to the title. Mr. Basingstoke had just returned from York, where he had been attending to family business since Sally's arrival here.

Despite Sam climbing on and off her lap at least thirty times, Sally listened attentively to the priest's sermon. She decided she liked the vicar. His homily on the Eighth Commandment was short, well prepared, and enlightening. She even detected his sense of humor and chuckled at one point while he was speaking. Unfortunately, she was the only one in the house of God to do so. Even George scowled at her. Mr. Basingstoke's voice was of moderate volume, which belied his small stature. It was difficult for Sally to believe the man was the same age as George, for with his thin frame and youthful, freckled face, he appeared far younger and far less masculine than the man she had married.

After the service, they gathered on the steps outside the chapel's timbered doors, and George presented the vicar to her.

She offered her hand, which he brought to his lips for a mock kiss.

"I regret that I was not here to welcome you to Tottenford when you arrived, my lady," he said.

"May I hope that your business in York was successfully concluded?" she said.

His lids lowered over pale green eyes. "Regretfully, my father, who had long been in ill health, died."

George moved to him and clapped a hand on his shoulder. "Charles . . . I didn't know. I'm sorry."

The vicar looked up at them and offered a wan smile. "It was for the best. He had been in frail health for a very long time." He eyed Sally. "I was the youngest of eleven children, so my father was not a young man when I was born."

Sally came to put a gloved hand on his arm. "I lost my father just last year. We were very close." She lowered her lashes. "It's rather difficult, is it not?"

His pale eyes sparkled. "I have every confidence

my poor parent is finally happy. He was given to self-sacrifice and religious fervor which, for as long as I can remember, prohibited him from ever enjoying anything. I truly believe he would have been in his element as one of those papist monks who slept on rocks and abstained from every possible pleasure."

It was all Sally could do to repress a giggle. Monks sleeping on rocks! Mr. Basingstoke really was enormously amusing.

He met her gaze, his lips sliding into a grin. "Thank you for understanding the humor I was unable to conceal in my talk this morning."

She laughed. "A pity everyone is always so somber in the sanctuary. My father was a vicar, and I must tell you he was given to inserting humor into a great many of his homilies."

Mr. Basingstoke directed his attention at George. "It's good to have you back, Sedgewick. How long before you return to Bath?"

"I'm not planning on returning there anytime soon."

"Willingham will, no doubt, be happy to know that."

George's mouth arched into a smile. "The man most likely finds me intolerable. I question every move he makes and offer suggestions that aren't likely welcome."

The vicar shook his head. "At one time you were the most knowledgeable landowner in England. Willingham's always commending you."

As he spoke, Willingham joined the group. Sally noted that he wore the same black frock coat he had worn that night he came to Hornsby for dinner.

The conversation immediately turned to matters of farming.

Sally glanced down at Sam, who tugged at her hand. He was tired of being on his best behavior. She bent down to sweep him into her arms before he got into mischief.

Mr. Basingstoke's eyes rounded. "Don't tell me, Sedgewick, this is your lad! I'd know him anywhere! He looks just like you, but he's certainly not a baby anymore."

"Exactly what I keep telling Lady Sedgewick," George said, shooting Sally an amused glance. "She's forever telling me he's just a babe."

Sally stroked Sam's curls as he poked his thumb into his mouth and contentedly laid his head against her modest bosom.

"You must have had children of your own, Lady Sedgewick, though I dare say you do look rather young," the vicar said.

She was utterly flattered. Not that she looked young, but that she looked maternal. "Only Georgette and Sam. I've known them all their lives."

"She was at school with my sister Glee," George explained.

"And how are your sisters?" Mr. Basingstoke asked. "I expect their nurseries continue to increase."

George turned somber. "Neither my sisters nor their nurseries are increasing, but my sisters are well. They're still in Bath."

Sally drew in a breath. Why had Mr. Basingstoke mentioned the nurseries, a sure reminder of Dianna's tragic death? Now George was likely to be morose all day. Even after all this time, he still had days like that. Days when she knew he grieved for the lovely woman who had been his wife and borne his children.

Her heart flinched. How could she ever feel truly a wife when she would never bear George children, never be physically loved by him? Now she was the one who grieved.

"Tell me, Father," George said to Mr. Basingstoke, "my wife says since Sunday is a day of rest, I'm to refrain from reading books on agriculture. Do you agree?"

Mr. Basingstoke smiled. "Reading the Bible—or other types of reading—are perfectly permissible on the Sabbath."

"You would tell Sedgewick that," Willingham said with jest. "The man is your meal ticket."

The vicar turned to Willingham. "As he's yours, but I daresay you wouldn't stay silent were Sedgewick desirous of turning Hornsby into a pineapple plantation."

At the unlikely prospect of growing pineapples in England, Sally pursed her lips, dimpling her cheeks.

Though both men spoke with good nature, the friction made Sally uncomfortable. " 'Tis a good thing all of you have been friends for a great many years," she said.

"Which reminds me of Blanks," Mr. Basingstoke said, his lips curving into a smile. "I suppose marriage and fatherhood has tamed him."

George shrugged. "He's still the hedonist, despite his marriage."

It wasn't always that way.

Mr. Basingstoke sighed and met George's gaze. "I thought if anyone could tame him, it would be that lively sister of yours."

Would the conversation always allude to Dianna's untimely death? Sally patted Sam's back and glanced at Georgette, then addressed the vicar. "The children grow restless. It's been a pleasure meeting you. You and Mr. Willingham must come to dine with us. Tonight?"

Both men looked at George.

"Do come. Lady Sedgewick sets a fine table."

"I don't doubt it," Mr. Basingstoke said, eying Sally appreciatively.

Unfortunately, Mr. Willingham did the same, and his dark, flashing eyes made her exceedingly uncomfortable. George's glance flicked from Willingham to Sally, and he placed a possessive hand at her waist and nodded. "Tonight, gentlemen." He reached for Georgette's hand, and they walked to the awaiting carriage.

The carriage had not driven over a thousand yards when a great commotion was heard. The coach lurched to a stop, and George flung open the door and sprang out. "What is it?" he asked, alarm in his voice.

John was running toward him, terror on his face. "They've all been slaughtered, my lord!"

George's stomach plummeted. From the pain on his tenant's face, George thought the man had lost his family. All those sweet little girls. His heart pounded nearly out of his chest. "Who's been slaughtered?" George demanded, surging toward John.

A shriek came from the carriage, and Sally burst from the coach, streaking toward them.

"The sheep," John rasped. His eyes filled with liquid.

It was as if George suffered a blow to the windpipe. "What sheep?" he finally managed.

Panting and laboring for breath, John slowed to a stop. "All of them."

By now, Willingham rushed up, shouting. "Our sheep, man?"

John nodded and spoke in a hoarse whisper. "All of them. Even the lambs."

Sally cried out, a long, sorrowful wail.

George moved to her, a million thoughts scrambling in his brain. He fleetingly thought of how Sally had begged to participate in the shearing. He swallowed hard. Now there would be no shearing. Now there was no herd. His brows drawing together, George said, "How? When?"

Sally's hand swiped the tears from her face. "Who would do this?" she asked in a shaking voice.

John shook his head. "I don't know. I live closest to the pastures, and I never heard nothin'. It musta happened in the middle of the night. Looks like some maniac came through there with a sword or dagger and embedded it in their bellies, one by one. He had to be one bloody son o' bitch. Beggin' yer pardon, milady."

Sally winced and her thin shoulders shook violently as she wept. Oddly, George was almost as upset over her grief as he was outraged over his loss. Damn, but he did not like to see her hurt. "Come, let's go. Perhaps we can save some of them." His arm around Sally, he hastened back to the carriage. "There's room for another," he called back to John.

"I'll gather some of the men and meet you there," Willingham said as he ran toward his tethered mount.

Once they were all settled in the carriage and the coach was speeding ahead, Sally gathered her composure enough to speak in a trembling voice. "We can't allow the children see it."

Of course she was right. "We'll drop you and the children off at Hornsby."

"Just the children," she said. "I might be able to help."

He remembered how fascinated she had been over the newborn lamb just the other day. Seeing all those slain creatures would be too much for her delicate sensibilities. "No," he said firmly. "I won't allow you, my lady."

"But George . . ." Her tears gushed forth.

He moved closer and set a reassuring arm around her. "I wish to God *I* didn't have to go, Sally. It won't be a pretty sight."

"They'll be needin' to be buried," John said. "By tomorrow, the odor will be overpowering."

A moan escaping from her, Sally buried her wet face into her hands.

"Who would do this?" George asked in a raspy voice, his head shaking from side to side. "Why?"

"The scarcer the wool, the higher price others' wool will fetch," John said. "It could be anyone."

"But not just anyone would be able to slay five hundred head of sheep," George said bitterly.

"Papa?" Georgette asked.

He glanced across the carriage where his children sat on either side of John. "What, love?"

"What does *slay* mean?"

His gaze locked with his daughter's, his stomach churning. "It means to kill."

Her little face clouded. "Someone killed our lambs?"

George nodded solemnly.

"How could anybody be that mean?" she asked.

From beneath lowered brows, his glance darted from Georgette's solemn face to Sally's tearful face, and he, too, felt like crying. But of course, he couldn't. What was needed in a situation like this was someone who could stay level-headed and make the painful decisions. Never mind that part of his own heart had been wrenched from him. "I honestly don't know, pet."

When they reached Hornsby, the coach slowed

only long enough to deposit Sally and the children, then it sped up again toward the pastures.

George and John were the first to arrive at the slaughter. Getting out of the carriage was the most difficult move he had ever made, but he would not allow John to know that. He wrenched the carriage door open and jumped down.

For a moment he froze. The silence was eerie. For as far as he could see, the fields were covered with the sprawled sheep. Most would have appeared to be asleep if it weren't for the blood staining their wool and running into red rivers. The grim scene turned his stomach. His fists clenched, and he spoke in a guttural voice. "I vow, whoever did this will pay."

John's voice choked with emotion. "Where do we begin?"

"Most important at present is saving any sheep which still might be alive."

John nodded.

"You take this pasture. I'll go across the hill." George directed the coachman, then jumped up on the box beside him.

After they rose over the crest, the coach came to a stop, and George, along with his coachman, began to search for signs of life from any of the hundred and fifty sheep which had grazed here. As George went to the east, southerly winds swept the sickening stench of death over the meadowland. Blood covered his boots as he make his way down the hill. As painful as it was, he studied each animal, grotesque in death, hopeful for signs of life. If only he could have been here last night, he might could have saved some of them. But it was too late now. The farther he went down the hill, the more hopeless his mission, the more his eyes misted.

Shaking their heads, he and the coachman met in the shallow valley. The horrible smell had become more powerful. George fought the overwhelming urge to get away from here. But he—more than anyone—must stay. The slaughtered sheep belonged to him. He was lord of Hornsby. No one else could make the decisions he would now have to make.

The sound of pounding horse hooves came from the crest of the hill, and George gazed up at Willingham and a half dozen other men riding toward them.

Willingham, pinching his nose in an effort to eliminate the foul odor that now permeated everything, came abreast of his employer and dismounted, a grim look on his face. "John said they're all dead back there."

George's lashes lowered and the muscle in his jaw tightened. "Same here."

"If it's permissible to your lordship, I would like to order the men to begin digging trenches."

George nodded somberly. "I'll send the coachman back to Hornsby to get handkerchiefs with which all the men can cover their noses."

"Have Lady Sedgewick sprinkle her perfume on them," Willingham advised.

"A good idea. We'll need all the hands we can get. I'll have my footman come assist."

"Your new groom's already here, offering to help." Willingham looked toward the hill he had just crossed.

His stomach queasy, George began to trudge back up the hill. When he rounded it, he saw Sally coming toward him on Thunder. *What the hell?* Impertinent wench! What was she doing here? The biggest bleeding heart there was. His eyes drilling into her, he picked up his pace.

She slowed as she came close to him. He saw that her tears were gone now.

"I don't want you here," he snapped.

"I know. It's just that I don't want to see you lose everything. Can't we still try to shear the sheep before we bury them? We won't get as much wool, but it would be better than getting nothing."

"Their wool's all bloody!"

"I know it's a lot to ask of the men, but Mrs. Mac-Mannis and I have agreed to boil all the bloody wool clean and lay it out to dry."

"I can't ask you to do that."

"You're not asking. We offered. It's the least we can do to help."

George glowered at her from beneath lowered brows. "I can't ask the men to shear dead, bloody animals."

"I spoke to Mr. Willingham. He thinks it's worth a try. Let him ask the men."

"That's not the point. It's too much to expect of anyone."

"But it's their money, too. You don't have to force them. Ask for volunteers."

By now, Willingham rode up to where Sally and George had gathered. "Lady Sedgewick's idea has merit, my lord."

"Then you'll ask the men to perform so gruesome a task?" George asked.

"I shall ask for volunteers, if that is agreeable with you, my lord?"

George's glance surveyed the macabre scene which surrounded him, choking him with total repugnance. His eyes moistened as he nodded. "I'll shear the first myself."

Chapter 21

That night Sally and George collapsed into their beds directly after George read to the children. He had earned the right to go to bed early, Sally thought. Though he was unused to physical labor, he had worked harder than any man that day, and when darkness came he was still laboring over dead sheep, eking out every ounce of wool that could be had. When the coal-like skies closed around him like a cave, Willingham finally forced him to quit.

Sally burst with pride in him—as well as in his workers, none of whom had refused to aid in the gruesome work. She, too, had done yeoman's work that day. Cook and the sturdy girl who helped her in the kitchen were the only household servants spared from lending a hand in some way with the grim task of shearing. The parlor maids carried baskets of the shorn, bloody wool from the fields to Mrs. MacMannis and Sally, who were cleansing it in cauldrons of boiling water. Other maids fetched more water, while still others laid out the clean, wet wool on Hornsby's dark green lawn. By nightfall only a hundred head of sheep had been shorn.

During the day Sally had been too busy to dwell on the savage, violent act that crippled Hornsby, but once she was in the sanctuary of her own bedchamber, she crushed her face into her pillow and wept bitterly. She had vowed not to cry in front of her broken husband. She would be strong for his sake. She would be his helpmate, but in the darkness of her room she would allow herself to weep. She wept for the poor creatures that had been massacred. She wept for the financial blow the disaster had struck. She wept for the unlikelihood that the stock would ever be replenished. Most of all, she wept for George. He had looked forward with unbounded pride to this year's crop, which was to have been the best ever.

She physically ached for George's hurt. Would this tragedy send him back to Bath? Back to the place where he couldn't be hurt because there he was devoid of feeling? She wept even more bitterly.

The next morning she met George at breakfast. He looked so much better than he had the night before. It was not just that he was clean-shaven and wore a fresh suit of clothing. Everything about him looked rested. A good thing, too, she thought, for today would be even harder than yesterday.

"Did you sleep well?" he asked.

She lied. "Yes. You?"

"I was asleep as soon as I hit the bed."

Her thoughts flitted to their bed in Bath. She could almost picture him removing his pantaloons before lying beside her. At the memory of his bare, muscled legs parallel to hers, her breath came a little faster. She poured herself coffee from the silver urn and sat down across from him. "Cook did a fine job of feeding everyone yesterday, especially considering she was unable to use the kitchen hearth."

His green eyes leveled with hers. "All the servants did a commendable job. I'm very proud of them." He took a sip of coffee. "And grateful."

She suddenly remembered something she wanted to share with him. "You know, George, I heard the most extraordinary story from one of the parlor maids yesterday." She stirred the cream she had added to her coffee.

He arched a brow.

"Estelle said she had difficulty sleeping the previous night, so she left her bed and began to pace her chamber. In the middle of the night, she peered from her window and was shocked to see a naked man walking toward Hornsby from the meadowlands."

George's eyes rounded as he whirled at her. "Did she see where he went?"

Sally shrugged. "No. She said she was too embarrassed to look. As soon as she saw his nudity, she began to tremble and spun away from the window."

His fist hammered the table. "Damn!"

"What's the matter?"

"He was the one."

Sally sat stunned for several seconds. "The one who slaughtered the sheep?"

He nodded.

"How do you know?"

"The person who . . . who killed the sheep would have been completely saturated with blood. If he had any sense, he would have taken off his clothes *before* the crime. The bloody clothes would have been evidence against him. I'm guessing he *did* strip first, then afterward he took a dip in the lake."

Her hand flew to her mouth and her eyes misted.

"Oh my God, you must be right! But who . . ." her voice cracked. "Who would do this awful thing?"

Anger flashed in his eyes. "Someone who hates me very much."

"But you haven't any enemies! You're amiable and well liked by all who know you."

His mouth went taut. "Obviously not all."

Adams entered the chamber. "Mr. Basingstoke begs a word with you, my lord."

"Send him here." George wiped a napkin over his mouth and got up to greet the vicar.

Mr. Basingstoke, wearing fawn breeches and riding boots, stormed into the room, his brow folded like a closed fan. "Sedgewick, I heard about the unspeakable act that's been inflicted upon you!"

George shook his head solemnly. "I seem to have made a dangerous enemy."

Sally winced, then addressed the vicar. "Would you care for coffee, Mr. Basingstoke?"

"No, thank you. I've come to work." His gaze locked with George's. "There are twenty men outside who've offered to help you today."

Unable to hold back her tears and unwilling to allow either man to see her cry, Sally brought her napkin to her face and dabbed at her mouth, then quickly wiped away the tears.

George nodded solemnly. "I don't know what I've ever done to deserve this, but I'm not too proud to accept help. We need every hand we can get. With twenty more men, I believe we'll finish today—and we must. The odor's already overpowering."

"Yes," Basingstoke said, wrinkling his nose. "I can smell it from here at the manor house."

Sally glanced at her napkin and jumped up. "You all need to use napkins around your faces to help stifle the smell. I'll just run upstairs for some perfume."

"Believe it or not, the perfume does help," George said, clapping a hand on Basingstoke's shoulder.

Basingstoke looked at George and solemnly shook his head. "The village folk are nearly as outraged as you. In fact, I've already got pledges from people who want to help you restock. So far, thirty sheep have been donated—and twelve new lambs can be spared by the good farmers of Tottenford."

"Then everyone must know that I've been wiped out," George said in a cracking voice.

The vicar shrugged. "I know because Willingham and I are close. I knew how important this year's crop was to Hornsby's fortunes."

George, his voice still cracking, turned his head away. "I'm moved by everyone's generosity." A pity it took a tragedy to show him that Hornsby and the people who inhabited it clasped his heart as surely as if bound by chains.

"It's your own generosity that's spurred this," Basingstoke said. "Never has anyone in Tottenford been in need that you've not come to their aid. I know that whenever I ask for your help, you'll do anything you can to assist. Now, for the first time, you need help, and it's time for others to help you."

"I daresay the old George would have been too proud to accept, but I have a family to consider now. You know, Charles, I had decided to stay at Hornsby. I wanted to make it a place my children would look to with pride." He laughed bitterly. "How in the hell I'll do that now without any money, I don't know."

There was pity on Basingstoke's face when he nodded.

By noon the wool that had been washed the day before was ready to be bagged, and new, wet wool replaced it in crooked, ever-lengthening lines across Hornsby's lawn. Those facts were conveyed to George via the maids who came throughout the day with empty baskets and left with full ones.

Not that George stood around talking. He spent the day bending already sore muscles over death-stiffened sheep. He had even mustered enough strength to single-handedly turn over a beast in order to shear its other side. Sweat clung to the napkin that was tied around his head to mask the foul odor. He worked without a break. He worked even when every limb cried out to be rested. He worked until the sunlight faded, then abandoned him altogether.

After shearing the last of the sheep, George winced in pain as he raised himself up from his bent-over stance and began to walk across the grim pastures. Now that his hands were free, he was at liberty to press the perfumed napkin to his face. He had inhaled the putrid stench for so long and his lungs were so permeated with the odor, he wondered if his breath would ever be free of it.

He heard voices and saw the forms of other men, but it was too dark to recognize anyone. He was almost too tired to walk, but he forced himself to climb the hill. With each step, he craved a ride upon a horse, but no such relief was available.

As he rounded the hill, he heard Willingham's voice and followed the sound.

When they met in the darkness, Willingham spoke in a weary voice. "We'll have to begin the trenches tomorrow."

"No," George said firmly. "We'll burn them. These men have worked hard enough."

"Burn the sheep?"

"Yes. With ropes and horses it shouldn't be too difficult to put them into piles for the bonfires."

"I wish I'd thought of that. It will be a lot less work—but a damn foul odor."

"The odor can't be any worse than it is now," George said.

For dinner that night George had invited to Hornsby as many men as could sit around the long dining room table, and he insisted that no man need dress for dinner this night.

"But we'll stink up your house," Willingham protested.

George shook his head. "The house already stinks. I daresay the wretched odor has reached as far as Tottenford."

Willingham shrugged. "I daresay you're right."

Sally saw to it their best wine was served to these loyal friends. Being the only woman at the table kept her silent throughout the dinner.

With the lion's share of their work now behind them, the men's thoughts turned to speculation over who could be responsible for the senseless slaughter.

George related the maid's tale about the naked man, and they all agreed that he must be the man responsible for killing the sheep.

"At least we know he was walking toward Hornsby—and thus, the village," Basingstoke said. "That should eliminate anyone to the north."

George's eyes narrowed, his voice lowered. "I would very much like to get my hands upon him."

"George!" Sally shrieked.

He spun toward her, his eyes wide with worry over the terror he heard in her voice.

All color drained from her face. "What about the children? If someone hates you that much—" Her voice broke.

A hush fell over the long table.

Dear God! He felt as if a giant had kicked him in the gut. His hand began to tremble so badly, he had to set down his fork. Could any pain be greater than seeing your child die? He spoke with barely controlled anger. "They are never, ever to be left alone. You will convey that order to the nurse and to all who serve at Hornsby."

Her eyes misted as she nodded solemnly.

Sally knew she would sleep well this night. She had been even more exhausted today than yesterday because of her lack of sleep the night before.

After dinner, when the men drank their port and smoked their cigars, Sally excused herself. "I'll run up and tuck in the children," she said. "Then I believe I'll go to bed."

As she went to leave the room, George took her hand. "Thank you for all you've done. You've made me very proud." He pressed a kiss into her palm.

That he acted and spoke so sweetly in front of all those men made his words even more appreciated. Sally favored him with a wan smile and left the room. Despite her fatigue, she felt feather light as she climbed the stairs. She could still feel the warmth of George's lips upon her hand.

After she read to the children and tucked them in—and honestly answered Georgette's question about the foul odor—Sally spoke privately with Miss Primble, instructing her to never leave the children unattended for even a moment. The young nurse was quick-witted enough to connect the vicious slaughter to fears for the safety of his lordship's children.

Before Sally went to her own chambers, she brought her maid to Georgette's room and explained that Hettie was never to leave Georgette alone at night. Hettie was a good girl. Sally felt confident knowing she was with Georgette.

As tired as she was, Sally took time to draft a letter to Glee to inform her of the wretched thing that had occurred at Hornsby. Then she climbed into her bed and immediately fell into a deep slumber.

Chapter 22

The stench went away. Not overnight, but gradually, as a person's hair grays—almost imperceptibly until one day the transformation is startlingly complete. Sally woke up this morning and realized the smell was gone. It was that morning she vowed to think on the tragedy no more. She had once told George she did not want him to ever go backward, only forward. Now she needed to heed her own advice.

For some peculiar reason, her husband had been better able than she to look to the future and refuse to dwell on the past that could not be changed. He rarely spoke of the tremendous setback, only of its perpetrator, upon whom he vowed to take vengeance. Some of the credit for George's remarkable recovery came courtesy of his two wealthy brothers-in-law, each of whom had pledged a hundred head of sheep from the herds on their respective estates. But most of George's endurance could be attributed to his own toughness and determination.

When she went downstairs for breakfast, Sally

did not expect to find her husband still at home. He was given to rising early and working long hours on the estate. But as she entered the chamber, he rose to greet her.

"Why are you still here?" she asked, her hand flying self-consciously to smooth her hair.

A sardonic look tilted his rugged face. "My presence offends you?"

She laughed. "Of course not. I'm glad you're here." She poured herself coffee and sat down across from him at a cloth-covered table that was placed beside a tall window looking out over Sally's kitchen garden.

"I've decided to spend the morning with you and the children," he said.

She arched a brow.

"The pony should be here shortly."

A smile wiped across her face. "Today?"

"The groom was to get it from Ilswitch this morning."

"The children will be so excited! We shall allow them to name him."

His lips puckered into a smile. "He's a filly, and I doubt that son of mine will have a hand in the naming." His brows folded, pinching the bridge of his nose. "I really think the boy should be talking. How old is he now?"

He knew very well how old Sam was! She frowned. "He's eight and twenty months."

"I'm sure something's wrong with him."

She scowled even deeper. "There's nothing whatsoever wrong with him! Surely you've been able to observe that he's possessed of a very keen mind."

George shrugged. "He does seem to be quick-witted enough."

"More than enough," she said through gritted

teeth. "For one thing, he knows all his colors. I have only to tell him to bring me the green cap, and he knows exactly which one it is—and the red, and the blue. Miss Primble has affirmed that there's not a color he doesn't know. Mrs. Howell's four-year-old daughter still doesn't know her colors."

He grinned. "Then your Sunday-morning conversations on the church steps are of some value."

"Don't be such an ogre. You know you wish for me to be accepted by Mrs. Howell—and everyone in the community."

"Oh, I don't have to worry about that. You've duly been approved by anyone who's within shouting distance of Hornsby."

She plopped a scone on her gilded porcelain plate and proceeded to slather it with soft butter. "You know, there may be a bit of a problem with having the pony."

"I know." He frowned. "I should have gotten two."

She nodded. "Sam is not likely to want to share."

"He'll have to learn that if he wants to ride the creature, he must be willing to share," George said in a stern voice.

After breakfast, they gathered up the children and began to walk with them to the stables. "Do you remember how the stables were in your childhood?" George asked Sally.

She was mildly piqued that he said *your* childhood—as if he wished to accentuate their age difference—and possibly the many other differences between them. She nodded solemnly and tried not to think of the sorrow she heard in his voice. The stable had once held racehorses and stallions and ponies and four matched bays for the carriage. Every stall had been filled. She hurt for George. "A pity your father changed so in the last years of his life and squandered away your birthright."

He gave a bitter laugh. "He did become rather a scoundrel after Mama died." His eyes met hers, and he reached to take her hand. "If it weren't for you, I would have done exactly as he did. I would have continued on my wayward path until there was nothing left for the children. There's not much now, but I vow to rebuild Hornsby."

She squeezed his hand. "Pray, do not credit me for turning you around! 'Twas your own decision to put your children first. When I realized you wished to"—finishing her thought would be difficult, but she needed to wedge the truth between them—"to sacrifice yourself, I've never been more proud of you."

He came to an abrupt stop and took both her hands in his. "Don't ever say that my marrying you was a sacrifice on my part. It was the best thing I've ever done."

Her heart expanded. Of course, he meant to say *for the children.* Still . . . he had no regrets. She met his gaze with watery eyes and reached up to stroke his chiseled cheek.

He covered her hand and brought it to his lips. "Thank you for everything," he said in a throaty voice.

The children's laughing voices and the happy yelp of their dog rang out as they ran across the sloping, verdant parkland, their parents hastening to catch up with them. It was a joy to watch Sam's little legs churning as fast as they could go. He knew as well as his father did the direction of the stables, and he was determined to be the first to see his new pony.

When they got to the stables, Ebinezer was rubbing down the gray pony.

"It shouldn't be too much for the beast to gently trot close by with a child on his back," George said for the benefit of the groom. He came and took the pony's lead line and began to lead it toward the open door.

Sam, anxious to come close to his wondrous new possession, nearly got stepped on by the pony.

George swung around to face the errant child and spoke angrily. "Don't ever come up behind a horse! You could have been hurt!" He bent to pick up the startled child.

His voice softened when he addressed his daughter. "Tell you what, love, I shall allow Sam to ride first, but I'll allow you to select a name for the pony. Remember, it's a girl."

Sally smiled at her husband's cleverness—and self-preservation. Of course Sam would have to ride first, and most likely longest, or his foul temper would make them all miserable.

Georgette's lovely little face brightened as she watched Sam being hoisted upon the mount. Sally took her hand, and they followed the males from the stable and continued to walk behind them as George patiently instructed Sam on how to sit a horse.

Seeing Sam's little body seated atop the mount filled Sally with fear. He was awfully small to ride alone.

George instructed his son on how to ride as if Sam were a little man, yet he was patient and his voice was gentle. As Sally watched George and his son, she came to a most shocking realization. George was enjoying this as much as Sam. And because she knew George so thoroughly, he could not hide that pride from her—it showed plainly in his demeanor. It was the pride a man takes in his son. She would have been at a loss to explain it, but his

Cheryl Bolen

proprietary manner with Sam was altogether different from that he used with his daughter.

Meanwhile, Georgette was so excited about naming the beast she lost all interest in watching her brother ride the animal. "Matilda is a very fine name," the little girl said.

"Yes, it is," Sally agreed as she stroked Georgette's rich, dark hair.

"Or I could call her Smokey because she's gray."

"You could."

The little girl giggled. "Or I could call her Baby because she's a baby horse."

Sally laughed. "Baby's nice, too. You've come up with some wonderful names, pet."

Georgette smiled up at her stepmother. "Which one do you like best?"

"I cannot say. They're all so good. You must decide for yourself."

"Oh dear, what a deminna."

It was all Sally could do not to burst out laughing. "You mean dilemma, pet."

With no falter in her composure, Georgette continued. "Such a dilemma to select a good name for our new pony." She wrinkled her little nose. "Perhaps Smokey isn't so good, after all. It reminds me of a boy horsy."

"You may be right," Sally agreed.

"I know! I'll ask Sam." Georgette ran ahead, her frilly white dress billowing behind her, her dark tresses waving like a flag. When she came abreast of her brother, his face was screwed up with concentration—and was not altogether free of fear. He had listened attentively to all the instructions his father had given him. Now he seemed afraid to glance at his sister.

"Sam," Georgette said, "should you like to call the horsy Baby? Or do you want to call her Matilda?"

Sally saw that George watched Sam's face intently. No doubt, he was in hopes Sam would reply.

Sam did not answer.

His sister was not dissuaded. "Baby?" she queried.

Sam shook his head.

"You want to call the horsy Matilda?" Georgette said in a sweet little voice.

Still not looking at his sister, Sam nodded.

"No wonder the lad won't speak," George said with amusement. "He doesn't have to. The little imp communicates exceedingly well without talking."

Georgette lagged back and looked up at Sally with a beaming face. "Matilda will be our horsy's name."

"I do believe that is my favorite one," Sally said decidedly. "But you are not to call it a horsy, pet. It's a pony. I know you only call it a horsy for Sam's sake, but he needs to learn the correct words. How else will he learn to speak?"

That night after they tucked in the children, Sally and George returned to the drawing room to face each other over a game table that was placed close to the fire. George began to deal two hands of piquet.

"I've been told you've managed to have a fire in every servant's bedchamber at night," George said. "Such a move seems at great odds with your economizing measures."

"Oh, I'm still economizing in every way I can." She peered over the top of her cards. "But I'll never sacrifice the well-being of anyone at Hornsby. It's my belief that every person should be entitled to sleep in a room free from chill and drafts."

"Commendable."

"The servants are so grateful for the *luxury* I've afforded them, they're more than willing to help me cut expenses in other areas."

"I don't know how you've done it, but I'm rather impressed," he said.

She set her hand on his arm. "Oblige me by not discussing money during our evenings. You deserve to have one portion of every day that is free from estate woes."

Another thing for which he was grateful to her. After the disaster with the sheep, he had briefly sunk into despair—a despair he hid from Sally. He had recovered completely. But now he had asked himself if losing his herd was the worst thing that could happen to him. *No, it isn't.* Losing someone you loved was worse. He knew that firsthand. And now he knew that losing Georgette or Sam or Sally was the worst thing that could happen. Sheep could be replaced—not easily, but they could. His loved ones could not.

These night meetings with Sally in front of the fire in his favorite room on earth had, indeed, become very special to him. In many ways, they were like the early-morning sessions he had enjoyed with Sally back in Bath. But they were somehow also different. Despite the two of them being far less intimately attired, he felt even closer to her.

They *were* much closer now—as two people who share the same hopes and dreams would necessarily be. And they shared the same love for their children. With Sally, he shared everything. Everything except his body.

His heart began to beat faster at the unlikely prospect of making love to Sally. He pictured her as she had looked in her thin night shift back in Bath. Hers was not a body to incite lust. It was too thin. But Dianna also had been thin, and his lust for her had been almost debilitating. At the memory of Sally's nipples pressing against the fine lawn of her night shift, he grew aroused.

Good lord, but it had been a long time since he had been sexually aroused over a woman. Perhaps that would explain the thoroughness of his erection. He could not speak. He could not concentrate on his cards. He could only feel. Feel the throbbing manhood nearly exploding under the game table. Feel a hunger to draw Sally into his arms. Feel a need to have her beneath him, to have himself sheathed within her. His breath grew ragged.

"George?"

He had stupidly brought the game to a halt. He tossed out the first card in his hand and gave her a shaky smile. He seemed unable to remove his gaze from her firelit face and its shades of honey and brown all feathering together, with her smoldering dark eyes the focal point. Willingham had been right. Sally was lovely. George had been so damned obsessed with Dianna he had not allowed himself to acknowledge Sally's attractiveness. Now he could only barely remember what Dianna looked like. He had tried to imagine the sound of Dianna's voice, but had not been able to. Did that mean that he no longer loved Dianna? Had she finally released her grip on his heart?

Perhaps the reason he had failed to notice Sally's modest beauty was because he had for so long pictured her with that wretchedly straight hair. Since they had married, though, Sally's hair was curly every day. He wondered how she had managed that. Did she do it to please him?

He was ashamed of his shallowness. That a

woman's hair was curly or straight should not matter in the least to him. Especially not with Sally. She was so much more to him than appearance.

"Do you know, George, what we must do with the children?" Sally asked, her dark eyes flashing with mirth.

He cocked an inquiring brow.

"We should take them out on the lake. Children do love to ride in boats, you know. And it would be ever so much fun to have a picnic. I remember how delighted I was as a child to come to Hornsby and go rowing on the lake. Of course, everything at Hornsby was so glorious! And I adored the folly."

"Then we shall picnic at the folly tomorrow. I'll collect the three of you at eleven of the clock."

He would never know how he finished the game or how he was able to climb the stairs beside her without the bulge between his legs giving him away.

When they came to the door of the viscountess's chambers, he said, "I've not seen these rooms since you redecorated. May I see them now?" Good lord, did he hope she would invite him to her bed?

A flitting look of some emotion crossed her face. Was it fear? "Certainly. Come in."

He knew the chambers would be different. Sally was wise to want to leave nothing here that would remind him of Dianna and all the intimacies they had shared within this chamber. And Sally had done a very good job. It was a totally different room. The scarlet had been eradicated. The bed— was it the same bed?—looked completely different. It was on a different wall and was draped in ivory silk. At least he thought it was silk. He was not very knowledgeable about fabrics.

The room reflected Sally's personality. Dianna's gilded writing desk had been painted ivory. Much more in Sally's understated style, he thought. The room was efficiently laid out, practical, not too elegant, nor extravagant. His gaze swept from the writing desk to the ivory draperies, to the bed—God, but he wanted to take her on that bed this very minute—then settled on Sally. "You've done an excellent job. It's quite lovely." *Like you,* he wanted to say.

Her eyes flitted to the protrusion between his thighs, and he was incapable of meeting her gaze. "Well, I'd best be off." He turned toward the door and left the room.

Once he was in his room and begging for release, he chastised himself for not making love to her. Hadn't her glance to his erection been an invitation to her bed? God, but he didn't know what to think. Sally was a virgin. Perhaps she didn't even know about erections.

And he couldn't just have taken her. With a person one cares about, one must slowly lead up to such a meaningful event.

Did he even wish to lead Sally in that direction? Would she have him if he did? Was his desire the result of deeper emotions, or was it a fleeting physical need?

Sleep would be a long time coming this night. He would close his eyes only to see Sally's deep chocolate eyes peering at him. He would turn in his bed and remember the gentle swell of her breasts beneath the gauzy linen of her night shift. And, God, how he wanted her!

Sally, too, lay awake long after George had left her. Because of what her brother David had told her, Sally did know about erections. Of course, she had never seen one. Until tonight.

What she could not understand—and probably never would—was if George had become aroused over her or over the memory of making love to Dianna in this very room.

Sally pounded her fist into the feather mattress and cursed Dianna.

Chapter 23

It was as pretty a June day as George could ever remember. The sun warmed him from the inside out, and he smiled from the inside out. Their outing had begun with each child taking a ride upon Matilda. After that, they walked the short distance from the stable to the lake, where they boarded the weathered little rowboat that had been moored beside a wobbly dock since George's own childhood. As he and Sally rowed, George watched his children's faces change from cautious curiosity to smiling, giggling approval. A pity he had not brought them here before. He vowed to make up for that omission. The well-worn oars plowed through the sun-dappled water, then reversed their direction.

They quit rowing, and the boat drifted toward the middle of the lake. George set up each of his children with the appropriate fishing gear.

But his daughter did not take to fishing. First, she was terrified of the worms. She calmed down when her father assured her she did not have to handle the offensive creatures nor would she even have to look at them since they would be down in the water. Then when her brother—with their father's help—reeled in a squirming trout, and Georgette saw the hook skewered into the fish, she begged her father to throw the defenseless creature back into the water.

The request threw George into a quandary. On the one hand he wished to please his daughter. Hadn't he always done everything in his power to make her happy? On the other hand, he was compelled to teach the boy manly pursuits. A sportsman simply did not spare the lives of the creatures he hunted, be they rainbow trout or richly pelted foxes. He finally decided that he was obligated to set an example for the boy.

George lifted his solemn gaze to Sally.

Without a single word passing between them, his wife knew he was imploring her to intercede with Georgette. After all, Sally was a female, too, and she would best know how to handle his squeamish daughter.

Sally moved to set a gentle hand on Georgette's shoulder. "I think, pet, that angling is a sport for men and lads. It is rather disgusting, is it not?"

Georgette's nose wrinkled when she responded. "It's odious."

A smile played at George's lips. His daughter's ability to mimic her elders belied her tender years. A pity one's children had to grow up so fast.

"Exactly," Sally said, picking up a pair of oars. "I believe we'll push off toward the shore, and you and I, pet, will go up to the folly. I shall need you to help me prepare the picnic."

Georgette's face brightened. "Can we have the picnic in the folly?"

"If you'd like, dearest."

A gentleman could not allow a lady to do all the rowing. George let his grip on Sam's fishing pole slide. "Hold the pole like a good lad," George instructed as he took up the other set of oars and began to row.

"You don't have to help," Sally said. "It's so short a distance I daresay I can easily handle it by myself." She eyed Sam. "You'd better help Sam. He's much too young for such responsibility."

"He'll do better if he's on his own."

As soon as those words were uttered, Sam's pole eased into the dark green depths of the lake. Sam grunted and spun around to his father, pointing his pudgy finger toward the ripple spiraling on the water's surface. He grunted again.

"Sensible Sal. Must you always be right?" George sent Sally an amused grin and exhaled with dramatic emphasis. He took the pole Georgette had tossed aside, and he baited it for Sam. This time he pulled Sam into the space between his own legs and pinned his arms around the intent lad, careful to keep one hand on the lad's pole. How foolish he had been to think a two-year-old capable of fishing alone!

While he and Sam attempted to fish, Sally rowed ashore. When she finished, he lifted Sam and stood him in the center of the boat. "Allow me to help the ladies from the boat." George proceeded to assist Georgette, then Sally to the wood dock before turning back to Sam. "Do you want to go with Mama?"

Sam shook his head and backed farther away from George.

"Fish?" George said to the boy.

Sam's head bobbed up and down.

Chuckling, George climbed back into the boat and placed the youngster once again between his legs as he began to row out to the center of the lake. There, he stopped and helped cast Sam's line into the lake. When no fish nibbled at their bait within a few moments, Sam grew impatient. He pointed to the water and with his hand made flipping images. Then he grunted.

George's eyes danced as he watched his determined son's pantomime. The lad really was rather bright. A most quick learner, to be sure. Without being aware of what he was doing, George pressed his lips into the golden curls on top his son's head. The lad's head was warm, as if the metallic glints in his pale hair imprisoned the heat.

It suddenly became clear to George that Sam was too young to sustain an interest in fishing. The lad liked action. He never tired of riding Matilda—what a horrid name for a pony. George fancied that Sam would never tire of rowing upon the lake. The little fellow loved movement. And the faster, the better.

It also became clear to George that his son was very much like him. His heart tripped over the realization. He swallowed. Again, without being consciously aware of what he was doing, George tightened his hold on the little scamp. The boy felt entirely different than Georgette had at the same age. She had always been feather light. Like her mother. But Sam was a sturdily built lad, to be sure. George's chest tightened. Didn't every man desire to have a son? A son in his own image? Dianna had died giving him this boy, and he had never—until this moment—valued that son. Suddenly his heart overflowed with this newly realized love he held for the boy.

A smile on his face, George watched Sam squirm loose from him and make his way to the discarded oars. As heavy as they were, Sam managed to pick them up and bring them to his father. Speed. That is what the boy wanted. He wished to go. And go fast.

George swiftly powered the oars from one side of the lake to the other. A look of sheer, wondrous glee settled on Sam's intent little face. When George happened to glance at his daughter, who had left the folly and come close to the dock, he realized she was jealous. Sally had been right. All children did indeed love boat rides.

He rowed to the rickety dock. Sally came down the knoll, the breeze molding her saffron dress against the gentle curves of her body. Silvery blond hair swept away from her smiling face. His breath caught. When had Sally become so lovely? As she came nearer, he was unable to remove his eyes from her, unable to dislodge the lump that stuck in his throat.

"Food's ready," she called.

Food? He had almost forgotten. Being in the sun always gave George a hearty appetite. Dispelling sensuous thoughts of Sally, he scooped up Sam and disembarked from the wobbly boat.

Georgette and Sam ran up the knoll to the folly, while George and Sally lagged behind. Where did children get so much energy? Would that he felt like running uphill. He took Sally's hand, a gesture that completed his total satisfaction. Being back at Hornsby with his children and the wife with whom he shared so much, his own life was finally, at long last, complete. What more could a man ask for? His heart drummed. There was only one thing. He wished to make Sally the wife of his heart. He wished to love her with his body and with his soul. His breath grew thinner as they reached the top of the knoll.

Sally had spread out the food on the benches,

just as they had done when the two of them had
come here before. Now he was sorry they had decided to eat here. Sitting beneath the trees held
much more allure than eating on marble benches
that reposed upon marble floors under a metallic
domed roof. They did not need the folly's protec-
tion today. There could never be a more beautiful
day than this lovely May afternoon.

"Would you mind greatly if we took our plates
down closer to the lake?" he asked Sally. "It's too
pretty a day to spend in this mausoleum."

"Not at all," she said as she began to gather up
the basket.

"Don't bother with that. We can each carry our
own plate."

She gave him a doubtful look. "I'm afraid every
morsel of food would slide off Sam's plate by the
time he reached the bottom of the knoll."

Of course she was right. "I'll take his." George
took both plates and began to walk down the
knoll, following his running, squealing children.

The four of them gathered together on the grass
ten feet from water's edge.

"I hope we shall not be bothered by ants," Sally
said before she bit into a hunk of cheese.

Sally worried too much. Ever since the business
with the sheep, she had been obsessed over the
children's safety.

Neither child had much of an appetite. There
were too many other distractions. Sam ate a total
of two bites, both of sweet blackberries. Georgette
dabbled at eating a bite from each food, but stopped
sometime after her nibble on the hard-cooked egg
and before trying the comfit Sally had insisted Cook
pack.

George and Sally exchanged amused glances over

the children's boundless energy. The children derived a great deal of fun from throwing stones into
the water. After that, they crossed and recrossed the
hump-backed bridge a dozen times before deciding to feed bread to the family of mallards that inhabited the lake. The children then walked up the
knoll and ran down, squealing all the way down.

"How can two such small creatures make that
much noise?" he asked.

She shrugged and handed him a hunk of bread.
"The bread's fresh."

His teeth sunk into a slice, and he nodded. "I
declare, all of Cook's food is fresher since you came
to us."

Sally laughed. "She must fear meeting the same
fate I dealt The Curmudgeon."

He loved to watch Sally laugh. He loved that she
had come out without a bonnet. So what if her
face darkened? He had come to admire her tawniness. He had come to realize there was much to
appreciate about the woman he had selected to be
his bride for all the reasons except love. His chest
tightened. He thought, perhaps, he had come to
love Sally. He nearly laughed out loud at the ludi-
crous idea that he had fallen in love with the former Sally Spenser.

He was rather glad the children were not un-
derfoot at the moment. He wished to have a very
serious conversation with his wife.

Georgette called to him from the bridge. "Papa?"

He glanced at her. Soil and grass stained her
lovely white dress with sky blue ribbands. A smile
tweaked at the corners of his mouth. "What is it,
love?"

"May Sam and I go feed Matilda a carrot?"

His glance darted from the children to the stables,

which were only a hundred yards away. Before he gave permission, though, his gaze met Sally's, soliciting approval.

She nodded.

Georgette went back up to the folly to fetch a carrot. When she reached the bottom of the knoll, she called to her brother. "Come, Sam!" She began to run toward the stables, and Sam ran after her, trying his determined best to catch up with her—which, of course, he never did.

"I believe Sam will have a very long nap this afternoon," Sally said. "He is most certainly wearing himself out."

George faced Sally, his back to the stables. He had never before noticed the metallic glints in her hair. They were just like Sam's. His eye took in the grace in her relaxed posture, the expression in her deep brown eyes, the slenderness of her person. He had come to love everything about Sally. His viscountess.

He moved closer to her and took her hand. She gazed at him with warmth and a shy little fluttering about her lips. His pulse accelerated. He wished to declare himself to this woman he had married. But what if she had no desire for him? His stomach lurched, then dropped. No woman had ever spurned him. Not for a minuet nor for a night of passion. Wherever the Viscount Sedgewick had cast his eye, the recipient had been only too pleased to accommodate the well-enough looking peer. He vowed to win his wife's love.

"Have you enjoyed our outing?" he asked her.

The glimmer in her expressive eyes was enough answer for him. She nodded. "Would that every day was this perfect."

His exact thoughts. He fleetingly recalled another comment she had made today that mirrored his own thoughts. She had said as a child she had loved everything about Hornsby. Did she still?

"Is Hornsby a place where you would be content to spend the rest of your life?" he asked.

Her slender face became serious. "Hornsby has always been my favorite place."

His heart tripped again. Did all of her thoughts so closely align with his own? Of course, it had not always been that way. The two of them had once collided. About small things. Not the big ones. With one exception. Sally had not approved of his coolness toward his son. And, as was most often the case, she had been right to chastise him.

He cleared his throat.

"George?" she said, sniffing, her nose in the air. "Do you smell something burning?"

He bolted upright. By God, he did! He spun around to look for the children at the very instant Sally shrieked. A blood-curdling shriek. A yellow flame leaped from the top of the stable's gabled roof. The stable was on fire!

He could not think. He could not speak. He could only react. He took off running with blazing speed. Sally, too, began running, but her speed could not match his. It was as if he possessed the speed of ten stallions.

He only hoped it would be enough.

As they neared the stable he called out his children's names in an urgent, strangled voice he could not believe was his own. "Georgette, Sam, get out of that stable!" Sally's calls echoed his own.

When he was within ten feet of the mews, Georgette stumbled out, coughing and rubbing her eyes. No sight had ever been more welcome.

"Where's Sam?" he asked in a cracking voice.

Her little shoulders shrugged.

And where was that damned groom?

George called over his shoulder to Sally. "You take her. I'll go for Sam."

With no decrease in his speed, George sprinted through the opened double doors and was immediately surrounded by thick gray smoke. He began to cough, and his heart pounded in fear. Where was his son? The damned smoke was so thick, he did not know if he would even be able to see Sam if the lad were five feet in front of him.

George's eyes stung and watered, and he couldn't seem to stop coughing. "Sam!" he called as loudly as his raw lungs would allow. The only sound was the crackling of burning wood and the frightening whinnying from the horses' stalls. Though he was standing in the middle of a burning building, a chill raced down his spine.

"Sam!" he yelled again as he pushed ahead toward the stall he thought was Matilda's.

This time he heard a faint, muffled noise. *Why in the hell couldn't the boy talk?* The sound came—he thought—from the pony's stall.

The loft—where the fire had started—snapped and crumbled away, igniting the stalls beneath it. A wall of flame leaped a mere ten feet from him. His hair singed. His hot skin felt like molten metal. His heart raced. He had to get out. Now, while he still could. But he could not leave without Sam.

It was hard to tell which stall was the pony's because of the heavy smoke, but he took a chance and threw open the door to the one he thought housed Matilda. His guess was right. The gray beast lunged from the stall and ran toward the light of day.

Terror like nothing he had ever experienced filled George's mind. *Where is my son?* He didn't see the lad. "Sam!" he called once more. Only a reduced sound came from his own lungs. Time was running out.

Then, from beneath the haystack at his feet, he saw a heart-wrenching sight. Sam's little head poked out, straw protruding from his hair at odd angles. *The babe had hidden beneath the haystack to get away from the fire!* He gathered Sam into his arms, convulsing into tears of joy.

Now to get out of here before the fiery building came crashing down on them! Cradling Sam tightly against him, George galloped down the center of the stable—only to find flames consuming much of the center. He could not go around them because the stalls would impede his flight. If he wished to live, there was only one thing to do. He would have to streak through the flames and hope for the best.

Burrowing Sam's face into the crook between his body and his shoulder, George ducked down low and bolted ahead. He knew he would have to go faster than he ever had. Like running his finger through a candle flame. The trick was to go so fast, the fire couldn't stick. Inhaling one final lungful of smoke, he started.

Fear made him want to turn back, but his mind was stronger than the fear. He had to save Sam. He ran straight into flames that towered over him. The first few feet into the fire's intensity he felt nothing. But by the time he could see the daylight, flames had taken hold of his coat.

He screamed the scream of a dying man, but could not allow himself to stop until he brought his son to safety. That first second he felt the flames licking against him, he felt no pain. But when he was more than halfway through the fire and close enough to smoke-free air to hope, pain seared

through him. He cried out like a woman but did
not slow down.

Then he heard Sally's cries. She was running toward him. The smoke was clearing. He must be
outside. But, bloody hell, he was on fire!

Her wet face collapsed in grief, Sally rushed to
him and took Sam. "Lie down, George! Smother
the flames!" she shouted.

He dropped immediately to the ground.

Chapter 24

Saving his son had cost George his life. That was all Sally could think of as she watched the ball of fire that was her husband stagger from the blazing stable and collapse, the life draining from him. She threw her own body on top of George in a final effort to smother the flames which charred the right side of his body. She would never remember the gamut of emotions that spun through her when she saw her husband on fire. She was certain he would die, and she could not allow that. How could she continue to live in a world devoid of George? Her attempt to save him was as feeble as offering the juice of a lemon to a man dying of thirst, but she had to try.

That was how Willingham found her: lying over her husband, weeping to the depths of her soul.

He lifted her, and she saw the flames had died. Her heart twisted. George's utter stillness told her he had died, too. With a ragged whimper, she heaped herself once again upon his heated body, placing her ear over his heart. Tears raced down her cheeks. She gazed up into the steward's face. "He's alive."

Willingham eyed the ragged holes in her gown and her own raw, swollen flesh where she had pressed herself into the flames. "You're hurt."

Her eyes wild, she shook her hand. "No! Not me! It's George!" She leaped to her feet and pounced on Willingham's chest, pounding it. "Please save him."

By now the farm workers had seen the smoke and flames and had gathered at the stable to put out the fire.

Willingham sent one of the gathering servants to fetch the doctor. "Lord Sedgewick's badly burned," he said. Then he requisitioned another servant to give him a hand carrying the master up to the manor house.

Sally was only too happy to place the hysterical children into Miss Primble's care as she hastened beside her unconscious husband and directed the men to take George to his own chamber on the second floor.

Adams and Mrs. MacMannus both gasped upon seeing their apparently lifeless master being carried by two men. Sally sped up the stairs to George's chamber and pulled back the silk bed covering just as the men brought in George's charred body and laid it on the fine white linen. She went to the window and opened the draperies to bright sunlight.

"Please," she said, looking up at the steward, "remove his clothing. I wish for him to be as comfortable as possible."

Willingham drew the heavy forest green velvet curtains around the bed. Sally's stomach turned when she saw the swath of crinkled skin on her husband's hips, back, arm, and part of his beloved face, but she could not allow herself to give in to the vapors. George needed her now, and she had to be strong for him. Since his back was the most damaged, the men turned him over on his stomach, his face turned toward them. The pain roused him from unconsciousness, and he screamed when they moved him. The agony that ravaged his face before he lapsed into unconsciousness again tore at Sally's heart.

With complete disregard for her own wounds or tattered dress, Sally stood at George's bedside, holding his limp hand within both of hers.

Soon the doctor came. He hurried to the bed and drew open the bed curtains. He winced when he saw the extent of the burns and gave Sally a look of sympathy. "I have a saying about burns, my lady. If they're on ten or twenty percent of the body, recovery's good. If they're thirty to fifty percent, recovery's not good. If they're over fifty percent, death is imminent. I'd say Lord Sedgewick's burns cover thirty percent of his body."

"I must ask that you be optimistic, doctor," Sally said firmly. "Tell us what we can do to speed recovery. We shall do everything within our power."

The old man nodded. "First, you'll need to send your servants far and wide to gather up as many burdock leaves as possible. It's best to have fresh ones every day."

"But what of the stickers?" she asked.

"Remove 'em! Then bruise the leaves with the white of an egg and lay the leaves on Lord Sedgewick wherever he is burned. I believe his lordship will have an immediate easing of the pain."

Her eyes filled with tears. "What if he doesn't regain consciousness?"

Doctor Moore gazed at her from above the rim of his spectacles, and he shrugged.

Sally felt like screaming. She felt like crying an ocean. She wanted to fall on her knees and beg Doctor Moore to make George well. Instead, she nodded. "Is there nothing else we can do?"

He was silent for a moment before he said, "Pray there is no fever."

The floor of her belly gave way. She could no longer see the doctor clearly for tears blurred his image.

He started for the chamber door. "I'll return tomorrow."

Willingham stayed. Not that his presence mattered to Sally. Nothing mattered except George. *He had to live!*

"There's something evil at Hornsby," she finally said to Willingham. "Someone is trying to ruin my husband."

Willingham moved to her and set a gentle hand on her shoulder. "I fear you many be right, my lady, but I vow that as long as I draw breath, I will not allow another evil thing to occur here. Hornsby's too fine a place."

"I always thought so." She ran a hand across her husband's burnished brow as her eyes lingered over his much loved face. Even his golden lashes were singed over his right eye. If he survived this . . . he would be scarred for the rest of his life. That face she had loved so thoroughly would never again look the same. But even were he to look grotesque, she would love him still. With all her heart. She regretted that they had not had the money to commission portraits. She would have loved having George's portrait.

If only he would live.

She suddenly spun toward Willingham. "Do me the goodness of having the servants gather burdock and oversee its preparation for Lord Sedgewick."

He moved toward the door, then turned back. "If there's anything else I can do . . ."

She met his solemn gaze with watery eyes and nodded.

Mr. Basingstoke came. Fiercely clutching her husband's hand, Sally turned to him. "It's good that you have come. George needs your prayers."

The youthful-looking vicar nodded as he came to stand at George's bedside. He looked at George lying there unconscious, burdock leaves lying over his swollen flesh, his face still a grimace of pain.

And Mr. Basingstoke began to pray aloud.

Sally bowed her head and prayed along with him.

After the prayers, the vicar's eye ran along Sally's tattered dress. "I understand, my lady, that you used your own body to beat down the last of the flames on Lord Sedgewick."

Without removing her eyes from George, she nodded.

"Allow me to stay with his lordship while you change your clothing, my lady."

"I cannot leave my husband."

"But surely you will allow me—or Willingham—or someone you trust to stay through the night with Lord Sedgewick?"

She spoke louder. "I won't leave him."

"But, my lady, he could be bedridden for weeks. You will have to allow others to stay with him. You have to stay strong. There are the children who need you."

"I cannot leave him."

His voice lowered. "Very well."

The door eased open. Sally did not turn to see who was entering the chamber.

"I've brought a tray of food for you, my lady." Mrs. MacMannus set the tray on George's writing desk.

Still Sally did not turn around. "That was very kind of you, Mrs. MacMannus. I'm not hungry at present, but perhaps later." She faced the house-keeper. "I should like a pitcher of water and a glass, though."

A few minutes later the housekeeper brought the water and set it on the table beside George's bed.

Sally poured three-fourths of a glass and held it to George's parched lips. "Please drink, dearest," she said to her unconscious husband, tipping the glass until the water touched his lips.

He did not heed her.

"I'm afraid he needs water," she told the vicar in a trembling voice.

"He'll let you know when he needs it."

For the next several hours, Mr. Basingstoke stood helplessly at Sally's side. He pulled up George's desk chair. "Please, my lady, sit down. You'll be just as close to him."

She shook her head. "I can't sit down. Perhaps later, when I'm tired. But not now."

Willingham entered the chamber and came to stand beside Sally and Mr. Basingstoke. "You must allow me to stay with his lordship tonight while you sleep, my lady," he said.

"Thank you for your thoughtfulness, sir, but I cannot leave my husband."

"But, my lady—"

Mr. Basingstoke shrugged with resignation. "She won't hear any of it, old fellow."

When the clock upon George's mantel struck midnight, Sally sighed. "I beg that you valued friends go to your own homes now." She turned to Willingham. "It's more important than ever that you be rested. George needs you to run Hornsby smoothly. That knowledge will help him recover." Then she turned to the vicar. "And I will need you tomorrow. Please come back." She offered her hand.

Both men kissed it and departed.

After the men left, Hettie came and begged her mistress to change her clothing, but Sally refused.

Sally grew tired and sat in the chair beside George's bed. The sounds of the house stilled. George's injured face—and the leaves that covered a portion of it—were only dimly illuminated by the light from the bedside candle. It was not a peaceful face.

If only he would make a sound. She squeezed his hand harder.

Finally he did begin to make noises. But they were the awful sounds of a man writhing in pain. Hadn't the doctor said the leaves would relieve his pain? Perhaps their effect was wearing off. What was needed was fresh leaves.

She rang the bell. Adams himself came. He wore his usual suit of black clothing, but it was wrinkled. Had he slept in it?

"I shall need fresh burdock leaves for his lordship," she said.

"Mrs. MacMannus has been keeping some fresh in a bowl of water. I'll just run and fetch them."

"Don't forget to rub them with egg white," she called after him.

Even after fresh leaves were applied to all George's burned areas, he still thrashed about in pain.

She was no longer able to sit in her chair. Every time he moved, she had to reposition the leaves over his burnt flesh, and in the dim candlelight it was difficult to tell the burnt skin from the unburnt.

He awakened at dawn.

He winced as he stirred, then he opened his eyes. "Sam?"

Her heart caught. She had feared she would never hear his voice again. "He's right as rain, my love. You saved his life."

He nodded. "I need brandy!"

"Oh yes, dearest," she said happily as she rang the bell rope once again.

A liveried footman answered it this time.

"I should like for you to bring the brandy from the drawing room," Sally instructed.

When the footman returned with the decanter, George attempted to sit up, but the pain prevented his movement.

Sally ran a gentle hand across his brow. "Does it hurt so terribly to move, my darling?"

He met her sympathetic gaze with watery eyes and nodded.

"The brandy should help," she said in a soothing voice.

His brows lowered. "Damn well better!"

Sally poured the brandy into the water glass and held it to George's lips. It hurt her to watch him ease up. The slightest movement set him wincing in pain.

With her help, he drank the entire glass, and soon was asleep again. Throughout the day visitors came. There was Willingham and the vicar and the doctor. George was in and out of consciousness. Even when he slept, his pain took no rest but caused him to cry out hoarsely. Sally saw to it the leaves were changed every few hours. She still refused to leave him, even for the few minutes it would take to change her clothing.

When night began to fall the second night, George's fever set in.

Chapter 25

When he had asked for another blanket, she had not been concerned. After all, there was a bit of chill in the air today. Not like yesterday. How could a day that had been so beautiful turn into such a nightmare? She fetched the counterpane from her own chamber and gently draped it over him.

His teeth chattered uncontrollably when he spoke. "It seems I'm in the best of hands."

She smiled down at him and moved to stroke his brow. His skin felt as if he had stood too close to the fireplace. Then she remembered the doctor's words. *Pray there is no fever.* The realization that fever had attacked her husband struck her like a galloping stallion. Her heart drummed. Her chest was too small. Tears pricked at her eyes. But she could not allow George to see her fear.

"Oh dear, you're hot." She tried to speak calmly. "Be a good patient and drink some water." She reached for the glass on the bedside table, and he attempted to sit up.

"No, my dearest husband, movement's far too painful for you. I'll hold the glass to your lips."

She tilted the glass to his parched lips, and he took a sip.

Even that slight movement caused George to wince with pain. "It's brandy I need," he grumbled.

Brandy was the only thing that would mask the pain. "Very well, dearest." She eyed the nearly empty bottle and poured the rest of it into his glass. As she held it to his lips, tears gathered in his eyes. *The pain.* If only there was something more she could do to ease his pain.

When the glass was empty, she said, "You had best try to sleep, dearest." She did not voice what was in her mind: the only time he was free of pain was when he was asleep.

But that did not prove to be true. His sleep during the next few hours was far from peaceful. He shivered almost uncontrollably. Sally pulled the counterpane over his shoulders and tucked it around his neck. A half hour later, he began to thrash about and threw off all his coverings, scattering the now brittle leaves. Sweat covered him.

Poor dear. If he was more comfortable without coverings, so be it. She would just have to see to it that his bed curtains were drawn when female servants entered her husband's chambers. She placed fresh leaves on him, but with his thrashing, such an act was futile.

Even with no covers, the perspiration continued to pop out on him. He thrashed about and was anything but quiet. If he was not moaning, he was screaming out. She had heard that same scream before. When he had been on fire running from the stable, cradling his son against him. She could not recall the horrifying event without tears coming to her eyes.

She rang for a servant.

Adams came, and she asked to have the basin filled and to have a cloth with which to rub down her husband.

For the next hour, she tried to bring down the fever by cooling George's skin with water. Never mind the leaves now. It was imperative she get the fever down. She would submerge the cloth in the water then gently squeeze it out over his muscled back until his skin shimmered under the golden candlelight.

But still his fever did not come down. Rather, it soared higher. It frightened her to touch his blazing skin. He began to tremble again. The chills had returned. She covered him, tucking the blankets over his broad shoulders.

A few minutes later, a quiet came over him. A peaceful look settled across his face. She gazed down at the damage done to his face by the fire. Were his face divided into quadrants, only the lower right quadrant suffered damage. His cheek was the worst. Like an injured knee, the outer edge of the wound was beginning to crust. Swelling and redness marked the center. She moved closer and saw there was yellow mucus around the wounded cheek.

Her whole being crashed. *Pray there is no fever.* Oh, dear God, there was fever! Would George die? She wanted to throw icy water on him, to slap at his good side . . . anything that would revive him. The alternative did not bear contemplation.

Her heart thudding, she began to talk aloud. As if George could hear her. "George Pembroke, the Viscount Sedgewick, so help me God, you have to get better! Do you hear me?"

The chamber door eased open, and she glanced

up at Willingham, whose countenance was grim. "How is he?"

She burst into tears.

He hurried to her and held her close, his arms closing around her.

Her shoulders shook and her voice cracked. "The fever's come."

The steward stiffened. "Have you tried bathing him in cool water?"

She backed away from him and nodded.

They both moved to George's bedside, Sally's hand gently stroking her husband's fevered brow as she cooed soothing words to him.

After a few moments, Willingham spoke. "Fever's not always bad. Sometimes it's a device nature gives us to rid our body of poisons. Once the body's cleaned of them, recovery can commence."

"Pray, I hope that you're right."

After a few minutes, Willingham broke the silence. "What your husband did yesterday was the bravest thing I've ever seen a man do."

"Running into the burning stable? Or running through flames to get out?"

"Both, actually." He cleared his throat. "His son will always look to his father with the greatest admiration, whether Lord Sedgewick lives or dies."

She spun to face him and glared. "Lord Sedgewick is going to live. I will not have any negative thoughts uttered in this sick chamber. Only healing ones. Do you understand me, Mr. Willingham?"

He swallowed. "Forgive me, my lady."

The two of them stood there the next few hours with little conversation passing between them. At midnight, she asked him to leave.

"I will—after you have changed your clothing, my lady. I will stay with Lord Sedgewick while you get dressed more comfortably."

She glared at the steward.

"I'm only thinking of his lordship," he protested. "What must he think when he wakes to see his wife in tattered clothing? Did you not say you want only positive thoughts in this chamber?"

She nodded. "Perhaps you're right. I hadn't considered what poor George might think." She moved toward the door. "I won't be more than a few moments."

To her astonishment, Hettie was waiting for Sally. "I hoped you'd come, my lady. Allow me to help you."

Sally collapsed into her vanity chair while Hettie took the pins from her hair and brushed it out. Sally would not have been able to summon the strength to have done so. A pity her curls were long gone. She would have liked to look better for George when he awakened, but her appearance was her last concern tonight.

She removed the sooty clothes, and Hettie helped her wash. Sally chose to wear a comfortable rose-colored morning dress.

"But, my lady, you will need a bit of sleep. I know you didn't sleep a wink last night. Should you not like to dress for sleep?"

"I cannot sleep, Hettie. My husband is gravely ill."

"But Mr. Willingham offered to stay with him at night and to come get you if a need arose."

"It was very kind of him, but I shall not leave Lord Sedgewick."

"But, my lady . . . you will give out."

"When I do, I suppose then I must sleep."

Sally stood silent as Hettie helped her to dress, then she returned to her husband's chamber.

Willingham's face brightened. "Allow me to say

his lordship should have a complete recovery when his eyes alight on you, my lady."

Sally bit at her lip. "Would that it were that easy . . ."

After Willingham left she continued to stand at her husband's bedside for the rest of the night. And a harrowing night it was. George thrashed about, screaming in pain, sweating with fever. He went from hot to cold. His wet coverings would be thrown off, only to be begged for with chattering teeth a few minutes later.

Most of the night he was unconscious, but occasionally he would stare at Sally and whisper his thanks. She knew he was delirious when he said, "My lovely Sally." Thank goodness he had not called her Dianna.

When morning came, the fever went away. A pity the pain did not.

Throughout the day, she continued to fortify George with brandy, but it helped only a little in diminishing the pain. Every time he would be about to drift off into sleep, the pain surged, depriving him of rest.

There were a few happy moments during the day. Once he said, "Oh, Sally, my love, what would I do without you?" And another time he said, "If I could move, I would kiss you. My angel Sally." A pity it had taken so grave a condition to summon such wondrous words from him.

The doctor came again. Sally told him about the fever the night before. "Thank God it's passed," she said reverently.

He leveled a solemn gaze upon her. "A penny to the pound says the fever will return tonight."

Sally gasped. How excessively she disliked Dr. Moore with his pessimistic sayings!

"And you, my lady," said the doctor, his spectacles slipping down the bridge of his nose, "you had better get some sleep today if you plan to be of help to him tonight."

She could no longer deny that she was exhausted. She had gone eight and forty hours without sleep. Her stores of energy had run out.

The vicar stood beside the doctor. "Please, Lady Sedgewick," Mr. Basingstoke said, "I beg that you sleep for a few hours while I stay with his lordship."

Sally had to be alert tonight. Tonight when the fever returned. George would need her. No one else could care for him as she could. She nodded and left the chamber.

That night the fever returned. And the next night. Whenever the fever came back, a horrible dread lived with Sally. She even tried to imagine life without George. As much as she loved the children, she would not wish to live if George weren't there to share her life with. How empty life would be without this wonderful, unselfish man. She marveled that a love as deep as hers hurt with such depth.

She kept thinking about the gloomy way the doctor had tried to prepare her for losing George. *Thirty to fifty percent, recovery's poor.* How could he—or anyone—discuss George's fate with such arbitrary numbers? Didn't that doctor know how . . . how irreplaceable George was? Was there not something else the doctor could do to promote greater healing?

She fell into a pattern where Mr. Basingstoke would sit with George during the mornings while Sally went to her chamber and slept. Each night she presided over the sick room. She made an effort now to wear a fresh dress each day, but she refused to take time away from George to have her hair curled.

Now that she was not needed at George's bedside every second, Sally finally gathered the courage to write to Glee and Felicity and inform them of their brother's brush with death. Glee fired a letter back immediately, telling Sally that Felicity had been terribly sick, but as soon as she could leave her, she would come to Hornsby.

On the second week, the fever went away. Sally prayed her thanks.

Though his pain was extreme, Sally knew that now George would recover. She continued to indulge him with brandy or whiskey to abate the pain. And she kept fresh leaves on the burn wounds.

Now that he was alert, his nudity embarrassed him. "I need to start wearing clothes," he told her.

"Perhaps pantaloons," she said, "but I'm afraid it will be too painful to wear clothing on your upper body."

He gave her a probing gaze. "When I had the fever . . . did I throw off my covers in your presence?"

"I am your wife, George."

"But . . ."

"Discussion closed. Unless my behaving like a wife offends you." She brazenly met his gaze.

"Of course not, Sally. I rather like having you for a wife. In fact, I cannot think anyone on the planet could be a better wife than you."

She could kiss him.

"Nor is there a man on the planet who is as brave and selfless as you."

He shook his head. "Pray, don't make a hero out of me. I did what any father would do."

"You're not like just any father. You're the most unselfish man I've ever known."

"And you're not equally as unselfish? I was told that you flung your own body over my burning body. That seems a most brave—and most foolish—thing to do."

"It was nothing. I've suffered no ill effects." Her voice cracked. "Not like you."

Anger flashed in his eyes. "I've tried to understand why I've been dealt more than a man should be asked to bear."

She set her hand on his. "But, dearest, the fire was an accident."

His voice went cold. "I wonder."

Her eyes widened. "What are you saying?"

"I don't trust the new groom. Nothing evil happened until after he came to Hornsby."

Her hand began to tremble. "But, George, the poor boy has no ax to grind against you! You'd never met him until he came to Hornsby."

"Came here and offered to work for no wages. I was a fool not to suspect something."

"There was no reason for you to expect something evil to come visiting you. You have no enemies."

He nodded solemnly. "I've probed my memory for anything I've done which would cause such hostility, but I honestly do not believe I've made such an enemy. In fact, I can think of no man who holds me in animosity."

"Because there is no such man," she said.

Healing was slow progress, but George's tolerance for pain increased weekly. Now he forced himself to do simple movements. He sat up in bed. "I wish to hold your hand, my lady."

She put her hand in his.

He gazed into her eyes. "I'm very grateful for your devotion to my sick room."

She wished she could tell him that she could not have left him, could never leave him, for she loved him with all her heart. But, of course, she could not blabber such silly feelings.

Now that some movement was possible, and now that George was able to hide his pain, Sally decided to allow the children to visit their father's chamber.

The first day they came, Georgette entered shyly, almost as if she was afraid to come into the sick room.

Not so with Sam. As soon as he realized this was the chamber occupied by his father and that it was his father who lay on the big full-tester bed, he ran to the bed and began to climb on it. When he met his father's warm green eyes, he spoke. "Papa sick?"

Her eyes moist, Sally looked from Sam to George and saw that huge tears had pooled in her husband's eyes.

Chapter 26

If only it did not hurt so damn much to move. He had grown bloody tired of lying on his stomach and bloody tired of that wife of his insisting on plastering him with those damned burdock leaves. The month of June had come and gone, and still George had not left this blasted bed. He had grown deuced sick of dark green, the color of the draperies at his windows and around his bed as well as on the velvet bedspread. He longed to be under blue skies, inhaling fresh air, and riding over the Hornsby estate.

A month previously he would not have believed a simple act like sitting up could bring such pleasure. When he sat up for the first time yesterday, the accomplishment filled him with pride. Once he was seated, the pain passed. A pity the stretching of skin while getting to the seated position hurt so wretchedly.

All the pain had been worth it, though, when his son had hopped on his lap and smiled up at his papa. The little scamp held the key to the innermost chambers of his father's heart. No words ever had affected George as profoundly as Sam uttering his first sentence to his father. It had not been much of a sentence, but it was a sentence, nevertheless. And he had uttered it not to his sister, nor to his stepmother, but to the father who had only recently come to love the sturdy little lad. Nothing could have aided George's recovery more quickly than his son's words. The lad had obviously missed him. By God, the boy needed him, and he vowed he would recover and be a good father to him.

Yesterday when Sally had poured a glass of scotch to ease his pain, George had declined to drink it. As a mother must wean a babe from her breast, George had to wean himself from the spirits. He could not allow himself to become dependent upon them. He had to force himself to conquer the pain on his own.

As bad as the pain was, he knew it had lessened each week. He would steel himself to learn to live with it. His next objective was to get out of the damned bed.

The other impetus behind his recovery was Sally. He wanted nothing more than to recover so that he could take her in his arms and love her to completion. Every time he smelled her light scent, his heart tripped. Whenever she would lapse and call him *my darling* or *dearest,* he allowed himself the luxury of believing she cared for him as a woman cares for a man. And every time she swept into his chamber directing a bright smile at him, he hungrily watched the smooth curves of her lithe body, and he became aroused. He had even come to appreciate her hair—without curls. His Sally, the Viscountess Sedgewick, had become an aphrodisiac to him.

Adding wood to Sally's bonfire was her complete devotion to his recovery. Perhaps she did not love him. She most likely did not. But in his entire life, he had never felt so thoroughly cared for. Everything that would make him happy made her happy. He knew without a doubt that at this point in their lives, he was the most important person in her life.

Perhaps that was not love, but it came dangerously close.

He asked himself, *What if it had been Sally who had been hurt?* The very thought of seeing her injured sent his stomach plunging. He would kill with his bare hands the person responsible for hurting her. And he knew that if Sally were the one hurt, he would be as devoted to her recovery as she was to his.

Is that what being married was about? His heart swelled. Good Lord, Sally *was* the wife of his heart. Whether she knew it or not.

When she swept into his chamber that morning, he watched her with a dry mouth and pounding heart. God, but he wanted her. Everything about her intoxicated him.

"How are we today, dearest?" she asked brightly.

Wincing, he scooted up to a seated position. To hell with all this damn lying about! He wished Sally to find him manly—not some bedridden bag of bones. "I shall be better with a good-morning kiss," he said with a smile.

He had never been so bold with her before.

She gave him a quizzing look, as if she were taken aback. Then a smile tugged at her mouth when she moved closer and lowered her lips to his.

Oh, the sweetness of her willing lips! 'Twas not a virgin's stiff peck. His Sally knew how to kiss!

He reluctantly pulled away. *Who in the hell had taught his wife how to kiss?* He hated the fellow. He took her hand and cleared his throat. "I thank you. For the kiss and for so much more. No man ever had a better advocate than I have in you."

Color tinged her cheeks as she contemplated his bed covering.

"I should like you to bring me a looking glass," he said somberly.

Fear flashed in her eyes. Did he look so hideous she did not wish for him to see himself? Dread choked him.

"Why do you need a looking glass? I swear that you're as handsome as ever."

Did she really think so? Hope bubbled within him. Was it possible that she was attracted to him? He could not deny her willing participation in the kiss. "Allow me to reassure myself," he said.

Her face was solemn when she replied. "Very well."

She went through his dressing room in order to reach her own adjoining one. It suddenly occurred to him that since they had come to Hornsby neither of them had used the adjoining chamber door. A practice he meant to change.

A moment later she returned with a lady's hand mirror and presented it to him. His heart pounded. Was he to be a freak for the rest of his life? Was he hideously deformed? He had not been unaware of the unattractive way the skin on his arms and shoulders had healed with a swirling, uneven surface resembling hardened lava. Would the flesh on his face also be twisted in such a manner?

With the greatest trepidation, he brought the mirror closer to his face. And he gazed at it with a sickening disbelief roiling his gut. How changed he was! And it was not a change for the better. Fortunately, the shape of his face had not been altered. And it was good that the fire had not reached his eyes. The matched set still looked perfectly normal—as did his nose. But there was a disfigurement about the mouth that was most unattractive. Rather like one with a hairlip. In the future, he must be more sympathetic to those so afflicted. He had been prepared for the deformity of the skin that would never again be smooth. The raw, reddened skin on his cheeks and neck much resembled the deformation on his arm.

His own reflection sickened him. He handed her back the mirror.

Sally must have sensed his disappointment for she ran a loving hand over his burned cheek. "How fortunate we are that it's still the same loved face."

Loved face? His heart drummed. Her words were so wildly welcomed, he almost forgot his great disappointment. His eyes misted. "I'm ugly." *Though, thankfully, she doesn't seem to agree.*

She scowled at him. "How dare you say that! Are you impugning my judgment?"

"Sally, I have eyes that, thankfully, still work."

She angrily thrust her hands to her hips. "So, what are you saying?"

"I'm saying my scars are quite noticeable, and they're ugly."

"Don't ever say that!" Tears came to her eyes, and her voice gentled. "I've never told you this before, but I still remember the first time I ever set eyes upon you. I thought you were the most handsome creature I had ever seen." She thrust out her chin defiantly. "I still think so."

Before his choked voice could respond, the chamber door was thrown open and a familiar voice boisterously greeted them. By Jove, it was his sister Glee, sweeping into the room, vibrant jade skirts trailing behind her—as was her husband, Blanks.

Damn, but it was good to see them. How good it was of them to come.

Glee scowled at Sally for a fraction of a second. "I'm upset that you did not notify me immediately of my brother's serious injuries, but I know, dearest sister, you had other things on your troubled mind." She took both of Sally's hands and smiled broadly.

Sally's eyes moistened. "We did not even know if George would live."

If only he could get out of this damned bed and comfort her! Every time she recalled that wretched day, she cried. And it tore at his heart to see his strong little Sally in tears.

Blanks came to set a hand on his wife's shoulder. "Then it's best you weren't here, my love. You're much too sensitive." Blanks faced George. "I must say, I expected worse, old fellow. You look awfully good to me."

Now Glee turned her full attention upon her brother. "Oh, dear me, I am so happy that you're still the same old George." She came to touch her lips to his forehead. "How are you feeling?"

"I've made good strides. Before yesterday, I couldn't even sit up."

Glee's green eyes began to swim in a pool of her own tears.

"Now, don't go being a watering pot on me," George chided. He closed his hand over hers. "It's good of you to come."

"Felicity wanted ever so much to come, too, but Moreland would not hear of it." Glee dropped her voice to a whisper. "She's increasing again, you know."

George's glance flicked to Blanks, then back to Glee. "Yes, I know."

"I don't know why you've had to bear so much," Glee said to George. "It's not fair at all."

George frowned. "My thoughts exactly."

Sally stepped up to the bed, the mirror still in her hand. "I do not wish for George to use his energies for negative thoughts. Only positive, healing ones."

"Of course, you're right," Glee said, taking her brother's hand. "When will you be able to get out of that wretched bed?"

He glanced at Sally.

"When he feels up to it, I expect," Sally said. "Now that the flesh is healing, his movements are less restricted."

"I believe by week's end I'll be out of this demmed bed."

"Watch your language, dearest," Sally said.

Bless her! *Dearest this, dearest that.* At least one good thing had come from this bloody accident. If it was an accident.

When Sally referred to her husband as "dearest," Glee's flashing eyes met Sally's. It was as if there were some secret between the two women. A secret that had something to do with him. Perhaps he needed a tête-à-tête with his sister.

Blanks came to stand to the left of his wife. "How long since you've ridden a horse, old fellow?"

"A month."

Blanks winced. "I vow, before I leave Hornsby, you'll be in the saddle again."

George offered a wan smile.

Miss Primble brought the children for their afternoon visit, and Sam came flying to his father's bed.

"I'm ever so sorry, your lordship," Miss Primble said, "I did not know you had visitors."

George imprisoned Sam with his arms and made silly noises upon the lad's neck, making him giggle. "It's all right, Miss P.," George said. "Allow them to visit for a spell with their aunt and uncle."

Glee intently watched the easy camaraderie that had developed between her brother and his son, and her eyes once again filled with tears.

"Aunt Glee!" Georgette said. "Where is Joy?"

"I shall not tell you until you present your aunt with a kiss," Glee said affectionately.

Georgette stood upon her tiptoes and Glee made herself even smaller by stooping low to accept her niece's kiss. "Now let me look at you!" Glee said. "I believe you have grown since the last time I saw you. Country life must agree with you, my precious niece."

Georgette frowned. "We were very happy here—until Papa got burned."

"Your mama won't allow allow us to speak in your father's chambers about the fire. We can only discuss his recovery—which I understand is coming along nicely."

Georgette nodded.

"I expect the carriage in which Joy and nurse are riding will be here any minute. Would you like to go watch for it?"

"Oh yes, ever so much." Georgette turned and skipped from the room.

Glee turned back toward her brother's bed. "I expect my nephew has forgotten me completely." She poked her nose into Sam's little face. "Hello, Sam."

Sam spun toward to his father, then back to her. "Papa sick!"

"Oh, George, he's talking! I told you not to worry about him."

George dropped a kiss on top of the lad's curly

hair. "I'm rather pleased that he chose to speak his first sentence to me."

"That's because," Sally interjected, "Sam was very worried about his papa. The two have become quite close."

"You're so fortunate to have a son," Glee said in a thin voice.

It hurt George when his sister hurt. And, whether Blanks knew it or not, he was hurting Glee with his unselfish love of her, his fear of losing her. George had his work cut out for him in helping to bring Glee and Blanks together again in that most important way. In the same way he hoped to be together with Sally. Soon.

Chapter 27

The next morning George decided he would be a cripple no longer. With his valet's help, he dressed. He tried not to think about that blasted cravat pinching against the tender burned skin on his neck. The doctor had said he could not go out in sunlight because the new skin was far too susceptible to more burning. More burning was the last thing in the world he wanted.

So he would have to content himself with walking down the stairs and busying himself in his library. There were many farming journals he had to get caught up on reading, and then there was Blanks. Just having his dearest friend under his roof sent a smile to George's healing face.

He had not counted on that slip of a wife of his having apoplexy when she saw him descending the staircase.

"Oh my goodness, George," she called up to him from the foot of the stairs, "are you sure you're up to it?" Her brows seriously rumpled as she watched him come down each step.

He would have liked for his progress to have

been faster, but the fact was that he was far weaker than he had expected. He became unbelievably winded, like an elderly person who could not walk and talk at the same time for lack of breath. Bloody hell, if he didn't feel wretchedly like an elderly person at the moment.

Glee came scurrying into the central hallway, her little face alight. "Bravo! George!" she said excitedly, gazing up at him with smiling eyes. "I'm ever so proud of you!"

His wife, on the other hand, had gone white with fear. "George Pembroke! Why did you not ask Blanks—or your man—to accompany you down the stairs? I declare, in my mind's eye I saw your weak legs giving out, making me a widow." She stomped her slippered foot. "And I assure you, I have no desire to be a widow."

When he came to the last step, he brushed his lips across Sally's smooth cheek. "Would you be a merry widow, my dear?"

She thrust hands to hips and narrowed her eyes. "I most certainly would not!"

He rather liked it when Sally was mad like this. It was a good mad.

Adams opened the front door, and Willingham came striding into the central hall.

"My lord! It's good to see you up and about." Willingham's eyes scanned those assembled around George.

"You remember my sister?" George asked Willingham.

The steward's eyes flashed. "How could I forget one as lovely as Mrs. Blankenship?" He bowed before Glee, and she offered him her hand.

George did not at all approve of the way Willingham positively drooled over married women. Including *his* Sally. The man needed to get his own wife and stop hungering after the wives of other men.

Willingham peeled his eyes from Glee and faced his employer. "Are you up to riding the estate yet, my lord?"

Sally answered. "He most certainly is not! Dr. Moore said George's skin will be extremely sensitive to the sun."

George gave a martyred expression. "I shall have to console myself by reading the new agriculture book by Hodson today."

"I did not know you had it. I was going to order it myself," Willingham said.

"Allow me to offer you mine—once I've read it."

Blanks came up and nodded at the steward. "Your servant, Willingham." Then he directed his attention to George. "I didn't know you were able to get up yet, old fellow."

"This is my first time. Come, let's go to the library." George raised a brow to his steward. "Willingham?"

"No, my lord, I've work to do. I only came to see if I could be of any use to you, and I see that I'm not needed."

Glee slipped her arm through Sally's. "I perceive this is your first day free of sick-room duty. Should you like to take a walk?"

"I would love to," Sally said. "Allow me to fetch a bonnet."

With unfurling pride, George watched Sally glide gracefully up the stairs. Only this moment did he become aware that she had ceased to curl her hair. A few months earlier he would have thought that straight hair of hers hideously unfashionable. Now he could scarcely remember what she looked like with curls. He had come to love the silvery blond wispiness of her hair. Even if it was as straight as a straw—her description, not his. He chuckled to himself.

In the oak-paneled library, George closed the door behind Blanks, drew open the olive velvet draperies, and went to sit on a sofa across from his friend.

"Has it occurred to you," Blanks began, "that someone is trying to ruin you?"

George gave an insincere laugh. "Is the sky blue?"

"Do you have any idea who it could be?"

George shrugged. "I have an idea, but it doesn't make sense."

Blanks leaned forward. "What doesn't make sense?"

"Nothing ever happened until a big, strapping fellow named Ebinezer showed up at Hornsby in May. He said he had experience working with horses, needed a job, and asked only for room and board— no wages."

Blanks's brows shot up. "No wages whatsoever?"

"None. I suppose a bell should have gone off in my head, but it didn't."

"Why should it? You don't have any enemies."

"I've combed my brain to think of anyone who has animosity toward me, but I can think of no one."

"I can't, either, old fellow, but it sounds as if someone *does* hate you and most likely hired old Ebinezer to destroy you. Why don't you just give him the boot?"

"I've thought of that, but I'm afraid it wouldn't solve anything. He could still get at me. Besides, I'd rather set a trap for him. That way I could learn who my enemy is, who hired him. The problem is—"

"It would be bloody difficult for you to stay

awake four and twenty hours a day to watch the bloke," Blanks said.

George's eyes flashed. "I know! A Bow Street runner!"

"An excellent idea. In fact, I believe you should ask for two. That way you could be assured one of them is always awake to keep a watch on the wretched groom." Blanks cleared his throat. "I understand money's rather thin this quarter. Allow me to hire the runners. You can pay me back next quarter."

"You're a good friend," George said.

"A brother, too."

George settled back into the sofa, but it hurt his tender back, forcing him to sit up ramrod straight again. "So Felicity's increasing again?" George said.

Blanks frowned. "Don't understand that Moreland. Would have sworn he worshipped the very ground Felicity trod. How can he risk . . . ?"

"They do love each other. Profoundly, I would say." George thought of how much he had come to love Sally. She was every bit as vital to him as Dianna had once been. The very thought of losing her was like a dagger to his heart. "When two people love each other, it's only a natural extension of that love to . . ." He swallowed hard. *To make love to each other.* He vowed that by week's end Sally would truly be his wife. His breath began to come rapidly.

"I know," Blanks said morosely. "I don't even want another woman. I want only my wife." His voice broke. "But I'm so bloody scared of losing her. I would not wish to live if I lost Glee."

As I would not wish to live without Sally. "You know, Blanks, a month ago I was almost killed. No one would have ever expected that—least of all me. Death can strike anyone at any time. You could be trampled by a stallion tomorrow. And what kind of memories would Glee have of you?" George grew solemn. When they were still in Bath, Sally had spoken of Glee and Blanks in a way that had rather shocked him at the time. It was so passionate a thing for a maiden to say. Or even to think. But now he had come to realize there was great emotional depth to this wisp of a woman he had married. "Sally once said something about you and Glee which I feel compelled to repeat. You do know that Glee confides in my wife?" Calling Sally his wife filled George with a heady sense of possession.

Blanks nodded. "What did Sally say?"

"She said Glee would rather die in your arms than live to old age without your love."

Tears sprang to Blanks's eyes. He stood up and walked to the window and watched his beautiful wife stroll the grounds of her girlhood home with Sally. "Daresay I need to dash off a letter to my own steward this morning," Blanks said in a raspy voice, then he turned on his booted foot and left the library.

It had been a month since Sally had set foot outdoors. The sun shone, and the weather was fair, with only a mild breeze. It was much like that horrid day that also had begun so beautifully—that day she could never recall without tears gathering in her eyes.

"Blanks has brought a few of his workers here to rebuild the stables for George," Glee said.

Sally sent her lovely sister a grateful smile. "You two are so kind to us."

"Was the stable completely destroyed?"

"I don't know." Sally refused to even look in the direction of the stable. "I shall never go there until the last remnants of it are gone. It's far too painful. I won't even ask about it. There's an aura of evil there."

"It does seem as if there's a black cloud over my brother's head."

"I cannot tell you how frightening it's been. . . . First the slaughter of all those sheep, then almost losing George. And I fear for the children excessively."

"I shouldn't have brought up the subject. You need to remove all those fears. After all, you can't do anything about it." Glee brightened and put an extra jaunt in her step. "I was delighted to see the transformation that's come over George when he's with Sam. I suppose you're responsible for it?"

Sally shook her head. "I don't think so. I admit I planned things that I thought might put them in close proximity with one another. Then George's own generous heart did the rest. He loves both the children terribly, and he's a wonderful father."

"I wish Blanks had a son," Glee said in a forlorn voice.

Sally cast a sideways glance at Glee. The breeze rustled in the other woman's curly auburn tresses. A pity she looked as if she had just remembered she was bereft of her greatest friend. In a way, she was. "You just might have to seduce the man," Sally said, turning back to the house, since the lawn was about to butt up against the wood.

Glee's mouth dropped open. "Sally! I cannot believe that word is even in your vocabulary. You must no longer be an innocent maiden."

For some reason, Sally felt compelled to withhold the truth from her best friend for the first time ever. "I declare, Glee, you shall put me to the blush!"

Glee came to a dead stop and stared at Sally.

"You goose, you don't have to tell me. I can tell by looking at you that you are a well-loved woman."

Glee did, indeed, put Sally to the blush.

That night the four of them played whist in the drawing room. Despite that George had been eager for a good game of whist, his mind obsessed over his life's partner who sat across the card table from him. The brush of her knee against his sent his heart racing. He watched her as she arranged the cards in her hand, and he remembered her gentle touch as she had bathed his fevered body. He imagined her hands gliding over his bare flesh, and he longed to stroke her bare flesh, to feel the gentle swell of her breast, to kiss a trail of butterfly kisses down to her navel. And below.

She caught him staring at her, and she smiled. The smile was like a beacon in a subterranean cave.

He and Sally barely won, and only because of Sally's skillful play. He had not played whist with her since they had married. Now he remembered her extreme competence at the game. No man could play better. Sally was so thoroughly competent in so many ways. He had come to love everything about her.

"No more games," Sally said as she stacked the cards into a deck and set it aside. "George has done far too much for one day."

"I'm fine. Really I am," he protested. He did not wish to go to his lonely chamber. He did not wish to part from Sally.

She shook her head firmly and stood up. "Come along, dearest. You must be exhausted."

"It appears the former Miss Spenser has made you an excellent wife, Sedgewick," Blanks said.

As George got to his feet, a crooked grin settled on his face. "I assure you, I have no complaints."

Sally slipped her slender arm around his back.

Good lord! Did she still fear he would fall down the stairs? Even more ridiculous, did she think she possessed the strength to prevent him from doing so? He shot her a mischievous smile.

They said farewell to Glee and Blanks, whose rooms were in the east wing, and began to mount the stairs.

The same thought resonated with each step up the staircase. *If only she were coming to my bed.* "You curled your hair tonight," he observed.

"Now that you no longer need me every moment, I shall start having my hair curled again."

He came to a stop and turned to gaze somberly at her slender face. "Don't."

"But I thought you liked me with curly hair!"

"I did, but I've come to appreciate you as nature made you, and no one could please me more."

Her hand brushed the burned side of his face. "Thank you, George, that's the nicest thing you've ever said to me."

He took her hand and pressed his lips into the cup of her palm. Her breath swooped. God, but he wanted to ask her to allow him in her bed tonight. But he knew he couldn't casually sleep with Sally.

He could only take her body after she knew she possessed his soul.

He started back up the stairs, an awkward silence engulfing them. From the top of the stairs, they walked midway down the hall to the viscountess's chambers and came to a stop.

"Good night, my lady," he said morosely.

She drew in her breath. "George?"

He brought her hand to his lips and kissed it. "What, my dear?"

"Please don't worry that you will offend me by refusing, and I shouldn't wish to hurt you or exhaust you for the world, but I thought, perhaps, you might wish to . . . to come into my chamber tonight."

He could sing halleluja to the heavens! Never had he felt so exalted. "There is nowhere on earth I'd rather be."

Chapter 28

Once inside her dark chamber, Sally turned to face him. Without removing his eyes from hers, he kicked the door shut behind him and greedily took in the loveliness of her slim body silhouetted against the firelight behind her. He moved to her, settled his trembling hands upon her shoulders, and gazed down into those soulful dark eyes of hers. His senses awakened to the rising and falling of her breasts, to her sweet floral scent, her warm breath. His head lowered to touch her lips, lightly at first, then with a deep and devastating hunger.

He gloried in the gentle whimper that shuddered through her as her arms came around him, as her mouth opened to him as hungrily as he tasted her.

This wasn't how he had planned their first mating. He was to be the master, patiently schooling his youthful bride in the ways of love. But he felt more like a green schoolboy than a master in the art of love. His patience was nonexistent. Her very touch set him trembling, and he was no more in control of himself than he was over that cat of his daughter's. He crushed Sally against him, against his arousal. His eager hands kneaded her soft breasts. Her breath came as fast and raspy as his, assuring him of her total compliance.

She was so utterly compliant he could have cried out his gratitude. Ever bolder, he slipped his hand beneath the silken bodice of her ivory gown. She drew in a deep ragged breath. Growing even more aroused, he traced the roughness of her nipples. She answered by swaying her lithe body to him—to his arousal—in a maddening, rhythmic motion.

He backed her nearer to the fire for he wanted his eyes to feast on her body. As he unfastened her dress, each new button seemed to take an eternity. The dress came to pool at the base of her lovely long legs, and his eyes greedily covered her. He took in the silvery highlights dancing in her hair. His eyes lingered over the gentle slope of her breasts, then her flat stomach that dipped in at her waist. His gaze came to rest on her drawers—damn the drawers! The sooner they were removed, the better.

He watched her solemn face, expecting embarrassment, but there was none.

"You are beautiful," he murmured in a hoarse voice. He came closer and dropped a kiss on one breast, then the other. When he reached beneath her drawers, she gave out a startled little gasp. His hand glided to the thatch down low. This time it was he who gasped. Gasped with agonizing anticipation.

Sally untied his cravat and tossed it to the carpeted floor. Then her gentle fingers slowly unfastened the buttons of his shirt. His eagerness to feel his bare flesh against hers raged like a wildfire within him. When she finished with his shirt, he stopped and threw off his coat and shirt, then kicked off his boots. He scooped Sally into his arms, carried her to the bed and laid her on the center of the silken spread. He stood gazing into her face, tenderly stroking it, appreciating her fevered look. He pulled back the bed's coverings on the outer side of the bed to enable her to move beneath them.

Sensitive that she was a maiden and unwilling to frighten her, he said, "I'm going remove the rest of my clothing now."

Her eyes smoldering, she nodded.

She turned her head as he undressed, but after he climbed beneath the covers she faced him, a hungry flame leaping to her eyes. He threw back the covers, then eased down those blasted drawers of hers and propped on one elbow to gaze over her slender body shimmering in the firelight. The hair at the juncture of her thighs was as blond as that on her beloved head.

He swallowed and spoke huskily. "I've wanted this for a very long time."

She answered by lifting her sweet lips to his for an open, demanding kiss.

He wasn't sure what should come next! Damn greenhorn! It was not as if he had not done this before. He had done it hundreds of times, most likely. But even with Dianna, who also had been a virgin, it was not like this. Now, he felt as if he could explode with his great need, yet he knew he had to be gentle. The last thing he needed was to frighten her.

He had thought to taste her. There, between her legs. To lubricate her virgin's crevice. The very thought sent his heart racing to the heavens. But were he to settle his lips there, he had no assurances his innocent wife would not leap from the bed in hysterics.

He decided against loving her with his mouth. Perhaps later, after she had become used to being with a man. Perhaps one day she would even taste him. There. He could scarcely breathe at the thought.

First, he would just savor the feel of his bare flesh touching hers, their mouths deliciously locked. His wife wildly exhilarated him with her own unexpected subservience to passion. He raised himself over her, and—to his utter gratitude—she had the good sense to part her legs for him. He grew even more breathless. Careful not to put all his weight upon her, he settled over her, his engorged need brushing against her sweet blond curls. With gentle fingers, he probed her seam. And deeper. Sweet God in heaven! She was ready for him.

He lowered his face to hers for a tender kiss and whispered words. "This may hurt you, my love."

"Oblige me by not stopping," she whispered in a breathless voice.

He had never thought to find one such as she in a lifetime. He stroked the moist hair from her warm brow before closing his mouth over hers. This time, the kiss was more urgent, almost frenzied as he lowered himself into her slick sheath, sucking her tongue into his warm mouth. She was tight. So blessedly tight. So far he hadn't hurt her. She rolled her hips up to meet his thus far gentle thrust. Then she stiffened, her hands digging into the flesh of his back. He went rigid and gently kissed her. "The worst is over, my dearest."

"Please don't stop whatever it is you are doing to me," she murmured in a hungry voice.

Her words were tinder to his fire. He came into

her swiftly and fully, and his lover pounded her torso up to meet his thrust after thrust until she cried out and trembled uncontrollably. He felt the warmth of his seed spreading in her molten crevice, and he had never in his life felt so utterly content.

"God in heaven, but I love you, Dianna!"

Dianna. Had her husband closed his eyes and imagined she was Dianna? With the satisfaction of a sated lover, her husband had uttered the only word that could trample the heart Sally had given him.

Those frank talks Sally had with her brother rushed back into her foggy mind. A man does not have to be in love with a woman to make love to her. When a man's need is great, he has to have a woman. Any woman.

That's all she had been to George. A willing body. A substitute for Dianna. And, oh, how willing she had been! She had allowed him complete access to her. His lips had caressed places she never imagined a man would venture.

Even now as she lay beneath him, wet with his seed, she shuddered at his touch. Waves of some powerful physical explosion washed over her.

For a few minuets she had allowed herself to think her husband had at last fallen in love with her. She would never forget the greedy way his eyes had raked her naked body before telling her she was beautiful. For those few moments she had allowed herself to believe she was beautiful.

George gently pulled away, brushing a chaste kiss on her brow. "I love you so very much."

As I love you, she wanted to say. But she must cling to her last semblance of pride. Tears gathered in her eyes. Just now . . . when he said those

words she longed to hear, longed to be true, were
his eyes closed? Did he pretend to himself she was
Dianna?

Within a few minutes she heard her husband's
steady breathing and knew that he had fallen
asleep. He truly had done too much on his first
day out of bed.

She lay there for a long time, remembering
every touch, every caressing word. Even if he did
not love her, she was now truly his. She possessed
his seed, a fact that gave her a wistful sense of in-
toxication. Dare she hope she would bear George's
babe? Her heart drummed at the prospect.

It was a long time after George went to sleep before she could detach herself from the feeling of
being one with him. What they had shared might
only be a physical necessity to him, but to her it
had been profound, uniting them not only in body
but also in soul.

But detach herself she must. She had too much
pride to degrade herself by allowing George to use
her merely for physical gratification. Never again
would she allow herself to be a substitute for
Dianna.

After more than hour had passed, she eased
herself from the bed and quietly opened the door
of her linen press. She selected a muslin morning
dress and dressed herself in the darkness. Once
she lighted a taper, she came to sit before her writing desk. With heavy heart, she began to compose
a letter to George. When she finished, she folded
and sealed it, addressed it to him, and propped it
against the silver candlestick before blowing out
the taper and leaving the room.

As the faint sun drifted into the chamber, George
lay in a blissful, half-conscious state. He knew something was vastly different from the other mornings

of his life. For one thing, this chamber was not as dark as his. For another, there was that scent he had come to love, the scent of Sally. He came fully awake, vibrant memories of the night before nearly overwhelming him with the tenderness he felt for Sally. He turned to her, wanting to feel her flesh once again, wanting to feel his lips on hers, wanting to continue where exhaustion had made him stop last night.

But she wasn't there. Perhaps nature had called. He lay there languidly, waiting for his wife to return. When she did not return after a considerable period of time, he propped himself up on his elbows and scanned the room for her. His heart pounded when he realized she was not there.

He was piqued that his wife had left him. More than that, disappointment filled his heart, and the euphoric feeling he had waked with vanished. This was not the way it was supposed to be. Something was wrong. His heart leapt. Had that evil force taken his wife from him? He bolted up to a sitting position. Where in the deuce was she?

He climbed down from the bed and into the pants he had shrugged out of the night before. There was nothing to do but get dressed, go downstairs, and find that wife of his. Something must have happened to her.

As he strode to his adjoining dressing room, he saw the letter propped against the candlestick. His name appeared on it in bold letters. His heart skidded. With shaking hands, he picked it up. He was afraid to open it. Instinctively, he knew its message would not be a welcome one.

Had he been that bad? It had been a very long time, but still . . . And his full strength had not returned, but still . . . She had seemed as satisfied as he.

And he had been extraordinarily satisfied. His breath came rapidly at the memory of his utter fulfillment.

He broke the seal, unfolded the vellum, and began to read:

Dearest George,

I am not going to say I'm sorry about what happened between us last night. How could a woman go to her grave without having experienced what I now know occurs between a husband and his wife? If I should be fortunate enough to be with child, I shall be most happy, indeed.

I regret, however, to inform you that such intimacy as we shared last night cannot continue between us. You see, I did marry you because I love you. But I love you as I love my brother. And under those circumstances, I feel it would be improper to continue to deceive you. My principal reason for marrying you was because of my love for the children. I thank you for allowing me to be a mother to them. And for pretending to hold me in deepest affection.

She did not sign the letter.

Pretending to hold her in affection! How could a woman be so blind? He fairly worshipped the ground she trod.

He read the letter over once again. Surely he had missed something. Some clue that it was a joke. That she cared for a him just a little bit.

But he thought back to her silence last night when he had proclaimed his love for her. Had she loved him at all, her physical state alone last night would have given voice to some kind of declaration. The fact there was no declaration, he admitted dejectedly, proved that she did not love him as he loved her. As he had hoped she would love him.

Running through flames had been far less painful than Sally's sudden coolness.

Chapter 29

A pity that women had such a beastly hold over men. Until today, George never gave a thought to what clothing he wore. His man was quite competent in that regard. But the navy blue coat Peters selected would not do at all. It had suddenly become very important to George that he look dashing. His sisters had always said that brown was an excellent color on him. If he were to wear the brown, perhaps Sally would find him more attractive. "The brown, today, Peters," he informed his valet.

But if a woman was not in love with you, it was deuced hard to force her to feel otherwise. No matter how becoming one looked in brown.

All the while Peters shaved him and helped him into his clothes, George's every thought centered on Sally. How could he force her to love him? The memory of the seductive way she had looked at him last night and the way she had responded to his every touch sent his heart racing. Sally must be a most accomplished actress.

He wished he could dislike her. It would make

matters so much easier, so much less painful. But, because of what she had given him last night, he loved her a hundred times more than he had loved her the day before. She was his universe.

Once he was dressed for the day, he wished to find Sally. Surely he could make her change her mind. Make her realize fate had made them man and wife.

He thought back to all the foolish girls who had thrown themselves at him over the years. Each of them had hoped to win his heart. But hearts were not easily given. Take that blasted Betsy Johnson, for example. Since before the girl had come out of the schoolroom, she had done everything in her power to snare his heart. She was pretty. She possessed great wealth. She adored him—or the prospect of being Lady Sedgewick. But she did not appeal to him on any level.

In the same way, he did not appeal to Sally. The realization was a cannonball to his gut. Sadly, there was nothing he could do to make her feel otherwise.

Simply put, his wife loved him like a brother. He loved Felicity and Glee dearly, but the feelings he held for them were in no way as powerful or consuming as the feelings he held for Sally—and certainly they were not sexual! Sally, who thought of him as a brother.

He suddenly wished he had stayed in bed. In his chamber. How could he face her knowing he would never again be able to hold her in his arms or feel her soft lips beneath his?

He had to shove numbing thoughts of her from his mind. He must think of something, or someone, else. His son. There was something he had been wanting to give Sam.

It took nearly an hour before George located

the silver spurs that his grandfather had commissioned for him when he was a small boy. Now they would be his son's.

After presenting them to a jubilant Sam, he asked that Matilda be brought around for the children. They had not ridden her since the day of the fire.

It was while they were waiting for the pony in the central hallway that Sally came up. His stomach churned, and he diverted his gaze from her.

"I cannot allow you to go outside today!" she said to him. "You know what Dr. Moore said!" Her eyes darted to the spurs. "My goodness, Sam, what do I see on your feet?" she asked in a honeyed voice.

"Papa give me," Sam said, pointing his little boots at her.

"They were Papa's when he was a little boy!" Georgette exclaimed.

Sally glanced at George. "I'm sure Sam will love them. I only hope he doesn't lose them. They are made of diamonds, are they not?"

George nodded. "So long as he enjoys them."

Adams opened the door as Ebinezer brought Matilda around. Sally glared at her husband. "I'll accompany them. I'm sure you have much to occupy you in your library, my lord."

So he had gone from being George—and even *dearest*—to being *my lord*. He watched dejectedly as his family left the house. From his library window he continued to watch them, a stubborn lump lodged in his throat. Sally was so happy when she was with the children. They, after all, had been her sole reason for marrying him.

*   *   *

From the morning-room window, Blanks watched his wife. She and that demmed Willingham were walking through the parkland. Did the man not have duties to perform? Surely Sedgewick didn't pay his steward to pay court to his sister. Did the snake Willingham not know Glee was a married woman?

The longer Blanks watched, the happier Glee looked. No less than five times—since he had been watching—she had lifted her laughing face to Willingham. And Blanks did not at all like the way she tucked her arm into Willingham's. It was far too intimate!

He could stand watching no longer. He stormed to the library and slammed the door behind him.

Sedgewick was sitting by the fire reading one of those blasted farming journals like the ones he read when he was at Sutton Hall. Sedgewick looked over the top of the page at him. "Pray, what is the matter?"

Blanks crossed the room and looked out the window. That deuced wife of his was still smiling up into the demmed steward's face. "Does that bloody steward of yours have nothing better to do than dance attendance upon my wife?"

George put down his reading and came to stand beside Blanks. "They say if one's mate is happy at home, there is no reason to ever stray. Can you honestly say you've made your wife happy?"

Blanks glared at him. "I love her, for God's sake. And she's well aware of those feelings!"

"I suggest you show her. My sister is desirous of bearing a son. Perhaps you can assist."

Good Lord! Did Sedgewick think Glee might go elsewhere for the physical love he denied her? Not his Glee. She was too fine a woman. "But she loves me!"

George faced him. His face was so deuced somber

the fellow looked tortured. "And that is all that matters. You'll never know how fortunate you are to possess your wife's love. Would that I possessed my wife's."

So he was tortured. As badly as he had been when Dianna died. Only now he had come to love again, and this time that love was not returned. If only Blanks could say something that would ease his friend's pain. But all he could do was to settle a hand on George's shoulder. "I am a most fortunate man." He turned away from the window, George's words guiding him. "I go to my wife now."

When Blanks came upon his wife and Willingham, the steward stammered a moment, then excused himself. Not missing a step, Glee tucked her arm into her husband's. "I should love above everything to go to the folly with you, my darling."

His thoughts flooded back to that long-ago day when he and Glee had taken refuge from the rain under the folly's domed roof. Her foolish actions that day had forced him to marry her. Looking back on it, he realized that had been the luckiest day of his life.

He placed his hand over hers and continued past the burned stable and on to the lake. "My men are getting the lumber today and will start rebuilding the stable tomorrow," he said.

Memories of his many childhood trips here swamped him. Looking back, he came to realize he had always been part of George and Glee's family. His happiest times had occurred here at Hornsby, not at his own Sutton Hall.

"Do you know, Blanks," Glee said, eying the placid lake, "that is the same boat you were sitting in the first time I ever set eyes on you."

"Is that so? Amazing it's still afloat." They began to mount the knoll up to the folly. His pulse pounded. His breath grew short.

"I'm ever so glad it's not raining today, dearest. Is it not a lovely day?"

He hoped she would not detect the tremble in his voice. "Indeed it is."

One minute they were in full sun, the next they were under the folly's shade. Now, he planned to take control. He took her hand and led her to the farthermost column and, with both his hands upon her shoulders, backed her into it, pressing himself against her as he lowered his head to hers.

She met his lips with a breathless passion. The intensity of the kiss deepened, and he was lost in a swirl of unleashed emotions. Encircling her in his arms, he crushed himself even closer to her. There was no way she could fail to feel the bulge beneath his breeches.

The next thing he knew, his little wife was rocking into him, slowly, languidly at first, but as their joint passion seared, their rhythm became faster, more urgent.

"Oh, please, Blanks, my love, come into me."

He could have stopped no easier than he could have summoned the night. He greedily lifted her skirts and pushed down her drawers, his precious Glee parting her legs for him at the same time she was attempting to release him from his blasted breeches.

When he was released, she caressed his swollen member greedily. If he did not stop her, he would come into her hand. That was what he had been wanting: to *not* come into her. He delayed making his decision, basking in her torturing touch.

Then he made his decision. He flicked her hand

away. And moving even closer to her, he parted her folds in preparation for him.

His breathing hitching ever upward, he came into his beloved wife, into her buttery warmth, panting as one who has just escaped death. His little Glee trembled uncontrollably. He held her close for a long time. Until long after their passion was spent. He dropped soft kisses into her glorious coppery curls.

She looked up at him, the vestiges of their passion evident in the moist tendrils of her hair, in the smoky look in her fevered eyes. "This is where you need to be, my love," she murmured.

He cradled her face within his palms. "I had almost forgotten the joy being loved by you brings me," he said in a raspy voice. As they stood there gazing at one another, he began to grow hard within her again.

Moments later, dazed with wet kisses and expanding emotions, he finally allowed himself to slip from her, and he readjusted his breeches. His palm wiped the wet hair from her sweet brow as he dropped a kiss upon her pert little nose.

She slipped both her arms around him just above his waist and settled her cheek against his chest. "Oh, my dearest, I cannot wait until tonight!"

Chapter 30

Blanks stayed in the library with George when the runners came from London. The two gentlemen, who were much the same age as he and Blanks, sat on the other side of the desk from him. George told of the sinister occurrences at Hornsby since the new groom had come. "I wish for you to observe the man every hour of the day. Oblige me by wearing less recognizable clothing, though," George said.

Neither man objected.

"Between my brother"—George indicated Blanks—"and me, we should be able to outfit you."

Blanks left his position in front of the window and came to address the men. "It's vital to Lord Sedgewick that we learn who employs this Ebinezer."

One of the runners withdrew a small occurrence book from his breast pocket and took up a pen. "We shall need a thorough description of the man."

"He's no more than five and twenty years of age," George said. "He's taller than I am, but built rather like me."

"The man is my height, with my brother's muscular build," Blanks interjected.

George got to his feet. "I shall have him bring around my horse." He glanced at Blanks. "For you to ride, since that blasted doctor and my wife have contrived to keep me indoors."

Blanks nodded. "That way you fellows can see for yourselves what the groom looks like."

"If the stables 'ave burned, where is the bloke stayin' at night?"

"Actually, he has insisted on staying in the burned-out stable," George said. "Claims he won't leave his animals. Don't know what the fellow plans to do in the event of rain."

The other runner glanced out the window. "Never ye mind about rain. We'll 'av 'im locked up tight by the time the next rain falls."

"If he is, indeed, the culprit," Blanks said.

George's brows dipped. "He's got to be."

Bonnets shading their faces, Sally and Glee spent the summer afternoon leisurely walking the parkland in front of Hornsby. Still refusing to go near the stable, Sally had balked at Glee's suggestion they walk to the lake.

"I understand the men have decided to build the new stable alongside the old one," Glee said. "There's enough of a shell in the old stable to house the horses and the groom until the new one is built."

"I cannot believe it's been almost two months since that fateful day," Sally said somberly. "So much has passed. I'm deliriously happy that George has recovered, but I'm ashamed to admit I miss those days in the sick room when I tended to him." Her voice lowered. "I loved being with him every waking moment and taking care of him. We became so close. We'll never recover what we then shared."

"Oh, pooh. It's as plain as the nose on my face that George has come to adore you. A pity he almost had to die to bring you to that state of closeness."

She knows. "I'm afraid that closeness will not ever come again."

Glee's lovely jade eyes narrowed. "Now, why ever would you say that? You've become his wife in every way."

Sally's face grew hot. "You don't understand. He pretended I was Dianna."

Glee came to a stop in the middle of the broad lawn and peered at Sally. "Nonsense! I know my brother, and I know he's in love with you. He has all the signs of a man who passionately loves his wife. Trust me, Dianna is long forgotten, rest her sweet soul."

Sally spoke in a choked voice. "He called me Dianna. When we were making love."

"Oh dear," Glee said, her face scrunching into a frown. "I daresay it was old habit. Was it during the first time?"

"The first time?"

"The first time you made love, goose!"

Sally swallowed. "Well, yes, actually."

"There you have it! Old habit for sure. Knowing my brother, I'd say he hadn't made love to another woman since Dianna, and it was only natural that her name would come to his lips—that first time—but, believe me, he loves you."

"I wish I could believe you," Sally said in a weak voice.

Glee's mouth puckered. "I think I can now understand everything."

"Everything?"

"The reason my poor brother behaves in so tortured a manner. After he called you Dianna, you put a stop to sharing a bed with him, did you not?"

Sally spun to face her. "How did you know?"

"Believe me," Glee said morosely, "I know the signs of a man terribly in love with his wife and deprived of her body. I've lived with such a man for more than two years."

They walked in silence toward the lane that ran in front of Hornsby.

"You didn't tell George, did you?" Glee said.

"Tell him what?"

"Tell him he called you Dianna."

"It hurt too deeply, and I'm much too proud for my own good."

"Just as I thought! Instead of apologizing for calling you by the name of his former wife, he thinks you've barred him from your bed because you don't love him. What *did* you tell him?" Glee tossed a quizzing glance at her sister.

"I . . . I didn't tell him anything. I wrote to him."

Glee turned to her, her eyes dancing. "What did you write to him?"

"I told him . . . we couldn't do that again." She drew in a deep breath. "I told him I loved him, but only like a brother."

Glee groaned. "That explains my poor brother's dejected behavior. It really wasn't a bit charitable of you to treat him so callously, you know. He's had a rough go of it."

Sally's stomach dropped. She wished she could believe her denial *did* hurt him—not that she wished to wound the poor dear. "Had I thought I was hurting him, I most certainly would not have behaved so *callously*, but I assure you, the only thing George loves about me is my too willing body."

"That's not true! I've known my brother a good

deal longer than you, and I'm positive he's in love with you."

Sally heaved her shoulders. "Would that I could believe there's truth to what you're saying. Unfortunately, you're only trying to make me feel better because you're such a very good friend to me."

"Pooh! I also love my brother, and I want him to be happy."

Sally could not discuss her strained relationship with George any longer. "Speaking of being happy, I could tell at whist last night that a big change has come over Blanks. And over you."

Glee smiled. A huge smile. Like the cat that caught the canary. "Yes, we are very happy indeed. We did it again, you know."

A crisp gust of wind slapped at Sally's face. "It?"

"You know, *it.*" Her smile gave no sign of lessening.

That which she had done with George. That glorious mating. No wonder Glee was so happy. Sally turned and took Glee's hand, covering it with her own. "I'm so very happy for you. And for Blanks."

"No one in the world is happier than I," Glee said smugly.

They came to the lane and turned back toward the manor house. Sally saw Ebinezer bring around George's horse. She was about to become angry until she saw that it was Blanks, not George, who mounted the beast.

"By the way," Glee said, "You did a most peculiar thing in the letter you sent me to tell me of George's accident."

Sally squinted against the sun to face her sister. "What?"

"You signed it *Sally Spenser.* I hope that does not mean you dislike being Lady Sedgewick."

"I suppose old habits are difficult to break. I'm

happy to be Lady Sedgewick, though I've never in
my life been more unhappy, if you understand
what I mean."

"I understand."

That night after dinner the four of them played
whist. This time it was females against males. Unfortunately, that put Sally next to George at the
table. He had hardly been able to utter a word to
her since reading her unwelcome letter. At the
same time, he had been unable to expunge her
from his every thought.

Most of all, he kept thinking of that blissful night
she had invited him into her chamber. How could
she have given herself to him so completely, then
turn around and abandon him? Every kiss, every
caress they had shared validated a most perfect
union. She couldn't be that good of an actress! Yet,
he had to accept that she did not really love him.
Except as a brother. *Damn it!*

Was it his recent deformity? He refused to believe he could have been that incompetent in the
ways of loving a woman. Besides, she was too inex-
perienced to feign the climax that had drenched
her, sending her into uncontrollable tremblings.
No, he had been capable of fulfilling her in that
way. Then, what was it?

"Your play, dearest," she murmured to him.

He glanced at her sweet face and noted she had
not curled her hair. Was that to please him? He
had told her he preferred her hair uncurled. His
eye trailed along her golden neck to the rising and
falling of her smooth little breasts. How he longed
to remove that gown! He shuddered, then tossed
out a card.

'Twas difficult to keep his mind on his play when

her presence continued to evoke her sensuality. Now he had some idea of the torture Blanks had put himself through these two years past.

Only today there was something different about Blanks. A self-satisfied composure. George glanced at his sister. She possessed that same telling smile.

And suddenly George realized that when Blanks had become jealous of Willingham yesterday and fled the library, he must have confronted Glee. And nature had obviously taken its course. Had they returned to the folly where Blanks had first compromised her? A smile hitched on George's face. One victory won. His own, unfortunately, would forevermore evade him.

"Dearest," Sally said to him, placing her hand on his sleeve. "Who were those men who came to you today?"

"No one you need be concerned with." He disliked excluding his wife from this business, but it was for her own good. Anything that related to the day of the fire still had the power to send her into hysterics.

After he and Blanks won the first game, he pleaded fatigue, though it was actually his wife's debilitating presence that made him wish to leave.

Sally mounted the stairs with her husband.

"You aren't still afraid I'll fall down?" he asked with a chuckle.

"No, you've quite satisfied me that you are recovered. I'm exceedingly happy, but I daresay I do miss your company."

He stopped and peered into her eyes. It was impossible for her to forget that other night when he had looked at her with such longing, so much that she had ventured to invite him to partake of her willing body. She could not allow herself to dwell on that night. It had meant nothing to him. He only needed a man's release, not a wife's love. "I rather thought you would prefer Glee's company to mine," he said.

She climbed to the next step. "I adored being with you day and night. I'm rather a controlling creature, and I daresay I was in my element ordering you about." *And being with you every moment and caring for you and loving you with all my heart.* None of those words would her pride allow her to say.

As they drew near her door, she stiffened and grabbed the knob. She would not allow herself to be used merely for his physical gratification. She flashed a smile and said, "Good night, George. I hope you sleep well."

He did not so much as even try to brush dry lips across her forehead. He spun on his heel and went to his chambers.

Once she was in bed, she relived the hopeful conversation she had with Glee. Then she remembered Glee telling her about the signature on the letter. *Sally Spenser.* An old habit that was hard to break. She no more wished to be Sally Spenser than she wished to be residing with her odious elder brother. Nevertheless, she had referred to herself by that name.

The wrong name.

Could George had done likewise when he called her Dianna? Could Glee be right?

Chapter 31

Given the fact that he had been able to sleep like a babe in the post chaise coming here, Lloyd had offered to take duty the first night. He was careful to dress all in black and even blackened his face so as not to be seen after dark when wandering about his lordship's estate. Once darkness fell, he left the big manor house, came to a thicket near the burned-out stable, and sat on a tuft of grass to wait. He wasn't sure what he was waiting for, but he would know when the time came.

His first observation came about six o'clock when the burly groom left the stable and went up to the big house for dinner. Lord Sedgewick had told him this Ebinezer took his meals at the big house. Abut half an hour later, the groom strolled leisurely back to the stable.

The next several hours were duller than a month-old razor. Waiting was the worst part of this blasted job. But the pay was fair, and Lloyd received a heap of pride in protecting the good and punishing the bad.

He glanced from the stable to the big house,

from the big house to the stable. He watched the candles in the big house being snuffed one by one until eleven o'clock, when the house was in complete darkness. He was getting sleepy himself, but he wasn't one to take a day's pay for not doing his job. So he stayed awake. Hard as it was.

Not long after the manor house went dark, he heard the soft pounding of horse's hooves. And they weren't going to the big house, either. He sat up straight, his ears perked. The horse kept coming right toward the stable without a falter in its stride. It wasn't until the horse stopped right beside the stable that Lloyd got a good glimpse of the rider. It was a lady! He watched as she dismounted and tethered her mount. Though he was some distance away, he could tell she was pretty. But something didn't seem right. She dressed like a real lady. Quality. Now, what would a lady of the *ton* be doing coming to visit with a groom?

It seemed to him a lady met a man at this time of night for one reason and one reason only. And Lloyd distinctly disliked the idea of spying on a pair of lovers. That weren't what he was being paid to do.

Sure enough, the Ebinezer fellow came out of the stable's shadows and kissed the lady. By the looks of the kiss, it wasn't the first time the two of them had met like this. He watched as the groom took her hand and led her into the ruined building.

Lloyd hated to pry into their doings, but he was receiving good compensation for doing so. He got up and quietly made his way to the dark side of the stable and bent down low. It was a very long shot, but there was the possibility the lady was the one what paid the groom, so Lloyd told himself he had to go listening to the two of them. Better that than watching!

It was the lady he heard first. "I see you've got fresh hay for us to lie on, Ebinezer. Have you missed me this past fortnight?"

"Aye, Miss Johnson," the groom said hungrily. "But I needs to get something straight between us, and I ain't talkin' about me cock."

The lady spoke real throatily like. "I love it when you say wicked things, Ebinezer. Come to me."

"Not until ye promise me I'm not goin' to have to do more killin'."

"I've been thinking about it, and I've decided Lord Sedgewick may have suffered enough for what he did to me. There's just one other tiny thing . . ."

"I don't want to do nothin' else. I want to come back to Bath, to Coriander House. I want to feel you lying beside me every night."

"You silly man. You know I'm always on top. Now come here."

Sweet heavens! Lloyd had just heard enough to convict the bloke! And the lady, too! Let's see, what were the facts he'd have to know? The lady was Miss Johnson of Coriander House in Bath. He could remember that without writing it down.

What he heard next was a bunch of grunting and moaning and some of the filthiest talk he'd ever heard in his one and thirty years! Thank the Good Lord he wouldn't have to repeat that part to his lordship.

Lloyd had a strong desire to run up to the big house this very moment and wake his lordship, but he felt he hadn't done much to earn his money. The thing to do was to follow the lady in order to get even more evidence against her.

But in order to follow her, he would need a mount. He got up quietly and went back to the manor house, where he woke up his mate.

"What goin' on?" Gordon said as he rubbed his eyes.

"I've got the lady."

"What lady?"

"The one that's tryin' to destroy Lord Sedgewick. I'll need to follow her when she leaves the groom. I think she's payin' the lad with her body. What I need you to do is to go find me a mount and wait for me at the lane—in the darkest place ye can find. Ye'll need to be quiet. We can't let her see you."

Lloyd hurried back to the stables, and the two of them were still going at it. He'd wager a quarter's salary he hadn't missed a thing except more dirty talk. He never heard of no lady talking like that one. She spoke more like a whore down at the docks than a lady living in a fine house with a name!

But he had to hand it to that Ebinezer. He could go many a round with the demanding wench. Lloyd wished he had half the stamina of the strapping groom.

After a couple of hours of that, the lady said, "You must help me dress now, Ebinezer. I have to leave before the light comes."

"Ye stayin' at the inn in the village?"

"Yes, but this will be my last time here. The innkeeper keeps asking what keeps bringing me to Tottenford. And Tottenford, my dear lover, is not exactly a metropolis."

"Don't know what no metropolis is."

"You're so blessedly simple. Wait a few days, then you'll be free to leave here and return to me." There was a pause, and Lloyd heard the jingling of coins. "Here's a few crowns for your transportation."

A few minutes later, they left the stable and the groom helped her mount her horse. Lloyd waited until she was almost out of his vision before he began to follow. He saw that when she got to the lane, she turned right. The road to Tottenford.

Gordon waited with the horse in a pocket of hedges. Lloyd took the reins. "Go back to bed. I can handle it."

Over breakfast the next morning, Adams told George that two men desired to speak to him in the library.

Could the runners have the information so quickly? George threw down his fork, got up and hurried to the library. "Gentlemen?"

Smug smiles met him. "We've got the information ye need," one of them said.

For some strange reason, his pulse quickened. "Who?"

The runner who kept the notebook replied. "A Miss Johnson from Coriander House in Bath."

George's heart pounded in his chest. Because he had the effrontery to marry a woman of lesser means and lesser beauty, and because he gave the woman a set-down at the Pump Room, Betsy Johnson wished to destroy him. "The slut! The bitch!"

"Aye, she's all of that and more," the runner said. "It's my belief she's been payin' the groom with her body."

George gave out a bitter laugh. "He could have such at any brothel."

"Ain't you right about that! I never heard no woman speakin' in such dirty language, much less a lady born."

"She's no lady," George said. He met the gaze of the man who had just spoken. "Forgive me for making you have to listen to the woman's foul mouth."

"It's all in a day's—or night's—work. I followed her to the Cock 'n Stock Inn, where the innkeeper confirmed that the lady's stayed there on three different occasions. Though she used the name Jones, the innkeeper can identify her."

"And Lloyd heard enough conversation between the lady from Bath and the groom to convict them," the other runner added.

"Gentlemen," George said, "I believe a trip to Bath is in order. First, of course, we shall arrest Ebinezer."

It was a couple of hours later before George returned to the house. Sally was waiting.

"George Pembroke, I declare, I am exceedingly mad at you! You know the doctor will not allow you out of doors. And why will you not tell me who those two men are?"

A sheepish grin on his face, he came to give her cheek a kiss. "I shall tell you everything when I return from Bath."

She seized his arm. "You are not going to Bath!"

"But, my dear, the Bow Street runners have already arrested Ebinezer and now plan to arrest Betsy Johnson for serious crimes committed against Lord Sedgewick, and I really must be there."

"Betsy Johnson!" she shrieked. "Bow Street runners? Oh, George, you're so very clever. And now everything falls into place so well." Until this moment, Sally had never thought she could hate Miss Johnson. After all, Sally was the victor, and she planned to be a gracious one. But anyone who could devise a scheme so sinister deserved Sally's hatred—along with a beheading. "You're not going to Bath without me! I don't trust you to take proper care of yourself."

George gave her an odd, pained look. "You're at liberty to do whatever you'd like, my lady."

"Then I shall gather a few things," she said as she began to run up the stairs. "Thank goodness I no longer have to worry about the children's safety. How long will we be gone, dearest?"

"We'll be back tomorrow."

"Then I shall leave the children in Glee's care."

As Hettie helped her pack, Sally's mind was a blur. The horrid past that the wicked Betsy Johnson had orchestrated mixed with the future and what Sally hoped to salvage of her marriage. Could she dare hope Glee was right?

There was only one way to find out. She would have to loosen her grip on her pride.

Chapter 32

The sun sliced into the carriage from the tiny side window, bathing George's poor, healing face in light while Sally, sitting opposite him, was in shadow. "Please come sit by me," she said. "You're in the sun."

He shot her a cold glance, then moved to sit next to her.

They rode on for some time without talking. Sally was much too aware of how close his knee was to her own. And the nearness of him flooded her with memories of that special nearness they had shared. That nearness she hoped to repeat.

In order to satisfy herself of his possible affection, she must throw her pride into the wind. Her pulse raced. She took in a deep breath, then began: "You know, George, I was greatly offended when you said you loved me, but then called me Dianna."

He spun to her, his eyes wide, his brows low. "I couldn't have called you Dianna! I haven't even thought of her in months. You must be mistaken."

"Does a soaring dove not know when it is felled by a musketball?"

A deep softness came over his still handsome face as he peered into her eyes, taking her hands in his and lifting them to his mouth. "I can't even picture Dianna. It's you and only you who relentlessly bombards my every waking thought and ignites my every desire."

So it had indeed just been an old habit! It really was she whom he loved! She now regretted the recent nights when her pride had kept her beloved from her bed. Her hand cupped his face. "And it's you and only you whom I've always loved."

His green eyes danced. "Always?"

She nodded shyly.

"Then may I suggest, Lady Sedgewick, that you sit upon my lap?" He cinched his hands about her waist and began to haul her to his lap.

She was seated atop him in a flash, circling her arms around his neck, lowering her lips to his for an unbelievably tender kiss. From her mouth he moved effortlessly to her slender neck, then he covered her bosom with gentle kisses. She sighed and arched, impatient for him to release her breasts for the more careful consideration of his mouth. As she felt the cool air rushing over her unbound breasts, she fleetingly thought of the coachman, of the impropriety of her near nakedness, but abandoned her inhibitions as George suckled on her hardened nipples, his gentle hand nudging upward from beneath her skirts, quelling any hint of rebellion as a deep need began to throb within.

"You're not wearing drawers!" he exclaimed.

She dropped a breathless kiss onto the top of his head. "Of course not! I had no desire to restrict you."

"Then you knew . . . ?"

She shook her head, sending her hair flying from its swept-up coif. "I didn't know. I hoped," she murmured, lowering her face to his.

"You little vixen!" he growled as he lifted her from the waist. "I wish for you to straddle me as if you were riding a horse bareback."

Smiling down into her husband's happy face, she fanned out her skirts, nudged one knee on either side of him, and faced him, forehead to forehead as she nibbled his lower lip into her mouth, her hips easing into a flowing rhythm against him. He crushed her to him and groaned his satisfaction.

A throbbing heat gushed at her core, expanding to fill every cell of her body with searing need.

When he released himself from his breeches, she trembled and stilled against him, her breathing erratic. His hands slipped beneath her skirts as he probed her opening, fitting himself to her before the first surge. Surge after surge spiked through her, and just as release was about to settle over her, another surge convulsed her until the surges were overlapping and she heard herself cry out over and over again.

When the surges ceased to slam against her, when she had no more air in her lungs with which to cry out, when she collapsed against his powerful chest, drenched as if she had been swimming, he drew her tightly against him and whispered throatily, breathlessly into her moist ear. "By all that's holy, my love, my Sally, I love you with all my heart."

He held her as if she were his most precious possession, and it dawned on her that her husband did indeed love her with the same debilitating intensity she felt for him. She lifted her face to his. "I'm ever so happy you decided to make me your wife and not your governess. What a wanton governess I would have been!"

He laughed as he drew her closer, and she pillowed her face into his chest for the long, joyous ride back to Bath.

ABOUT THE AUTHOR

After careers in journalism and in teaching English, Cheryl Bolen published her first book *(A Duke Deceived* with Harlequin Historical) in 1998 and was named Notable New Author.

Cheryl lives in a suburb of Houston with her professor husband. They are the parents of two sons who claim to be grown. An antiques dealer, Cheryl travels to England whenever writing deadlines permit.

Readers can write to her at Kensington Books or through her website, www.cherylbolen.com.